RETURN TO BONNYBRAE

A breathtaking and powerful historical saga

GWEN KIRKWOOD

Sinclair Family Saga Book 3

Revised edition 2023
Joffe Books, London
www.joffebooks.com

First published by Romaunce Books in
Great Britain in 2016

This paperback edition was first published
in Great Britain in 2023

Cover art by Jarmila Takač

ISBN: 978-1-80405-853-4

I would like to thank Morag Williams, retired Health Board archivist, for her time and patience in providing information and literature concerning the early days of hospitals and nursing.

CHAPTER ONE

All day the sky had been a sullen grey with a biting wind stinging the face and hands. In the kitchen at Bonnybrae farm Jamie Sinclair gazed at the glowing embers of the fire, glad to be indoors with the day's work finished, but he could not banish a feeling of unease. Miss Catherina Capel had covertly slipped a piece of paper from her glove into his hand at her grandfather's funeral. At twenty-two Jamie did not usually dwell on the past but tonight he was in contemplative mood as he considered the funeral of the old laird, Sir Reginald Capel of Stavondale Tower. He had accompanied Uncle Jim, Aunt Maggie and Uncle Joe. They had been joined by two of his other Sinclair uncles, who were also tenants on the Stavondale Estate. He had been amazed by the number of people who were there to pay their last respects, although his grandfather had respected Sir Reginald as a gentleman and a fair landlord. At eighty-five he had outlived most of his peers, as well as ex-president Roosevelt. He had done better than either of Jamie's grandfathers in that he had lived to see the end of the war, though that must have brought a mixture of relief and sorrow considering his only grandson had been killed in the trenches barely ten months ago, in March 1918.

Peace had been declared in November, almost three months ago, but the labour on most farms was still scarce. Jamie knew his Uncle Jim was exhausted when he had gone to bed early. He was forecasting snow by morning. If he was right, there would be extra work feeding and breaking ice to water their cattle and sheep. The fiery embers stirred in the grate. Jamie leaned forward and added another log. He was not ready to sleep. His thoughts were on Catherina and her pale, grief-stricken face. She had always looked young for her years with her wide, infectious smile, sparkling dark eyes and unruly curls. Today she looked older than eighteen, clad as she was in a long black coat and a hat which hid her luxuriant dark hair and shadowed her elfin face. She had looked frail, not a description he would ever have applied to the cuddly, rounded girl he had first met the day he ran away from his home in Yorkshire and arrived here at Bonnybrae to seek a home with Aunt Maggie and Uncle Joe. How thoughtless, how reckless he had been at fourteen. Rina, as she preferred to be called, had given him a ride up the road on the back of her pony. She had felt soft and round when he put his arms around her to hold on. He had felt like crying because she reminded him of his little sister, Marie, and the rest of the family he had left behind, and he was deadly tired and anxiously praying Grandfather Sinclair would allow him to stay and work for him at Bonnybrae.

He knew Rina had loved her grandfather deeply and sincerely. As he expected, the funeral had been an ordeal, filled with grief, yet she was determined to show a brave face to the world. He wondered who would comfort her now. Early in their youthful acquaintance Jamie had learned that Sir Reginald was her friend and confidant, as well as being her grandfather. She admitted he was always loving and understanding while her parents had little time for her. News of Sir Reginald's rapidly deteriorating health had cast a shadow over his tenants and consequently they had discussed it at the weekly cattle market and at the railway station while they were loading their milk churns onto the train to Glasgow.

When Uncle Jim returned from the station with the news Jamie had written to Rina at once, offering what little comfort he could. Now he was anxious. Had he been wrong to write? He had certainly been wrong to assume her parents would have informed her of her beloved grandfather's rapid deterioration.

Theirs was a long-standing, if unusual, friendship, ever since Rina had pleaded with him to write her a weekly letter during her time at boarding school in Edinburgh. She was ten years old and he had done as she asked, but even then he had been aware of the difference in their status. At sixteen her parents insisted she must attend a school for young ladies in Gloucestershire and he had deliberately written only an occasional letter. Had he been presumptuous in writing now? Belatedly he had learned Mr and Mrs Capel — or Sir Roger and Lady Capel — as they were now, had not mentioned her grandfather's failing health. His letter would be a shock. Had he caused her unnecessary distress?

Rina had been a frequent visitor at Braeside, the home of his Aunt Maggie and Uncle Joe, ever since her grandfather had suggested she call there so she could tell him about their restoration of the house. Over the past eight years both Joe and Maggie had developed a warm affection for her, regardless of the difference in their background and education. She had first arrived riding her pony bareback and wearing her brother's baggy breeches, and with a smile to melt the hardest of hearts.

Joe Greig was a partner in the factory where he had worked since leaving school and he travelled to and from work each day on the train. Miss Catherina Capel happened to be travelling home on the same local train, the last leg of her long journey from Gloucestershire. Joe had automatically dealt with her heavy suitcase and she had settled herself in the seat beside him as instinctively as a lamb runs to its mother. Oblivious to other passengers she poured out her distress, telling Joe she had known nothing of her grandfather's deteriorating health until she received a letter from Jamie.

'I didn't want to leave him after the Christmas vacation but Mother insisted I must return until my eighteenth birthday in June. They should have told me he is worse. They don't care if I never see him again, or to talk to him.' Her voice shook and Joe was afraid she might burst into tears. He patted her hand awkwardly until she regained control. 'After I read Jamie's letter yesterday I stayed up most of the night. I packed my trunk and some boxes. My friends have promised to send them on by rail. I shall refuse to go back whatever my parents say.' Her soft mouth trembled.

'Dinnae distress yourself, Miss Catherina,' Joe pleaded. He hated to see her so upset.

'You never call me that.' She turned to look at him almost accusingly. Joe smiled.

'I know you prefer Rina, but you're a young lady now. Your parents will not approve of me being familiar.'

'Grandfather calls me Rina and he liked me being friends with you and visiting Braeside. He said it was good for me. I don't care what my parents say.' Joe knew her parents would strongly disapprove of her even sitting beside him on the train. Mrs Capel had wanted her to attend a finishing school in Switzerland when she was sixteen but Sir Reginald had refused to entertain the idea while there was a war. Since he was expected to pay the fees he had his way. He had compromised by agreeing she could attend a finishing school for young ladies in Britain, but he had forecast changing times ahead when the war was over.

'Things are changing now the war is over,' Joe said gently, unwittingly echoing her grandfather's view, 'but your parents will still want you to mix with people from your own class.'

'Class!' Rina muttered. 'I hate the hypocrisy and the stupid things we learn . . .'

'I know. Maggie and I will always be your friends. Jamie too, although he is a young man now and neither of you can remain as close as you were as children.' Rina was silent, then she turned to Joe.

'My parents didn't want me to come home,' she said urgently. 'Mama insisted Father should cut my allowance. I didn't have enough to pay my train fare. I borrowed it from three of my friends. I-I must repay them. I-I hope Grandfather is well enough to give me the money. He doesn't like people who have debts.'

'Don't worry about that, Rina,' Joe said kindly. 'I'm sure your parents will repay your friends.'

'I don't think they will. They will be angry because I have returned unexpectedly.'

'If they refuse you must come to me or Maggie. We'll give you the money. Good friends are precious. It is too easy to lose them. We must repay our debts.' Joe glanced at her pale face and wondered if she had had anything to eat on her long journey if she was so short of money. There were no shops at their little country station. 'Do you want a piece of Maggie's toffee? She always gives me a packet to eat on the train but we were so busy talking I forgot.'

'Oh yes please!' Joe smiled. She looked almost like the eager child he remembered.

'You take it then. This is our station.' He guessed she was hungry when she hurriedly put the largest piece into her mouth and crammed the rest into her pocket without hesitation. He lifted her case onto the platform. 'This is very heavy to carry all the way to Stavondale Tower,' he said.

'I know but I shall need some of my clothes and things until my trunk arrives.'

'Shall we leave your case at the station? If no one has collected it by morning I will ask Jim or Jamie to collect it when they bring the milk to the train tomorrow.'

'Yes please. Could you do that for me?' She looked young and pathetically grateful Joe thought. When he had placed her case in the care of the stationmaster she said, 'I do hope Grandfather is not as ill as Jamie seemed to think.' Joe shivered inwardly. He had been at work all day so he had not heard today's news but it was possible Rina would arrive too late to see her grandfather alive. Yesterday's reports had

5

been grave indeed. They walked together until they reached the lodge at the entrance to Stavondale Tower then Rina stopped and gave Joe an unexpected hug before she turned away to hide her tears. She hurried away up the long avenue.

Joe had told Jim and Jamie about meeting Rina on the train that evening. He was anxious about her and the reception she might find when she arrived at Stavondale Tower. It was this which had worried Jamie and caused him to think he might have made a mistake in writing to Rina. Would she tell her parents who had sent her news? Had he distressed her unnecessarily? What if the news had been exaggerated as rumours often were? But they had proved to be true. Surely it was better to be prepared?

He could still recall his own grief when Grandfather Greig died in his sleep the year after he had come to Bonnybrae. He understood how much worse it must be for Rina when her grandfather had played such a big part all her life. He had not intended to interfere but surely it would have been worse if no one had mentioned Sir Reginald was dying? Jamie chewed his lower lip.

He remembered how homesick he had felt the day he arrived at Bonnybrae, even though it was his own decision to run away from home. Rina had started coming to the farm to see the animals the day after he started work, always eager to help him with the young lambs and pigs. He remembered Grandfather Sinclair's dismay when he discovered the young girl they were entertaining in their farmhouse kitchen was the granddaughter of Sir Reginald Capel of Stavondale. He would like to have forbidden her to come back but he found her innocent charm as irresistible as Maggie and Joe. Jamie enjoyed her company. She was young and cheerful, like another sister at a time when he was missing his own brothers and sisters so badly, especially Meg who was only a year younger than him and had always been sweet and cheerful.

Grandfather Sinclair had constantly issued warnings that no good could come of fostering friendship between his grandson and a granddaughter of the landed gentry.

'They're only bairns, and the wee lassie craves friendship and affection,' Maggie defended them with a smile. 'She loves animals. She always asks about them in her letters. She asks about you too, Father.' She beamed at him and it occurred to him that Maggie and the bairn had the same beguiling smile and look of wide-eyed innocence, although they were from different generations.

Jamie had replied to Rina's letters throughout her schooldays but he knew his grandfather's warnings had been justified when Rina was sixteen. She was dreading the move to the ladies' college and making new friends. When she had come to say goodbye she had clung to him. He still recalled how her soft mouth had trembled with the effort of holding back her tears. He had intended to give her a comforting kiss on her cheek but she had flung her arms around his neck and turned her mouth to his. Their kiss was no longer one of childish affection. He remembered the stirrings of desire Rina's soft curves had awakened as she pressed herself against him and he understood his grandfather's misgivings.

As he continued to stare into the fire in the Bonnybrae kitchen that night after the funeral Jamie felt a pang of anxiety for Rina. He reached for the poker and gave the burning logs a fierce jab. His affection for her was deep and sincere. He didn't want to cause her any trouble. After the funeral service the mourners had filed past Catherina and her parents. He thought they looked more grim than sad. He was following Aunt Maggie and Uncle Joe and he was not surprised when Maggie paused a few yards further along the path and whispered in a choked voice, 'I longed to give wee Rina a comforting hug but we weren't even allowed to touch their hands.' Jamie didn't say anything. It was then Rina had leaned forward and pressed a small square of paper into his hand, her eyes pleading for secrecy as she held his gaze before he moved on. He had not told anyone. Later he had opened the neatly folded paper which looked as if it had been torn from a diary and scribbled in haste. 'I am troubled and shamed. Truly I did not know. I am sorry. I will come to Braeside tomorrow and hope you can forgive me.' What could possibly be so serious, or so urgent?

The following day was Saturday. As usual Maggie cooked the dinner for all of them together. Since the war finished there was less demand for soldiers' uniforms so Joe's workload had become easier. As manager he stayed at home on alternate Saturdays and they all ate their lunch together in the Bonnybrae kitchen. Jamie was glad his two uncles got on so well, strengthening the bond between the Greigs and the Sinclairs. His mother and Uncle Joe were Greigs, his father, Uncle Jim and Aunt Maggie were Sinclairs. Grandmother Sinclair had bitterly opposed his parents' marriage and he wondered how she would feel if she could see them now with Uncle Joe and Aunt Maggie so happily married.

Maggie was just carrying a large bowl of mashed potatoes to the table when a tentative knock sounded at the back door. Joe was nearest and he opened the door.

'Why, Rina lassie, there's no need to knock,' he said. 'Come away inside out of the cold wind. We thought there would be snow but it's holding off.' Maggie set down her bowl and hurried round the table. Something in the girl's pale face and wide anxious eyes told Maggie she was needing some kind of reassurance, though why she should she had no idea. Instinctively she opened her arms and Rina almost ran into them. She clung to Maggie for a moment, then slowly straightened.

'I'm so sorry,' she said, looking around. 'I-I'd forgotten it would be lunchtime for you all. I should have remembered when I called at Braeside and there was no one there.' Jim had drawn another chair up to the table and Maggie hastened to assure her there was plenty to eat for everyone.

'Sit ye there, lassie,' Jim said. 'It's a bitter wind outside and whatever might be troubling ye it's always better with a good meal inside ye.' Rina was surprised. She didn't know Jim Sinclair as well as she knew Mr and Mrs Greig, but he had a welcoming smile and his eyes were kind. She hoped he would still be the same when she told them her news but she was terribly afraid none of them would want to see her again, including Jamie.

CHAPTER TWO

Rina's healthy appetite had disappeared during the past week but Maggie was an excellent cook and soon they were all tucking into the steak and kidney pudding, potatoes and sprouts and buttered carrots. A little while later she stared at her empty plate. She had believed her stomach was tied in so many knots she could never face food again, but when Maggie brought a creamy rice pudding with a dish of bottled raspberries she knew she would eat that too, and Mr Sinclair was right, she did feel better. Maggie moved to set the kettle on the rib for a cup of tea but Jamie looked across at Rina, seeing the haunted expression had returned to her elfin face. It suddenly struck him what a small heart-shaped face she had for a girl with such a cuddly figure, yet even that looked thinner.

'I think Rina wants to talk to me but it's a cold day for walking. Is it all right if we go through to the living room Aunt Maggie?'

'Of course it is, but don't you both want a cup of tea first?' Jamie looked questioningly at Rina and saw the colour ebb and flow beneath her fair skin, leaving her far too pale.

'I-I thought I wanted to tell Jamie alone b-but you have all been so kind and when you hear what I have to say you will probably never speak to me again if — if Grandfather was speaking the truth. My father . . .' her eyes filled with tears and she gulped. 'My father says he was deranged and didn't know what he was saying b-but we had had several good talks when we were alone. I-I think he did know what he was saying, and — and I think he wanted me to know.'

Maggie poured tea for them all. It was her soothing remedy for all ills and Joe said gently, 'So you arrived home in time to see your grandfather, and talk with him, Rina?'

'Oh yes.' She turned to Jamie. 'I can never thank you enough for writing to tell me he was so ill, Jamie. I would never have known.' Her soft mouth hardened. 'I would never have seen him again.'

'I thought I might have overstepped our friendship.' Jamie said slowly. 'I've been worried in case my letter had distressed you, though I didn't mean to.'

'It was the best thing anyone could do for me. I shall always remember, and treasure, those last few hours with my grandfather, whatever he did in the past. I didn't tell my parents how I knew he was so ill. They were furious because I had come home.' She shuddered.

'Drink your tea, Rina, then tell us from the beginning,' Joe said kindly. 'It's usually easiest and remember we're none of us here to judge whatever you have to say.'

'Grandfather said you would understand,' she said gratefully. 'But F-Father said I must never repeat what he said because he was crazy and w-when people are dying they don't know what they are saying. After I left you, Uncle Joe, I met Ernest coming out of the stables. He promised to get my case from the station so I went straight in to see Grandfather. My parents didn't realise I was home.' She frowned. 'Mrs Moffat was still there. She cleans and washes for Grandfather but she always goes home at midday. She said she had stayed to keep an eye on Grandfather to let Mrs MacCrindle, the housekeeper, have a sleep because she had looked after him all day and then stayed up all night with him. I could tell Mrs Moffat was annoyed. Neither Father nor Mother had been to see him or to help. She said Father had looked in for a few minutes the previous afternoon. He said Grandfather was sleeping away and better left in peace. They refused to hire a nurse. He had not eaten anything during the past few days, she said, but she agreed with Mrs Mac that it was important to keep giving him wee drinks from the feeding cup.' She looked up at Maggie. 'I hadn't seen one before. It looks just like a small tea pot without a lid and it has a handle on the side and a tiny spout. Grandfather must have recognised my voice because he opened his eyes and asked . . .' she bit back a little sob, '. . . he asked "Is that ma lassie? Are you here at last, Rina?" Later Mrs Mac told me he had been asking for me for several days and especially during the night when he was very restless.' She turned to Jamie. 'He would have died without seeing me if you had not written. I told Mrs Moffat I would stay with him but I asked if she could bring me something to eat because I hadn't had anything since a slice of bread for breakfast. She said there was some chicken soup and she would warm it and bring me some soda scone and cheese. She was astonished when Grandfather said, 'Bring a drop for me, please, Annie. Rina will help me drink it.' Mrs Moffat sieved it into the cup and a wee while later I held him up with one arm and the cup thing with the other and he drank it all. Mrs Moffat said that was the most he had had in the last three days. I am so, so very glad I arrived in time,' she said fervently and squeezed Jamie's hand.

'Grandfather kept closing his eyes as though it was an effort to keep them open but he was not sleeping and we talked about all sorts of things. I told him I had had to bor-row money from my friends to buy my train ticket so he told me where to find the key to his desk. He gave me money to buy three postal orders to send to them, then he gave me a leather purse containing twenty-five guineas. He told me to keep it safe. He — he said it was our secret because it sounded as though I might need it.' She caught her lip between her teeth. 'I think he only meant I should keep it a secret from Mother. When Mrs Mac came down she said I was the best

11

medicine he could have. Grandfather said she was right about that. She brought him a cup of blackcurrant tea. She had made it with some of her jam and sieved out the currants. When she saw how well I managed to hold Grandfather and the cup, and how much he had drunk she said I was a fine nurse and she was thankful I had come. When we were alone Grandfather began to talk again. He said things had changed during the war and they would never be the same again. He believed working for a wage had shown a lot of women what they could achieve and given them independence and if I wanted to do something with my life I should do so, and not be rushed into a marriage I don't want. He was perfectly lucid. Honestly,' she insisted vehemently. 'He knew I love animals but he thought the time was not yet right for me to work with sick animals, but he thought nurses must be in demand with all the wounded men and then the terrible flu epidemic. He thought there must be hundreds of children who needed care if their fathers had died in the war. Then he said there was no need for me to go back to Gloucestershire, even though he had paid my fees until the summer.' Rina's face looked grave. 'He said I should not be concerned what Mother thought about me working for a living, especially if I was helping people, b-but- he hoped I would always keep myself pure as all young ladies should. I-I didn't tell him some of the young ladies who executed the finest curtsies and the most graceful dances boasted about the . . . er the things they had done with young men when they went home.' She frowned. 'I shall tell Mama if she tries to send me back.'

'Oh my dear, would that be wise?' Maggie said, reaching across the table to take her hand.

'Mama thinks everything is good at the school for young ladies but it is not. I shall never be one of the primping women who take tiny steps and pretend to faint at the smallest vulgarity, but I am better than all of them at adding up figures and speaking French and reading.' They were all silent in the face of her scorn for the institution where she had been forced to spend most of the past two years. She took a long drink of tea and Maggie automatically filled her cup again.

'After talking so long Grandfather seemed tired. Mrs Mac had come in again by then. She was really pleased I had come. She said she would stay with him while I had a sleep but she promised to waken me at midnight and take a rest herself. It was one o' clock before she came for me. She said Grandfather had had a restful sleep and now he was asking for me. I went downstairs and he asked for another drink. He seemed very alert. He was alert. I know he was,' she insisted. Maggie reached across and patted her hand and smiled so Rina went on. 'When Mrs Mac had gone to bed he began to tell me about the provisions he had made for the future. He said Mrs Mac had been a loyal servant and friend for many years and she must have her cottage without rent for the rest of her life and if ever I thought his wishes were not being carried out I must go to see Mr Neil MacQuade, his lawyer. He told me about other bequests he had made and that the lawyer had a note of everything. Then he said he was sorry he could not leave me a large fortune but he was sure I would learn to budget better than my parents and he had left me enough money to let me study for whatever I decided to do.' Her eyes filled with tears but she blinked them away. 'I told him he must not worry about such things but he said there would be death duties to pay and my father would probably sell some of the farms.'

'Aah,' said Jim. 'Is that what you were afraid to tell us, Miss Rina?'

'He didn't mention Bonnybrae. He has always said it is one of the best farms. He did say Stavondale Tower might have to be sold because it costs a lot to maintain. Then he sounded angry. "Your father blames me, Rina, because I had put some of the bigger farms in Jonathan's name to preserve his inheritance. Don't believe all he tells you. MacQuade assures me Jonathan's share of the death duties will not be a great amount because parliament is passing a law to give a discount for young men who died fighting for their country.

There will be taxes to pay on my death. Your father will have to sell some farms to pay them because he has been over-spending for many years." He explained things so clearly to me I'm sure he knew what he was saying. Truly he did.' Rina stopped talking and looked at the faces around the table. Her small face crumpled but she strove for control.

'Of course he did my love,' Maggie said gently. 'We all expect changes to the estate.'

'Of course we do, lassie,' Jim said. 'If your father raises the rents it will not be your fault.'

'Oh.' Rina seemed surprised. 'He didn't mention rents, or things like that, only that my parents lived beyond — beyond their income, I think.' She frowned and looked at Maggie. 'He — he said if ever I needed a friend to give me advice, or comfort, he was sure you would do your best to help if you could. B-but that was before . . .'

'Did he really say that?' Maggie asked, surprised but pleased.

'Yes, but he admitted he didn't really know you, except through me visiting you at Braeside, but he remembered you when you were a young girl at church. He — he said we b-both resembled the portrait in the dining room. It is a picture of my great-grandmother, his own mother.' Maggie caught her breath, wondering what else he had said. Had he needed to unburden himself, as her own mother had done before she could die in peace?

Rina chewed her lower lip, wondering if they would banish her from the house if she tried to tell them the rest, or would they believe her grandfather was crazy as her father said.

'He . . . he said he was s-sorry for things that happened in the past when he was a young man. He . . .' she looked Maggie in the eye but the colour had drained from her face, '. . . he said he is your father, your real father b-by blood.' She went on hurriedly. 'He did not know when he married my grandmother that — that the — the young lady was expecting his child. He said she married his friend, James

14

Sinclair, and they had a baby a few months later. He knew he was your father when he saw you later.'

'That can't be true!' Jamie gasped. 'Surely he didn't mean the old woman in black who was my grandmother? The one who . . . ?'

'I-I think so,' Rina said in a small voice. 'He asked if I would like Mrs Greig for my aunt. I said I couldn't think of anything I would like better, except for him to get well again. He talked some more, telling me about the young men he had known in his youth but it seemed to exhaust him. He said James Sinclair was one of the kindest and most genuine men he had ever known, as well as being the best farmer on Stavondale Estate. He said he had done all he could to make sure h-his daughter and Joe Greig could keep Braeside, and he hoped the Sinclairs would always farm at Bonnybrae. Then he went to sleep.' She looked across at Maggie with troubled eyes. 'I thought and thought about it and I'm sure he was speaking the truth. He said he hadn't meant to be wicked or to treat the lady badly.' There was pleading in her dark eyes as she held Maggie's gaze. 'When he wakened again it was daylight. Father came in. He was angry because I had come home and I had stayed all night with Grandfather. He was furious with Mrs MacCrindle too until Grandfather opened his eyes and said he had asked me to stay with him. Then . . . then I'm sure he had a mischievous gleam in his eyes like he used to have when he was teasing. He said, "Before I went to sleep, lassie, did I tell you Mrs Margaret Grieg is your aunt?" Then he looked up at my father and said. "I'm Mrs Greig's father you know. She's your half-sister." He sighed and sank against his pillows. My father began to shout but Grandfather seemed very weary. He closed his eyes but I know he heard my father shouting that he was raving mad and such a thing couldn't be true, and . . . and . . .' She burst into tears but she blew her nose and brushed them away determinedly. 'Mrs Mac came in to see what all the noise was about. She went to the bedside and she said . . . she said, "He's gone." F-father went quiet. Then he turned to me and hissed "Don't you dare breathe a word of such nonsense." He — he didn't seem sad or upset, not like Mrs Mac. She sobbed and hugged me against her.' Abruptly Rina pushed her chair back. 'I will go now. I'm sorry if I have upset you. I understand if you — you never want to see me again,' she added in a choked little voice. Maggie hurried round the table and drew Rina's trembling figure into her arms.

'Hush now, lassie, hush ye. We have heard something of this before. It is no surprise, but . . .'

'You have? You don't believe Grandfather was crazy, as Father insists? You're not angry with me for telling you? Nor with Grandfather for behaving badly and not being a gentleman to — to your mother?'

'Of course not, lassie,' Maggie said gruffly. 'I don't blame anybody, least of all you.'

'Whatever the truth is, Miss Rina,' Jim said, 'it's all in the past and none of it is your fault. Anyway, I reckon Maggie will be pleased to have another niece. She loves young folks around her, don't you, Maggie? Are you coming through to the room, Joe? You too Jamie? I can see you're bursting to say something but Miss Rina can't tell you anymore.'

Maggie flashed her brother a grateful glance. Joe followed him to the door but he paused.

'If you want to know anything else, Rina you could ask Mr MacQuade. He dealt with Braeside and he approved of your grandfather giving us the land. I had a feeling then he knew more than he was saying. Maybe this is the reason Sir Reginald encouraged you to visit us. Whatever you discover we shall always welcome you. Isn't that right Maggie?'

'It certainly is,' Maggie agreed and gave Rina another hug, something she had often wanted to do and never dared in case she overstepped her place. Rina turned into her bosom and allowed the silent tears to fall. She had bottled them up since her grandfather closed his eyes for the last time. Her house mistress had stressed all young ladies should control their emotions at all times, and her mother considered it unladylike to shed tears, but her grief for her beloved Grandfather could not be brushed aside.

Maggie was a great believer in keeping busy and when Rina began to help her clear away the dishes and picked up a tea towel to dry them she did not protest as she might have done at one time.

'Mr MacQuade spoke to me at Grandfather's funeral. He seemed friendly,' Rina said uncertainly. 'He wanted me to be there with my parents when he read Grandfather's will. He said there were things which would concern me in the future, but Father refused to have me in the room. He said I was still a child but I shall be eighteen in June and I don't feel like a child, not anymore.'

'You're certainly not a child when you can organize all your belongings and have them sent by train and travel all that distance on your own. I could never do that,' Maggie said with a shudder.

'I'm sure you could if you had as good a reason as I had,' Rina said wanly. 'I can't tell you how glad I am that Jamie wrote to tell me. I know he does not write so regularly now and I expect he has other friends to see, but I do love to get his letters. He never treats me like a child, or as a silly girl.'

'That is because he knows you are sensible and intelligent and you share his love of animals. I think he does meet other friends sometimes and I know he saw a lot of our half-cousin's daughter the last time he went to Yorkshire to visit his family.'

'I see,' Rina said a little forlornly and Maggie wondered if she was wrong to try and steer Rina away from her close friendship with Jamie. She thought of her father's warnings. Rina was the daughter of their landlord and he was now Sir Roger Capel of Stavondale. Her parents would expect her to make a suitable marriage to one of the other wealthy landowners.

* * *

As soon as the door closed behind them Jamie turned to his two uncles and demanded to know the truth about his Grandmother Sinclair.

'Is it true that the old woman who called me a — a bastard . . . ?' how he hated that word. 'Is it right that she had been — been with the son of the laird? And then — then married Grandfather Sinclair and didn't tell him? How dare she marry him when the laird didnae want her?' Jim looked helplessly at Joe and shrugged.

'Well is that what happened?' Jamie asked furiously. 'How dare she call me a — a bastard and tell me I'm not a Sinclair? Why was she so cruel to my mother if she had committed a worse sin herself? It was all her fault that I was born before my parents could marry. Grandfather Greig and Grandfather Sinclair explained about that but — but . . .'

'Whisht, laddie, calm down now,' Joe said. 'We all agree it was wrong of Mistress Sinclair to talk to you as she did when you were too young to understand, but remember she was your Uncle Jim's mother, and he has been good to you. She was Maggie's mother too, and she will tell you herself that Mrs Sinclair was not thinking clearly by then. Tell him Jim.'

'We-ell it's true my mother was greatly disturbed for some time before she died, but once she had confessed and told Maggie the truth, and she realised my father had always known her secret, and understood, then she seemed to be at peace. Maggie and my father both forgave her for any sins she had committed,' Jim said slowly. 'We have to do the same,' he held up his hand to silence Jamie's indignant protest. 'You're right, Jamie, she should never have talked to you as she did, especially when you were too young to understand. I realise she cast a shadow on your young life, but in a way it was that which brought you here and I am thankful for that.'

'And so are Maggie and I,' Joe added quickly, warmly.

'But she was so horrible to my mother,' Jamie insisted, but with less anger. 'I don't think my father ever forgave her for that, even though he was her son — her own flesh and blood.'

'Aye we canna blame your parents for feeling bitter, but I believe they have put the past behind them. The lesson ye need to learn from all the heartache, Jamie,' Jim said gravely, reminding Jamie of his grandfather, 'is not to let your own passions and desires get the better of you. You're still too young, and your life has been too sheltered, for you to meet such temptations, but you're a man now. I see a change in Miss Rina too. She seems to have become a woman overnight. Don't let yourself be tempted by desire even though she needs your strength and comfort. It's friendship she needs. Never forget she's the daughter of Sir Roger Capel. He would be an implacable enemy. He might find a way to put us out of Bonnybrae if he thinks your relationship with his daughter is too serious.' Jamie flushed and stared at his uncle. He had been well aware of Rina's feminine attraction for some time now. As for being tempted he had gained a little experience on that front on his last visit to Yorkshire to see his family.

'Above all, laddie,' Joe added interrupting his thoughts, 'don't be tempted to try anything in the name of revenge by using Rina because you think the old laird used your grandmother. Maggie and I could never forgive that. We love both of you.'

'Uncle Joe! I would never think of such a thing,' Jamie said indignantly. 'Rina has been my friend since the day I came to Bonnybrae on the back of her pony.'

'I'm glad to hear it,' Joe nodded. It had crossed Joe's mind that old Mrs Sinclair's blood ran in her grandson's veins and Joe knew well how vengeful she had become in her old age. 'I would hate to see either Rina or you forced into a marriage of convenience. The war might have changed many things but there is still a wide gap between the classes. If rumours are true about Sir Roger and Lady Capel being short of money they will be looking to their only daughter to marry a wealthy husband.'

'Well good luck to them! If I can do anything to keep Rina from being unhappy then I shall, but I would never do anything in revenge. I am angry because my grandmother thought she had the right to judge when she had committed the same sin herself.'

CHAPTER THREE

As Maggie finished putting away the dishes and tidying the kitchen Rina mentioned Mr MacQuade again, even more diffidently this time.

'Do you think it would be alright for me to write to him myself without telling my parents?'

'You did say he had wanted to speak to you so I don't see why not,' Maggie said slowly. 'He probably wanted you to hear your grandfather's last wishes.'

'He said they concerned my future. I have been thinking about it a lot. Mother is annoyed because I refuse to go back to Gloucestershire. She says my keep has been paid for and I should be living there.'

'Surely she must welcome your company, as Joe and I do.'

'I have always loved coming to see you both but Father will be furious if he discovers I have been here today, especially if he suspects I told you what Grandfather said about him being your father. I think he is afraid you might claim some of Grandfather's money.' She pulled a face. 'Money seems to be all my parents think about,' she added in exasperation.

'I would never dream of claiming money, even if I had any proof,' Maggie gasped. 'I had my mother's word for what happened, as you have your grandfather's, but I think we should forget about the past and concentrate on the future.'

'I know that, and I'm sure Grandfather knew too.'

'But how awful if your father believes such a thing. He will never want you to come near us again,' Maggie said in distress. Rina moved closer and took her hand.

'So long as you want to see me, I shall always come. Would — would you mind if I call you Aunt Maggie, as Jamie does? After all you are my aunt. That is the best thing Grandfather could give me.'

'I would be honoured if that is what you want, my dear.'

'It is. I think Grandfather knew I would need your advice and help. May I ask a favour?'

'Of course you may. Anything I can do . . .'

'I do want to write to Mr MacQuade. There are things I need to know but I am afraid Father might open any letters I get in reply. He may even prevent me reading them. Could I ask the lawyers to send any letters to your address at Braeside? I would collect them from you.'

'Oh Rina, my dear . . . Are you sure your father would be so — so strict?'

'He can be d-devious . . .' She clamped her teeth over her lower lip and blinked back tears. 'I expect you think I'm disrespectful. I don't mean to be but Grandfather told me there would be a little money to help me until I train for work, if I decide to do that, but Father has not mentioned anything about that. Instead he keeps telling me how much it costs to keep me in food and clothes and it is time I was married. Twice he has mentioned the name of a man he considers suitable. I met him once when he came for the shooting. He is almost as old as Father, but he is much wealthier. Some of the girls at the school for young ladies think the only thing they want is to marry a wealthy husband.'

'I see.' Maggie was lost for words. Joe had voiced his fears that Rina would be married off to the first wealthy man who offered for her, especially if the rumours of her parents' debts were true. She moved closer and gave Rina a hug.

'If I receive any letters for you I shall keep them safe until you call for them. Meanwhile I think it would be a good idea to make an appointment to meet Mr MacQuade at his office so that you can speak to him in private and ask him any questions.'

'Oh thank you,' Rina said, her eyes shining, her smile more like the young girl Maggie knew and loved. 'I feel as though a weight has been lifted away. I was so afraid none of you would want to see me again. It was wicked of Grandfather, wasn't it?'

'I suppose it was,' Maggie agreed, 'but these things do take two people, Rina. Girls must learn to say no, just as young men should restrain themselves. At least everything has turned out well.'

'You're very forgiving. I am so happy to have you for my aunt.'

* * *

Rina called at Braeside to see Maggie the following day but it was only a brief visit while she was out exercising Duke.

'I wrote a letter to Mr MacQuade last night,' she said, 'but I needed a postage stamp so Duke and I went down to the post office at Locheagle, where Mr Greig used to live. I bought two so I shall have a spare one and I posted my letter straight away.'

'But why did you go all the way to Locheagle, Rina?' Maggie asked. 'What's wrong with the post office at East Lowrie? That's where people usually go from Stavondale Tower, isn't it?'

'Yes, that's why I didn't want to go there. Miss Jamieson knows everybody's business and she would probably have told my father I had been there.'

'You really are anxious about your parents intercepting your letters aren't you?' Maggie murmured with a worried frown. 'I'm sure they must realise you are no longer a child.'

'Mmm, maybe,' Rina said as she turned Duke to canter back home. 'They don't want to admit it,' she muttered to her pony. It was dreadful to think you couldn't trust your own parents but she was sure they were hiding something from her. In any case they flatly refused to discuss her future, other than to say they expected her to marry and be off their hands soon. Her happiness didn't seem to matter.

Both Maggie and Rina were surprised when a letter arrived from Mr MacQuade by return of post. It was short and written in his own hand. He had made an appointment for Rina to call at his offices the following day. He had checked the times of the local train and he asked her to be there for eleven o'clock. Afterwards he suggested they should go to lunch at his home with his wife and younger daughter. He would see she was back at the station in time to catch the afternoon train back to Stavondale. Rina scanned the letter quickly then read it aloud to Maggie.

'I don't know how I shall explain my absence all day if my parents ask,' Rina said anxiously, 'but I'm sure they would prevent me going if they knew I was going to talk to Mr MacQuade. I must ask Mrs MacCrindle to help. She is very worried just now because my mother has locked up Grandfather's wing of Stavondale Tower so neither of us can get in. I kept some of my own things with Grandfather. He set aside a room for me. Mrs MacCrindle can't get in to clean so she is afraid she will not earn any money.'

'Perhaps you could tell her where you are going?' Maggie suggested. 'Tell her you will mention her worries to the lawyer. After all you said your grandfather had provided for her future, didn't you, Rina?'

'Yes. You're right, he did.' She hugged Maggie exuberantly. 'Grandfather will never know how right he was when he said I would need you for my friend.'

Rina arrived at the lawyer's offices on time. The elderly woman in reception seemed to be expecting her and escorted her to one of the doors. Rina knocked and waited for an instruction to enter.

'Thank you, Miss Fellowes.' Neil MacQuade was seated behind a wide oak desk when they entered but he rose to

23

greet them at once. 'Will you bring in three cups of coffee and ask my son to join us, please?'

'All right Mr MacQuade, but Mr Charles is dealing with a client right now.'

'Very well. Ask him to join us as soon as he is free.' He turned to Rina and drew one of the brown leather chairs nearer the fire, indicating she should take a seat. 'It is a cold day Miss Capel. Come and warm yourself beside the fire. I am so very glad you were able to come. I felt you should have been present at the reading of your grandfather's will but presumably your parents have now informed you themselves about the provisions he has made for you?'

'No. No they have not mentioned Grandfather since he died and there are so many things I wanted to ask. He talked to me a lot before he — he died. I'm sure he was perfectly clear in his mind all the time, even though my father says he was speaking nonsense and his mind was deranged.'

'He always had a very clear view of things any time I spoke to him and I visited him only four days before his death. He was certainly mentally alert then, although easily tired.' He paused while another young woman brought in a tray of coffee and a plate of small biscuits. She arranged the cups and saucers and poured the coffee from a large silver coffee pot.

'Mr Charles says he will be with you in a few minutes, sir.' Neil MacQuade nodded and thanked her. 'My father and your grandfather were very good friends as well as doing business together,' he told Rina. 'My son is called Charles after my father. He only joined us last summer but if ever I am not available and you need to speak to me you can ask for Charles instead. I have filled him in on the Stavondale affairs. I think it is what your grandfather would have wished. Did you know he made me trustee for you, instead of your parents, until you are twenty-five?'

'No, no I did not know that. Why should I need a trustee?'

'He wanted to be sure his wishes for you were carried out. He — he didn't want anyone to cheat you out of your inheritance, even if it is a small one.' He flushed slightly. 'Cheat was your grandfather's word not mine.' He sipped his coffee.

'I see,' Rina said thoughtfully. 'Then I was right to come. I have a feeling my parents are withholding things from me. They refuse to mention anything to do with Grandfather's affairs. All they want is to see me married to someone who can afford to keep me,' she said in a low voice but Neil MacQuade heard the faint bitterness in her tone. The door opened and a younger edition of himself joined them. Charles MacQuade greeted her pleasantly before taking a seat and lifting his cup and saucer from the tray. Conversation became general but Rina liked Charles MacQuade's ready smile and she judged him to have a sense of humour, something which seemed to be completely lacking in her own father.

When Charles left them to attend to another appointment Rina set down her empty coffee cup ready to hear whatever Mr Neil MacQuade had to tell her. Her stomach was churning with nerves.

'I noted that you asked me to send any communications to you via Mrs Greig at Braeside. I assume you are friends with Mr and Mrs Greig? Do you want me to send your letters there in future?'

'Yes please. Mrs Greig is really my Aunt Maggie. I did not know that until just before Grandfather died. He told me he was her father. It is true we both resemble the painting of his mother, but my father refuses to believe it. He said it was nonsense and his mind was deranged.'

'He was telling you the truth. He confided in my father about his past and he asked me to make sure the Greigs owned all legal rights to Braeside and the land on which it stands. I think he was afraid your father might try to reclaim the house once it was rebuilt but we made sure he cannot do that. Anyway, I am pleased to hear you have a friend you can rely on between now and your eighteenth birthday. By then you may have decided what you would like to do with your life.'

'I shall be eighteen in June and I have already decided I would like to train to be a nurse,' Rina told him in a determined tone which made him smile and reminded him of her grandfather.

'He did mention that possibility to me. He said you care deeply for all living things.'

'I do, but I am not sure what I need to do to train to be a nurse. I know there is a Royal College of Nursing which was established three years ago in 1916 but I need to find out more. I may need money for food and clothes until I am trained enough to earn my living. I tried to tell my parents but Mother flew into a rage and Father says he cannot afford to keep me any longer because Grandfather has left a lot of debts which he must pay. Is — is that true?' she asked in a small voice, reminding Neil MacQuade she was still very young, even younger than his own daughter. He frowned and hesitated before he began to tell her about her grandfather's affairs.

'May I speak frankly, Miss Capel?'

'Yes, please do. I need to know the truth if I am to decide what to do. And my name is Catherina, but my friends call me Rina.'

'Very well, Rina,' he said with a smile. 'It is true there are always taxes to pay when a landowner dies. Death duties we call them. Usually the estate will have accumulated capital from the rents and other income from the estate and set enough aside to pay death duties. Unfortunately, your parents lived beyond their income so there is little money left for paying taxes. Your grandfather was aware of this so he tried to protect his estate by putting the larger farms in your brother's name. We could not have known he would die fighting for his country, and at such a young age, but any death duties he would have had to pay will be greatly reduced due to the government's recent legislation. Even so it will be necessary to sell some of the outlying farms. Your grandfather thought it likely that your parents will sell Stavondale Tower and possibly buy a house in London or Edinburgh. He said they enjoy city life.'

'Buy a house in London?' Rina echoed, her eyes widening in dismay. 'But I don't want to live in London. I should hate living in a city all the time.'

'I suspect your parents know that, my dear. It is probably one of the reasons they would like to see you married.' He didn't tell her that her father had frequently run up gambling debts during his sojourns in the city, while her mother spent lavishly on the latest fashions and entertaining some of the gentry who were well out of their league. Her grandfather had known of his daughter-in-law's extravagance but he had discovered his son's weakness by accident a few years ago when some of his friends had come up to Scotland for the shooting. It was then he had changed his will in favour of his grandson. More recently he had changed it again to make what provision he could for his granddaughter's future and to give her some independence. Now she was looking at him with distress in her large dark eyes and the colour had drained from her rounded cheeks.

'What can I do?' she asked in a low voice.

'Your grandfather understood how you would feel if your home was sold or if you were forced to marry. He has done his best to ensure you have a choice. I expect you know your grandfather always employed a land agent. He used to live at Stavondale Manor. Your grandfather has recently modernised it.'

'I didn't know that,' Rina said. 'I haven't been to Manor Farm recently, except for the two paddocks nearest Grandfather's stables. I keep my pony there. Father says I must sell him now.' Her voice shook. 'Mother forbade me to go near any of the farms. She said it was not ladylike but grandfather always took me with him to visit his tenants if I was home for the holidays when he was still able to ride. He knew about Mother's instructions but he encouraged me to visit the Sinclairs at Bonnybrae. My parents will be furious if they discover I still visit regularly.'

'I see. Since your parents have not informed you themselves let me tell you the plans your grandfather made for you.' He looked down at his papers. 'He added a large

27

extension to Stavondale Manor with two extra bedrooms and a large sitting room. He raised the roof to make a third floor for servants and nursery accommodation and he installed plumbing and a hot water system, as well as two new bathrooms and a modern kitchen. You probably know he left Mrs MacCrindle the use of her cottage for her lifetime and a small income. He thought she would probably be happy to keep the house aired for your use whenever you want to stay there. He was adamant you must have a place you could call home, where you could be happy. He stated in his will that the income from Manor Farm should be paid to a trust account with my firm. Normally I would have expected him to name your father as your trustee instead of myself. We are to pay you a monthly sum from the farm profits to allow you to train as a nurse, if that is what you decide to do. And also for the upkeep of the house. He also left you the contents of his wing at Stavondale Tower. He thought you might choose some of them to furnish Stavondale Manor.'

'Oh!' Rina gasped and her eyes filled with tears. She blinked rapidly. 'Grandfather understood so well. He has thought of everything.' She frowned and looked up at Neil MacQuade. 'I have not been allowed in that wing since his death. Mother locked all the doors. Mrs MacCrindle is upset because she is not even allowed in to dust.'

'I see.' Neil MacQuade said shortly, his mouth tightening. He didn't know how valuable the contents would be but he would take steps to find out before Lady Capel disposed of them. 'I shall call to see your parents without delay. The house contents will be listed and valued. Meanwhile I hold a key for the front door.' He frowned. Had the old laird guessed the lengths his son and daughter-in-law might go to in order to deprive their daughter of her small inheritance? He wished Sir Reginald had added Manor Farm itself to the trust now, instead of waiting until Miss Capel reached the age of twenty-five. At that time the farm was to be put into her name in its entirety and she could run the farm as she wished and all the income would be hers.

'I don't know much about farming, Miss, er, Rina, so I have asked Mr McGill to supply me with quarterly accounts for everything which is bought and sold and produced at Manor Farm. I would be pleased if you would take an interest in them too. I hope to prove worthy of the trust your grandfather placed in me. I want to see you are treated fairly.

'Grandfather prided himself on being a good judge of men. I'm sure you will do your best for me.'

'I understand your parents are continuing to take beef, lamb, bacon, butter, milk, eggs and vegetables from Manor Farm, even though they are aware the income should come to you. And . . .'

'Maybe they don't know yet. Do they know Grandfather has arranged a small income for me?'

'Oh yes, they know,' MacQuade said darkly. 'I read the will to them. They should have informed you themselves since they prevented you from being present at the reading in person. However small your grandfather's legacy proves to be it means you can choose what you do with your life. I don't want to influence you or cause a rift between you and your parents but don't let anyone talk you into doing something unless your heart is in it.'

'It is a great relief to know I have a choice.'

'I'm afraid your parents will not be pleased to hear I have discussed the will with you.' He wondered if they had hoped to draw the income from Manor Farm themselves and give Rina a mere pittance. Maybe they intended to cheat her of the Manor House too if she married. The old laird had been wiser than he, or his late father, realised. Or maybe he understood how selfish and hard-hearted both of Rina's parents were. He wondered how any parent could fail to love their own child, especially one as intelligent and pleasant as Rina, with her bright eyes and wide smile. He was looking forward to introducing her to his younger daughter, Melissa. Maybe she was just the sort of friend his timid offspring needed.

'Now that I know it is possible I must find out how I can train to be a nurse.'

'Melissa, my daughter, may be able to help. She would like to be a nurse herself but she is rather shy and very lacking in self-confidence, quite unlike her elder sister and my son. She was a twin but her sister died when they were three years old. My wife and I have often wondered if it has had a lasting effect.'

'How sad,' Rina said sincerely. 'I would have loved to have a sister. How old is your daughter Mr MacQuade?'

'She was eighteen in January, six months older than you are, but she has never lived away from home. I confess her mother and I are anxious, wondering how she will get on living in a nurses' home but it is the only thing she wants to do. She is a very caring person. If she is very quiet it does not mean she is unfriendly. I hope you will excuse her if she seems so.'

'I am looking forward to meeting her and hearing what she has discovered about training.'

'In that case if you think of any questions we will discuss them over lunch. I will drive you to my home now.' He led her outside and to the side of the building where he opened the door of an automobile and indicated she should get in.

'Oh my! Is this yours? I have never seen a motor car so close before,' she said excitedly.

'So you cannot have ridden in one then? You may find it a little noisy compared to riding your pony but I hope you will not be afraid.'

'What kind is it? Have you had it a long time?"

'It is a Vauxhall. It was designed by an engineer called Pomeroy. This model did well in trials in Scotland. I was lucky to be able to buy it from the parents of an old friend. He was killed during the war. The Vauxhall firm are not making any more like this since the war.' Rina could tell he was very proud of his mode of transport, but as they drew onto the street and zoomed away, she clung on nervously.

'You don't need to be afraid,' MacQuade said with a grin. 'I am perfectly in control. It will not buck and throw you off as your horse might do.' Gradually Rina realised he really did seem to be in control of this iron monster and she relaxed her hold on her seat and began to enjoy the ride. How envious her father would be if he saw this. She knew he had wanted a motor car for some time and he had blamed her grandfather because he could not afford to buy one.

They drew into a street of large sandstone houses and Neil MacQuade drew the car to a halt on the roadside. All the houses had steps at the front and small, neat gardens.

'These houses and streets were built before anyone ever dreamed of motor cars being invented but we have a large garden at the back and a stable with a small barn where we kept two ponies and the trap. Eventually I shall make changes to house my car there but very few of the residents own a motor car yet. There is still room for the milkman and the grocer to pass by on the road with their horse and cart.'

'I had not considered that a motor car might need a stable,' Rina said with a smile as he led her up the steps and into a wide hallway with doors on either side and a wide staircase in front of them which curved to left and right at the top. Two doors at the far end obviously led to the kitchen and other back premises, including a small family parlour she learned later. A short plump woman with rosy cheeks and a welcoming smile came to greet them and Mr MacQuade introduced her as his wife. Rina was always quick to assess people and she knew she was going to like this motherly, comfortable woman. Her own smile was wide and friendly as they shook hands.

'It is kind of you to invite me to lunch, Mrs MacQuade but I am afraid I am a bit untidy.' She tried to smooth down her dark curly hair. Mrs MacQuade chuckled.

'No one ever emerges from Neil's monstrous machine looking tidy.' She raised her voice. 'Mel dear, will you come and show Miss Capel to the bathroom so that she can wash and tidy herself. I have put clean towels out.'

'Oh please call me Rina.'

'Rina? That is an unusual name, isn't it?' Mrs MacQuade said.

'My proper name is Catherina, and my parents call me that, but all my friends call me Rina.'

'Ah, here you are, Mel. Rina, my dear, this is Melissa, the youngest of the family. I'm afraid we all call her Mel.' The girl came forward shyly. She was small in stature and rounded like her mother but with a timid smile and rather anxious blue eyes. Her hair was brown and it hung down her back in a thick shining plait, making her look younger than her eighteen years.

'Hello Mel,' Rina smiled warmly and shook the hand which Mel held out so diffidently. 'I am really pleased to meet you. Your father says you want to train as a nurse and that is what I would like to do. I hope you will be able to tell me how I should go about training?'

'I will try.' Mel's eyes shone with a new radiance and her smile widened a little. 'First I will show you the bathroom so that you can tidy yourself. I will wait on the landing and show you down to the dining room.' A little while later as they descended the stairs together Mel said, 'We only use the dining room when Father brings his clients or other business-men people home. When we are on our own we use the small family room next to the kitchen.'

'Oh, I wish I had known. Sometimes, in fact often, I have had meals at Bonnybrae farm where the Sinclairs live, or with Aunt Maggie at Braeside, and they always eat in the kitchen. It is so warm and welcoming there.' She lowered her voice and said in conspiratorial tones. 'Mother would not approve of me saying so but the truth is I am so tired of learning what ladies are supposed to do, or not do, and how the gentry should live and all the etiquette.'

'Really?' Mel stopped halfway down the stairs. Rina saw relief in her eyes. 'I, er, we, Mama and I, we thought we should treat you like a lady. Father said you had spent a lot of time at a finishing school for young ladies and you will probably marry a rich lord.'

'I can't tell you how much I have hated these past two years,' Rina said vehemently. 'Everything seems so — so false and insincere. Truth didn't seem important so long as you gave the correct impression.'

'Oh! I had no idea. I-I thought you would be very er sophisticated.'

'I'm afraid not. I am a great disappointment to my mama. She is furious with me for even mentioning wanting to be a nurse. She is convinced such work must be too menial for any daughter of hers. That is what she says. I shall get no support from my parents but I hope your father will be able to give me advice. He said you may be able to help too.'

Waiting in the dining room Neil and Mary MacQuade raised their eyebrows at each other in astonishment. They could hear the murmur of the girls' voices and guessed they must have paused halfway down the stairs to continue their conversation. It was so unlike their mouse-like daughter to respond with more than yes or no in conversation with strangers, or even people she knew well. After lunch they were even more surprised when Melissa invited Rina to her bedroom to see the information she had received with her nursing application. Neil MacQuade had intended driving Rina back to the station on his way to the office but instead he said he would come back later and take her to catch the later train.

'It is more than we could ever have hoped that Mel would feel at ease with someone she has only just met, let alone a daughter of Lady Capel,' he said. 'This is a welcome surprise and Rina seems a delightful young person. I know her grandfather was afraid she would get a raw deal from her parents and I believe he may have been right.'

'All the more reason we should befriend the child then. If Mel should benefit as well it would be a blessing. I must confess the thought of her going away to live among strangers and being lonely and miserable is worrying me dreadfully.'

'I know. Me too. We'll take things slowly and see how they get on. Rina is not at all like Lady Capel as far as I can see.'

In the middle of the afternoon the two girls appeared in the kitchen and Mel pushed the kettle on to boil.

'Mel! Whatever are you doing, bringing Miss . . . er, Rina into the kitchen?'

'We're going to take afternoon tea in the wee parlour. Are you going to join us, Mama? I have so much to tell you.'

'Yes, but we should take tea in the drawing room when we have a guest dear.'

'Oh no, Mama. Rina says she much prefers a homely kitchen and she often shares a meal with the Sinclairs who are tenants of her father, and she has even discovered she has an aunt called Mrs Greig. Isn't that amazing?'

'I suppose it is. Didn't you know your aunt before Rina?'

'Oh yes, I knew her and I really liked her. Grandfather knew I used to visit her and he said she would probably prove to be a good friend to me if I needed one, and she has. I didn't know she was Grandfather's daughter though, but he told me himself before he died. He said he had not behaved like a gentleman should in his youth and Mrs Greig is father's half-sister, although she always believed Mr Sinclair was her father.'

'I see,' Mary MacQuade said slowly, as she processed this news, wondering whether Rina really understood the situation.

'My father refuses to believe it. He would be furious if he knew I had told anyone, but Mel's papa already knew. He has also told me Grandfather has left me a little money to let me train to be a nurse and I'm to get the Manor House to make my home if my parents sell Stavondale Tower and move to London. He says I can furnish it with things I like from Grandfather's wing. He is going to come himself and talk to my parents and do an — an inventory.' She frowned. 'I'm not sure what he meant.'

'And Mama,' Mel butted in with excitement. 'Rina has invited me to go to see her empty house and help her choose furniture to put in it if Father will take me there when he goes, and she has a pony of her own called Duke. She is going to give me a ride on him.'

'A ride? But Mel you never wanted a pony when Vicky and Charlie learned to ride.'

34

'That was because they were bigger than me and they made fun because I was nervous. Rina says Duke is very quiet. She will hold his bridle while we walk round his paddock.'

'Well! I can't believe this, but I am very pleased my dear.' She sighed happily. 'Life is a continual discovery. Now for tea. I have fresh scones and chocolate cake. Will that suit you both?'

'Oh yes please!' they chorused in unison, then both burst into laughter. Mary MacQuade was bemused. Mel was acting as a normal young girl should but she had never made friends easily, or wanted any of her school friends to come to the house. They were just finishing tea when Neil MacQuade arrived.

'Oh Daddy, you've come much earlier than we expected,' Mel cried. Her expressive face registered disappointment.

'Well I'm sorry if I have interrupted your girlish gossip,' he said with amusement and raised surprised eyebrows at his wife. 'As a matter of fact I had to come early because I have made an appointment for Rina with Mr Dixon, the bank manager. We are going to set up an account in your own name, Rina. It will not contain a lot of money but you may need some for household expenses if you do move into Stavondale Manor. Mr Dixon feels you are very young to have an account of your own but I have assured him your monthly income will be small and you seem to manage your own affairs already. He would like to meet you and explain how things work.'

'I did borrow money from three of my friends to pay for my train ticket from Gloucestershire,' Rina admitted reluctantly. 'I didn't like to borrow. Grandfather says it is not good, but I am so glad I arrived home in time to see Grandfather one last time. He gave me enough money to buy postal orders so I could repay my friends immediately. Mr Greig sent them off for me from the post office.'

'Did he? Have you heard from your friends since?'

'Oh yes. They all wrote to thank me for returning their money so promptly and to say how sorry they were to hear about Grandfather. Er . . . Grandfather also gave me a leather

35

purse containing twenty-five guineas. He said it was in case I needed anything until his affairs could be sorted out. He said it was a secret between us so I have not told Mama or Papa. I had to use one of the guineas today to buy my train ticket. I have more shillings and some florins and half crowns in my reticule now than I have ever had. I feel quite rich.' She grinned mischievously.

'Your grandfather obviously trusted you not to spend foolishly then, Rina. He must have guessed you might need money without asking your parents, or maybe he thought they might refuse.'

'He knew they had cut my allowance almost to nothing. That's why I had to borrow from my friends to pay my train fare home.'

'Then we shall tell Mr Dixon your grandfather had faith in you. It will reassure him.'

'Will he tell my father?'

'No. A good bank manager knows when to be discreet.'

'In that case I will bring twenty of the guineas to add to my new account to keep them safe.'

'That is a good idea and it will impress Mr Dixon. Your parents moved their account to a different bank when your grandfather first became ill.'

'I see,' she said slowly. She looked up at him then, her eyes troubled. 'Grandfather was worried because he suspected my parents were owing money. He blamed Mama but I don't think she could have spent money without Father's agreement, do you?'

'I don't think so, but I don't know your parents very well, Rina. You are my client now and it is your interests I must look after. I shall call at Stavondale on Monday.'

'Can I come with you and Rina to the station, Father?' Mel asked eagerly.

'Of course you can dear. The two of you can ride together in the back so long as you tie your hats on securely.'

Rina saw Joe Greig on the train but the seat next to him was already occupied so she waited until they both got off at their local station. She told him of her day's events as they walked along together. She was excited about having a bank account so she could get her own money when she needed it.

'And I have made a new friend called Mel MacQuade and she is going to train to be a nurse. I do hope we can go together. Will you give Aunt Maggie all my news?'

'I will,' Joe promised with a smile, 'and she will be as pleased as I am to know things are working out well for you after all.'

'I shall have to persuade Jamie to start writing letters to me again when I have to stay away.'

'I'm sure he will do that but I expect you will be too busy working to miss Jamie.'

'Oh no, I always miss him when I'm away. He is my very best friend.' As they drew near the small lodge house on the drive up to Stavondale Tower she said. 'Mr MacQuade is coming to spend most of the day on Monday at Stavondale so I shall be unable to call at Braeside that day. Will you tell Aunt Maggie? He is going to talk to my parents and I think Mel may be coming with them. He is bringing another man to value things in Grandfather's wing of Stavondale and make an inventory.'

'I suppose everything has to be valued for death duties. I hope it will not be too distressing for you Rina,' Joe said as they parted company, 'but you know where to find us if you need a bit of comfort. Maggie and I are always pleased to see you.' Rina looked up at him with a grateful smile. 'I know you are and I can't tell you how much that means to me, especially now Grandfather has gone.'

She had almost reached the stables when she saw Ernest, her grandfather's stable boy. He seemed agitated.

'Hello Ernest. Is Duke all right? Did you exercise him while I have been away?'

'Oh yes, Miss, and he's fine. It's your father, Miss. Sir Roger is in a terrible temper. He has been down here twice searching for you but none of us knew where you were. He even went to Mrs MacCrindle and Mrs Moffat to ask if they had seen you. At first he thought you must be out on Duke and had maybe taken a tumble but I told him you had not ridden Duke today. I hope that's all right, Miss?' He looked at Rina anxiously.

'Of course it is, Ernest. I wonder why my father needed to see me. Most days he doesn't care where I am, or what I do.' She frowned, knowing she ought not to have said that to the stable boy, and knowing too that he probably sensed her bitterness at her parents' neglect. 'Perhaps there's something wrong with Mother. Lady Stavondale hasn't had an accident has she?'

'Oh no, it's nothing like that Miss. There was a Lord, er . . . somebody or other, visiting for his dinner and your father wanted you to be there.'

'Ah, now I see.' Rina's face paled. Surely Lord Tannahill had not been to visit? Why would he come without warning? Or had he been invited? 'I had better hurry up to the house then.' She gave Ernest what she hoped was a reassuring smile but her heart was thumping as she entered the spacious front hall of the east wing of Stavondale Tower. Immediately her mother bustled from one of the rooms. Rina had never seen her look so angry. Lady Capel was one of those people who could be coldly cutting but she believed in keeping her dignity at all times. Today her cheeks were flushed with anger, her eyes narrowed.

'Where have you been? Why didn't you tell us your plans? How could you disappear for a whole day? Lord Tannahill called specially to see you?' She didn't wait for answers. She was too overwrought, but she had to pause for breath.

'I did not know Lord Tannahill was coming.' Rina knew she should have left it at that. 'But in any case, I have no wish to see him.'

'No wish to see him! You will never get another offer of marriage as good as his, you ungrateful, wretched girl! Your father searched everywhere for you. You made us look foolish when we could not find you. Lord Tannahill could not wait any longer. He was catching the train to London.'

'Neither of you usually care where I am, or what I do, so long as I don't get in the way of your own enjoyment with your friends.' Rina tried to keep the resentment out of her voice, but it was true, her parents had never spent time with her for as long as she could remember. She had had a nanny, then a governess, then boarding school when she was ten. It was her grandfather who had kept her company, teaching her to ride as soon as her short legs could straddle the pony's back, taking her with him to see his agent or visit his tenants. Her mother spluttered with anger, so unlike the lady she claimed to be that Rina almost laughed aloud. Her mother glared furiously.

'Well? Where have you been all day? Answer me! We know you have not been galloping round the countryside on that stupid pony, as you usually do.' Rina was not a coward and she hated telling lies but instinct warned her not to divulge all her business, exciting though it had been.

'I visited a friend.'

'A friend? You have no friends round here. They are all at the finishing school still, as you should be. I hope you have not been seeing any of your father's tenants?'

'No, I had lunch with Melissa and we spent a very enjoyable afternoon.'

'Melissa? Who . . . ?'

'Mel MacQuade. I went on the train. We had lunch at her home with her mama.'

'MacQuade?' Rina spun round at the sound of her father's voice, also raised in anger. 'MacQuade the lawyer?' he demanded.

'I believe Melissa is his daughter, yes,' Rina said quietly, biting back a smile.

'Her grandfather! He must have introduced them!' Lady Stavondale hissed. 'I told you he was a bad influence. He always has been. Now he's interfering even from the grave.'

'Don't talk rubbish, Helen,' Sir Roger snapped, making Rina's mother tighten her thin lips in fury. 'Have you told her she missed Lord Tannahill's visit? Does she understand what we expect her to do when he returns the weekend after this?'

'I have not had time to tell her anything. She has only just appeared.'

'Well tell her now. I'm going to change for dinner. And make sure she understands her duty.' No one would believe she was their only daughter the way they referred to her, Rina thought. Then it hit her what her father had said. What duty? And why was Lord Tannahill returning to stay for a weekend? Her heart began to thud. She stared at her mother.

'What does he mean?' she asked, her voice barely a hoarse whisper.

'Lord Tannahill wants to marry you as soon as it can be arranged. Since you have insisted on leaving the finishing school, even though we have paid your fees, we think it is time for you to marry before your rebellious spirit gets out of hand. He wants a son and heir before he gets any older.'

'But I don't want to marry anyone! I don't even know Lord Tannahill except as an acquaintance of my father's . . .'

'You will get to know him. That is the reason he is coming to stay. Entertaining him in the way he is accustomed will be very expensive so you must make the most of it and be sure to do as he wishes. We must order two new dresses for you for the evenings and . . .'

'No! No, I will not marry him.' Rina's face was white now but her dark eyes sparked with anger and indignation. 'I wanted to recoil when he kissed my hand. I felt the whiskers on his upper lip. It was revolting.' She shuddered, remembering some of the intimate things the older girls had revealed about their meetings with the men they were to marry.

'You will have to get used to more revolting things than that. It is what your father and I insist you must do for your own sake, and ours,' she added, barely aware she had said the words out loud until she saw Rina's mouth tighten, her expression set. 'And don't put on that mulish face with me, Catherina!' she said sharply. 'You are like your grandfather. He always wore the same stubborn look whenever your father demanded more money from the estate. At least you will have no worries regarding money. Lord Tannahill has a beautiful mansion in London. He will spend more time there when he has a wife so . . .'

'London! I don't want to live in London with anyone . . .'

'Of course you do. You will move in the same circles as your friends from the finishing school. You will be able to see them whenever you like, especially once you have provided an heir to the Tannahill Estates. Your father and I will be staying with you often. We enjoy the life in London.'

'Aah . . .' Rina muttered under her breath. That was what her parents wanted — a free house in London to enjoy the city life at someone else's expense. They didn't care about her, or her happiness. Rina was not given to self-pity but in her heart she knew it was only themselves her parents were thinking about. She sought refuge in anger and blinked rapidly to disperse the tears which were stinging her eyes.

'Grandfather was an old man but even he could see things are changing. He said the war had given women more independence. We no longer need to . . .'

'Your grandfather! Don't mention that man to me! You will do as we tell you.'

'No! I do not want, or need, marriage, especially not for your convenience. I told you I intend to train as a nurse. Even if . . .'

'A nurse,' her mother spat. 'If you want to care for somebody you can look after Lord Tannahill's six-year-old daughter. I didn't think you would want to be bothered with someone else's child so I told him he would have to send her to boarding school. He has agreed.'

'Lord Tannahill has a daughter?' Rina asked her eyes widening.

'Yes. I thought you would know. His first wife was wealthy but she was not young when they married. She died in childbirth. That's why he wants a young wife to bear him several sons.' Rina gasped at her mother's nerve. Her sheer arrogance in arranging the life of a six-year-old child, as well

41

as the life of her own daughter. Even amidst her tumultuous thoughts she spared a moment for the six-year-old who would be banished to a strange school with no one to care if she was unhappy.

'You're the most callous, selfish, hard-hearted person I know.' She ran from the room.

'Catherina! Come back here at once. I have not finished our conversation.' But Rina ran to her room, closed the door, and for the first time in her life, she turned the key in the lock. She flung herself on her bed and let the tears fall.

CHAPTER FOUR

Rina was not given to self-pity. She sat up and dried her eyes. She would run away. But where could she go? She knew Aunt Maggie and Uncle Joe would give her shelter but they were too near. She could not involve them. Her parents would seek revenge and probably tell the Sinclairs to leave the farm and deprive them of their livelihood. 'Why, oh why did you have to die and leave me with them, Grandfather?' she muttered aloud. Her parents really didn't care for anyone except themselves. She remembered what it said in the Bible about honour thy father and thy mother and for a moment she was filled with remorse, but then she remembered her father had done nothing to help her beloved grandfather. He had not even hired a nurse to care for him in his last days. They had not called in to see how he was. They had left his care to Mrs MacCrindle, his housekeeper, knowing she was powerless to remonstrate with them or make demands. Her young heart hardened against her parents. Thank God for Jamie, she thought. At least she had arrived home in time to share her grandfather's final hours. She bit hard on her lower lip to stop the tears falling again. What could she do? There was a tap on her bedroom door.

'Ye're to come down for dinner, Miss Rina. Your father is waiting. He — he said to come at once . . .' It was the diffident voice of Amy the young kitchen maid.

'Tell them I do not want any dinner, please Amy.'

'Sir Roger sounds very angry, Miss.' The young maid sounded anxious.

'Say I am not coming down again today,' Rina called back. It was true she felt she could not swallow food sitting at the same table as her parents while she felt so angry with them, so let down, so used. At least she had enjoyed a substantial afternoon tea with Mel and her mama. At the thought of Mel she sat bolt upright. Mr MacQuade had promised to call on her parents on Monday, as well as look at Stavondale Manor and spend time looking round her grandfather's wing of Stavondale Tower so that he could advise her how to proceed. Maybe he would be able to help, though she couldn't think what he could do. He couldn't prevent Lord Tannahill from coming to stay for the weekend.

Rina was surprised to find she had slept soundly in spite of her inner tumult. Daylight was illuminating her bedroom although it was still early. Her mother always had her breakfast in bed and never appeared before ten o'clock. Her father had no set routine but he always ate in the dining room. Rina knew it was terrible to regard her parents with contempt but she couldn't help it. Her father liked to act as though he was a great lord, even though he had done nothing to earn such status. She knew her mother had been bitterly disillusioned when she discovered he did not have a vast fortune compared to many gentlemen. Rina poured cold water into the basin and washed her face and hands. She felt wide awake and more cheerful when she was washed and dressed. She crept down to the kitchen to make herself a boiled egg and toast.

'Good morning Miss Rina,' Mrs Bell, the cook greeted her. 'I'll cook you some breakfast. What do you fancy?'

'That's all right, Mrs Bell, but thank you. 'I will make myself an egg and some toast and eat it in here if you don't mind,' The cook shook her head.

'Amy is busy cleaning out the fires. You know I don't mind you eating in my kitchen but what will your father say? He was very angry last night, Miss.'

'He will not know. If he asks where I am you can tell him I have gone for a ride on Duke.'

'Very well, Miss Rina. I'm sorry you're in trouble. If there is anything I can do . . . ?'

'There is nothing anyone can do.' Rina's mouth set firmly. She looked up at Mrs Bell. 'Did you see the gentleman who called unexpectedly yesterday?'

'Oh yes, Miss. But we did expect him. Lady Capel ordered a special menu the day before.'

'I see. Did you see him?'

'Yes Miss. I think he's a friend of your father's.'

'He is the man my parents want me to marry.' Rina said flatly, knowing her parents would be furious with her for discussing such a matter with the servants, but Mrs Bell had always been kind to her, and to Nat. She had rescued them both from various punishments more than once when they were young.

'Oh Miss, you must have misunderstood. The gentleman who came yesterday was an older man.'

'I haven't misunderstood. It is true. I have never defied my parents before, even when I thought they were being unfair.'

'I know you haven't Miss Rina. You were always a happy, smiling wee lassie.'

'I didn't know Lord Tannahill was to visit yesterday. They were angry because I was not here to entertain him. I don't want to marry anyone yet. I want to be a nurse and help people who need me.'

'That would certainly be worthwhile work,' Mrs Bell said slowly, 'but your mama?'

'She is very scathing about such occupations. Now, I have eaten a good breakfast and I shall go for a gallop to brighten my spirits.'

'Do be careful, Miss Rina. We wouldn't want anything to happen to you. Would you like some food to take with you?'

'Dear Mrs Bell, you're very kind, but I don't need food today. I want to call on Mrs MacCrindle.'

'She will be pleased to see you Miss. She is feeling very low since your grandfather's funeral. She can't even get into his home to dust his wee treasures.'

'Well maybe I shall be able to cheer her up a little.'

Mrs MacCrindle was certainly pleased to see her and she made no secret of the fact.

'Your father came here looking for you yesterday, Miss Rina. He was in a fine fury when none of us could tell him where ye were. He said they had a special guest he wanted you to meet.'

'They knew Lord Tannahill was expected so they should have warned me. Though, come to think of it I'm glad they didn't. He is the man they want me to marry so I'm pleased I missed him.'

'Ah, Miss . . .' the older woman wrung her hands. 'Your grandfather was afraid your parents might marry you off to some wealthy man at the first opportunity. He said he would do his best to help you. He wanted you to be happy and live your own life.'

'And that is exactly what I intend to do, Mrs Mac. Grandfather has done the best he can for us all. Can you keep a secret?' Mrs MacCrindle looked at her and smiled sadly.

'Aye, lassie, I can. Your grandfather would have told you that.'

'Well I went to see his lawyer yesterday, Mr MacQuade. He said I was to assure you that your legacy will be paid as soon as Grandfather's affairs can be sorted out and the death duties settled.'

'Oh, I'm not worried about that, Miss Rina. I do have a wee bit put by and he made sure I would have a roof over my head, but . . .'

'But you don't know what to do with yourself?' Rina smiled. 'Well, Mr MacQuade has a key to the front door of Grandfather's wing of Stavondale Tower and he is coming on Monday. He is bringing a man to value the contents in case

46

any of them are valuable for death duties but he says I can take anything I want from the carpets and furnishings and pictures and move them to Stavondale Manor. That's the house where the land agent used to live, when we had one.'

'I remember. Before he died your grandfather made great improvements. I wondered why he was going to so much trouble to make it so big and so grand.'

'He believed my parents will sell Stavondale Tower and move to the city. Mr MacQuade agrees. He thinks they want to move to London.'

'Move to London? To live, Miss Rina?'

'Yes. Grandfather understood how much I would hate to live in a city. He has done his best to make sure I have a home of my own. He thought you might be happy to keep it clean and aired until I need it?'

'Oh I would, Miss! Indeed I would. That's the best news I've had since Sir Reginald died. The manager at Manor Farm is anxious about his job too and he says a lot of the tenants are worried they will not be able to pay their rents now your father has increased them so much.'

'He has raised the rents already?'

'I think he must have been planning to do it ever since your grandfather first became ill, Miss.'

'I see.' Her first thought was for Jamie and his family. 'I'm glad you told me. You can tell Mr McGill his job at Manor Farm will be safe for some years, so long as I am allowed to stay here and train to be a nurse. I don't want to get married, especially to a man I barely know. I hope Mr MacQuade can help me persuade my parents, or find a way to defy them. They don't know he is coming on Monday. He thinks they will be annoyed with him for discussing Grandfather's will with me. I pray he can help. I don't want to marry Lord Tannahill.'

'I wish there was something I could do to help ye, Miss Rina.'

'There is, Mrs Mac. Miss MacQuade will be coming with her father. I'm sure you will like her. I know you will not have much time because we have to wait for Mr MacQuade to come with his key and let us in but I wondered — could you make luncheon for us please? I can give you money to buy what you need but there will not be much time to cook anything.'

'Oh Miss Rina, I'll be happy to do that,' Mrs Mac said with pleasure. 'That will be four of you?'

'Yes, if the other man stays for lunch.'

'Then I shall make a pot of vegetable soup and bake fresh bread at my own cottage. And I'll have a rabbit pie ready to pop in the oven as soon as we can get into the kitchen at Stavondale Tower. There's plenty of fruit and I'll bake fresh shortbread and ask Mr McGill to save me some cream. How will that do?'

'It will be absolutely splendid.' Rina demonstrated her delight with a hug for the plump little woman she had known all her life. She didn't care what her lady mother thought about not being familiar with servants. They were human beings, just as she was. 'Now I'm going for a ride on Duke. I need a good gallop so I can forget my fear of the future and cheer my spirits.'

Rina did exactly that. She believed Duke always knew how she was feeling and he greeted her with a friendly nicker, blowing his warm breath in her ear as though telling her he understood. Almost instinctively horse and rider found themselves on the track up to Braeside and Bonnybrae. Joe was a conscientious man and there was a problem with one of the looms so he had elected to go in and supervise its repair and make sure it was safe to operate even though it was his day off. Consequently, Maggie was on her own and it was no time at all before Rina was confiding her troubles, sitting at the kitchen table, drinking hot coffee and nibbling buttery shortbread fingers.

'I have never seen Mother so angry,' she confided. 'I didn't know Lord Tannahill was coming to visit but I'm glad I was not at home. I don't want to see him, but he is coming back on Friday evening and he will be staying over the weekend.'

'But surely you parents can't force you to marry a man you scarcely know, Rina, especially if he is as old as you say?' Maggie said slowly, her face troubled.

'He is forty-one, five years younger than Father. I thought of running away but I don't have anywhere I can go where they would not find me, and I really do want to train as a nurse. You would like my new friend, Melissa MacQuade. She is a little older than I am but she is very shy and quiet, or so her father said, but we talked all afternoon. She is coming to see me on Monday when Mr MacQuade comes to value the contents of Grandfather's house. I wish I could bring her to visit you but she can't ride and it is too far to ask her to walk. Why, oh why will my parents not let me choose my own friends and my own life?'

'I expect they think they know what is best for you, dear. Will you walk up to Bonnybrae with me?' Maggie asked. 'I'm going to make the dinner for Jamie and Jim. You can bring Duke and turn him into one of the paddocks while you eat with us.' So Rina led her pony and they walked together up the track. 'If Lord Tannahill is a reasonable man, and sensible, he will understand you don't wish to marry yet,' Maggie mused, searching her mind for a solution. 'Perhaps you should introduce him to your own friends, share your own interests with him. Make him see you may be young but you have a mind of your own. Show him how much you enjoy riding for one thing. Ask him to accompany you. Get him away from your parents. You might like him better than you think.'

'Not with a moustache that feels like a toothbrush!' Rina shivered.

'Maybe he will shave it off if you ask him.' Maggie was trying to be optimistic but she felt anxious for Rina with her lively mind and her love of life.

Later, eating dinner in the Bonnybrae kitchen, Rina was surprised when Jim gave much the same advice as Maggie had, especially since he was usually a man of few words.

'Be yourself, lassie. Ye're a fine young woman,' Jim advised. 'Let him see you can think for yourself. Tell him you want to make decisions about your life. Don't pretend to be different to please him or even to please your parents. We all respect you the way you are. Maybe he will see for himself that you're not ready to be his wife.' It warmed Rina's young heart to know they all cared deeply for her and for her future. Only Jamie was unusually quiet. He seemed subdued, almost moody.

'He has a daughter, six years old,' Rina remembered. 'Mother told him he would have to send her to boarding school out of the way. I think that would be cruel and I shall tell him so.' Jim bit back a smile. He had a feeling if Rina got this Lord Tannahill away from her parents she might express many more of her forthright views. It might be no bad thing to let him see she was no milk and water Miss, or the primping, flirtatious young thing he was probably expecting.

'If he has a daughter he must have had a wife.' Jamie had barely spoken until now. Everything would be different if Rina married her wealthy lord. He didn't like the idea at all, even though he knew it was not his business. 'Why does he want another wife?'

'She died when the wee girl was born,' Rina told him. 'Mother says he wants a young wife who will give him sons.' She shuddered. 'I don't want to give him sons, even if I knew how.' Maggie's heart ached for her. She was so innocent in many ways.

'You know Rina dear, if there is anything we can do to help, we will.'

'Would you let me bring him here? I shall tell him you are my very best friends in all the world.'

'I doubt if he would believe that,' Jim said wryly, 'and I can't imagine he would want to meet the likes o' us, but ye're welcome to bring him if that's what ye want.'

The meal was over and Rina had helped Maggie clear the table and wash the dishes, as she did automatically these days. Maggie had learned to accept her help. Jamie came through from the scullery.

'We have a pair of lambs needing fed from the bottle, Rina. Do you want to help with one of them?'

'Lambs already? Oh lovely! Of course I would like to feed them.'

'They're not easy fed. They're small and weak. The ewe lambed early so they got a bit starved.'

Maggie smiled as she watched the two young friends go out to the barn, each carrying a bottle of milk under their coats to keep it warm. The lamb teats were bigger than baby teats and tougher. She wondered if these two puny lambs would have been better learning to feed with baby teats.

'They may not survive in spite of Uncle Jim's efforts,' Jamie warned Rina as they approached the barn, 'but we couldn't leave them to die. It takes ages every day to give them feeds. We have to dribble it slowly into their mouths until they get stronger and learn to suck.'

'Oh they are tiny!' Rina exclaimed. 'They're adorable. I have never seen any so small and it is nearly eight years since I first helped you feed lambs.'

'I remember,' Jamie said with a sigh. 'Such a lot has happened since then,' he reflected as they settled themselves on a heap of clean straw each cradling a lamb on their knees. Rina saw at once it would take a lot of time and patience if these two were to survive.

'I will come as often as I can and help to feed them,' Rina volunteered, 'but I can't always get away. My parents, well my mother especially, is being difficult. She's desperate for me to marry Lord Tannahill because she thinks she will be able to stay in his mansion in London whenever she pleases if I am his wife. She doesn't care whether I'm happy or not. I think she will be glad if they sell Stavondale Tower. She prefers living in a city and entertaining all the time.'

'Sell the Tower? Would you like living in London?' Jamie was appalled at the thought.

'You know I would hate it. Grandfather knew too. Mrs Mac told me he has been making the land agent's house more modern. He renamed it Stavondale Manor. He wanted to be sure I would have a place to call home and be near people I know. Mr MacQuade knows I would like to train as a nurse.

We would not be paid for our first year of training but he says I shall get a small income for a few years once grandfather's affairs are sorted out. My parents didn't want me to know because it would give me a choice.' She sighed heavily. 'But they have authority over me until I'm twenty-one. I'm so afraid they will make me marry.'

As they talked the two lambs gradually swallowed enough milk to keep them going for another few hours. They set them back in the small straw pen beside their mother. She barely moved but she nuzzled them closer with her nose.

'She's still very sick,' Jamie said, watching her carefully. 'That's why she hasna much milk, but Uncle Jim hopes it will come if the lambs keep suckling her a bit.' When he turned he found Rina close beside him. He was surprised when she put her arms around his waist and laid her curly head against his chest. He could smell the lavender and lemon she used to rinse her hair and he felt a mix of emotions; desire stirred in his loins as well as the tenderness he had always felt since the first day they met. But Rina had been a ten-year-old child then. She was a young woman now, and a pretty one, and he was no longer a homesick boy.

'Rina?' he said softly. 'You know we shouldn't be . . .'

'Oh Jamie, I would be happy if it was you they wanted me to marry. I would love you and help you care for the animals, and. . . .'

'Rina,' Jamie gasped as she pressed her soft body close against him. He struggled to control his desire. Uncle Jim could come into the barn at any moment and see them together. He held Rina's shoulders gently so that she had to look up at him. 'You know your parents would never let you come here again, even to see Aunt Maggie, if they saw us together like this. In fact, if they knew we are alone together they would be shocked.'

'But don't you see Jamie, if you — if you,' she frowned uncertainly, 'if you did what my grandfather did to your grandmother they would have to let me marry you instead of Lord Tannahill. Grandfather said he didn't know he had

52

given your grandmother a baby until it was too late. He was already married when he knew, but I would tell Lord Tannahill and he would go away and never come back.'

'You know we couldn't do that, Rina. I have nothing of my own. I could not even provide a roof over our heads, let alone give you the sort of life you are accustomed to.'

'I don't want to live like a lady. Mother complains how difficult it is to get servants since the war but she should understand people fought for freedom and surely that means choice.'

'Your father would be furious. He would probably terminate the tenancy for Bonnybrae and put Uncle Jim out of the farm. It is the only home he has ever known. I would not even have a job.' He was horrified at the prospect of causing Uncle Jim so much trouble after he had taken him in and taught him how to run the farm and plough and sow and look after all the animals. 'Uncle Jim asked for me to be included as a joint tenant on the new tenancy agreements . . .'

'Did my father agree?'

'Yes, provided we agree to the increased rents and I take responsibility for paying all the rent if Uncle Jim became ill or circumstances change.'

'I see.' He felt Rina's body tremble against him. She sniffed hard and he knew she was struggling to hold back tears. She dropped her arms from around his waist but she kept her head bowed and would not look at him. He wanted to hug her, to comfort her. He wanted more than that but . . .

'You don't love me enough to want me for your wife,' she said in a low, wobbly voice.

'Oh Rina, I think I have always loved you since the day you gave me a lift on your pony, but it's because I care that I cannot take advantage of you. I promised Grandfather Sinclair I would never do that. He guessed I cared for you and it worried him because he knew you were a different class to humble farmers and your father's tenants. If I married you and gave you children and a life of poverty you would grow to hate me and . . .'

'I could never hate you, Jamie.'

'Oh yes you would, especially when your old friends disowned you.'

'If anyone did that they would not be worthy of being my friend.' She thought of Melissa. They had only just met yet Rina was sure they were going to be firm friends whatever happened — except perhaps if she married Lord Tannahill and had to live in London. She shuddered.

'I can't take that risk. I care too much for you to want you to live in poverty. Grandfather was a wise man. He read a lot and he was convinced farming will go back to being a struggle now the war is over and the government can bring in food on the big ships again. It was only when the Germans sank so many and the food stocks dwindled to starvation level that the politicians guaranteed the prices until 1922.'

'Oh Jamie what am I to do. I know you care for me really but . . .'

'I do, truly I do, Rina. I always will. You must be brave. Do as Aunt Maggie and Uncle Jim suggest and let this Lord Whatshisname see the real you. If you barely know him he can't know you either.

'My parents don't care. It is themselves they're thinking of. Grandfather said they spent too much money whenever they went to London.'

'We ought to go in or Uncle Jim will begin to wonder what's keeping us,' Jamie said gently. Rina rubbed her eyes, then nodded, giving him a wan smile.

'I will come again whenever I can to feed the wee lambs and I will not make any more demands.'

'Oh Rina, if only I could do what you want and marry you I would do it tomorrow, but I can't. One day you will thank me for not taking advantage. You're brave and strong and you must stand up to your parents if possible. I can't imagine any man wanting to marry a young girl against her will. You must make him see it is your parents' who want this marriage, not you.'

'I will try. Maybe they're rushing him too,' she added with a spark of hope.

* * *

When Neil MacQuade and Melissa arrived, Rina was already waiting on the stone veranda of her grandfather's wing at Stavondale Tower. He unlocked the heavy oak door and swung it open. The old house already had a fusty smell. Rina hated the forsaken, unlived in atmosphere and quickly opened several of the windows. Mel helped her. Rina lost no time in telling the lawyer of Lord Tannahill's proposed stay with them the coming weekend.

'My parents say I am underage and I have no choice. I must obey their wishes and marry him,' she told him. Her voice wobbled in spite of her determination to stay calm. Her dark eyes were wide and troubled as she gazed hopefully at the only person left who might be able to help.

'I see,' Neil MacQuade said frowning. 'Your grandfather feared you might be forced into marriage against your will. He did his best to make sure you had a choice. It is true, you are still very young and under your parents' care, but I would have expected them to wait a year as a mark of respect before planning a wedding. I think I had better call on them. Mr Fell, the valuer, has a pony and trap so he will be here soon to value the contents of this wing of Stavondale Tower. It is better if you stay here to show him round. I will deal with your parents on my own.'

'Thank you,' Rina breathed with relief. 'Would it be all right if Mel and I run down to Mrs Mac's cottage and help her carry the food she is preparing for our luncheon? We shall not be more than ten minutes.'

'Aah, that is a splendid arrangement. Thank you Miss . . . thank you Rina.' He smiled warmly. He had known they would not be welcome for lunch at Lady Capel's, especially when she knew he had informed her daughter of nearly all the provisions surrounding her legacy. It gave Rina options for a future of her own choosing — so long as she was not rushed into marriage before she was of an age to make decisions. 'I will wait here for Mr Fell until you return. I will take a look around. Is there anything you would particularly like to keep for yourself, Rina?'

'Oh yes. I would like to have the painting of my great-grandmother. She was Grandfather's mother. She is also the grandmother of Aunt Maggie. You know, that's Mrs Greig?'

'Aah yes, I remember hearing of a connection . . .'

'Grandfather said we both resemble his mother, or at least Aunt Maggie did when she was a girl. She had dark hair like mine then but she has wavy white hair now.'

'I see.' Neil MacQuade bit back a smile at Rina's innocent acceptance of the situation. In his granddaughter's eyes Sir Reginald could never have committed any real sin, but it was a skeleton in the Capel family cupboard which her father was at pains to deny.

He was right when he surmised Sir Roger and Lady Capel would not be happy with him for discussing Sir Reginald's will with their daughter. They were absolutely furious but he stood his ground, his mouth tightening as he listened to their abuse.

'I was employed to handle Sir Reginald's affairs and I shall do so until his estate is finalised. Miss Capel should have been here for the reading of the will. He wanted her to know of the provisions he had made. He wanted to give her a choice to follow a career if that is what she wished. Above all he did not want to see her forced into marriage with a man old enough to be her father.' He had not intended to say that but they had roused his temper. He understood now why Rina was so anxious.

'That has nothing to do with you. We are her parents and she will do as we tell her.'

'Her grandfather hoped to prevent this situation. He knew about your gambling debts, Sir Roger and he predicted that Lady Capel would want to sell Stavondale Tower and move to the city.' MacQuade did not bother to conceal his contempt. 'I have not told Catherina yet that she will own Manor Farm when she is twenty-five, but she knows she can make the house her home and she will have a small income from the farm produce. Mr McGill has agreed to supply quarterly accounts to my office so in future you will be required to pay for any produce you use from there in order for your daughter to draw an income while she trains as a nurse. I believe you already know that is what she wants to do.' Lady Capel's face went white.

'A nurse!' she hissed in contempt. 'It is no more than a childish whim. She arrived in time to see her grandfather during his last days and her head is filled with nonsense. She should never have been here. No doubt you are responsible for that too!' MacQuade's eyes widened but he neither admitted nor denied it.

'It is more than a childish whim. She has asked me and my family to help in any way we can to find a hospital where she will receive good instruction and be able to take examinations.'

'No!' Lady Capel almost screamed with rage. 'No daughter of mine will do such menial work. Who knows what illness she might contract? She will do as we say. She will marry Lord Tannahill before her eighteenth birthday in June.' Neil MacQuade looked from one to the other, his mouth tightening. Sir Roger Capel had barely spoken since his gambling debts had been mentioned. He looked pale and strained. Surely he had not believed his father was completely ignorant of his feckless ways. An idea was forming in his own mind. He doubted whether he could make it stand in a court of law but when he thought of Rina being used as a sacrificial lamb in a marriage she did not want — all for the sake of her selfish parents, well he would take a risk.

'Are you aware that Sir Reginald Capel appointed me, and my firm, which now includes my son, as trustees for Miss Capel until she is twenty-five? He said he considered it necessary for her own sake. I'm beginning to realise it was not to protect her against her own youthful whims and desires, nor against possible fortune hunters as I had thought, it was to protect her against her own parents. If you insist on your daughter marrying against her will, I shall apply to have her made a ward of court to protect her.'

'You can't do that!' Lady Capel had been standing, facing up to him like a cock in combat. Now she flopped onto a nearby chair. 'Say something Roger! Tell this — this upstart lawyer . . . Tell him he can't tell us what we can do with our own child. He can't, can he?'

'I don't know,' Sir Roger said a trifle wearily. He pushed his fingers through his hair. 'You know I am not happy about forcing Catherina into a marriage with Tannahill. He is not the soft option you seem to think. He will rule his own roost, and those in it. I'm not saying he wouldn't look after her but you think you can set yourself up in his London mansion on the pretext that Catherina is a young wife and needs help. I don't think he would allow you to take over so easily, even if Catherina wanted us there, and I doubt if she would. She has too much spirit. Too much of my father in her to accept things without a fight. Why do you think she has already sought the help of MacQuade here?'

'She's ruined,' Lady Capel almost sobbed with frustration. 'Your father spoiled her from the day he saw her. Like his mother, he said. Now he's still interfering in our lives from the grave.'

'Unless you have any questions?' Neil MacQuade interrupted, 'I shall go and oversee the valuation of the contents of Sir Reginald's home. You are aware that he left them to his granddaughter of course, as stated in his will, but they do need to be valued for death duties. He told me he had a rare collection of jade which he inherited from an uncle, or great uncle, I think.' He watched the colour drain from Lady Capel's face and her lips became a thin line. He knew then why she had locked the doors of her late father-in-law's home and prevented anyone from entering, even Catherina, who had every right. 'He also mentioned two valuable Chinese vases. He wanted to be sure Catherina understood their value. He thought we should take them to the bank for safekeeping until she has a home of her own and can appreciate their value, unless she finds herself desperately short of money at a later date then he gave his blessing for her to sell them.'

'I removed the jade pieces,' Lady Capel said sullenly, her eyes full of malice.

'Did you, Helen? You didn't say,' Sir Roger remarked in surprise.

'Yes,' MacQuade said mildly, 'I though the cabinet looked emptier than usual but I have not had a close examination yet. I thought I should inform you we were at the house before doing so. Sir Reginald gave me a key.'

'He had no business to do that! I was going to keep the jade safely.'

'I'm afraid I shall need to take the collection with me now for the purposes of the valuation.' He guessed she had intended to turn the jade into cash the next time she was in London. He doubted whether she would even have told her husband. His contempt increased and he was more determined than ever to protect Catherina and her interests in any way he could.

CHAPTER FIVE

Rina was filled with dread at the prospect of seeing Lord Tannahill when Friday dawned. She had been back at Bonnybrae to help Jamie with the lambs every day since the valuation on Monday, a day which she had enjoyed due to Melissa. She thought Mel had enjoyed it too, helping her choose the furniture and carpets which could be moved to Stavondale Manor. Mr MacQuade had given her a copy of the valuation, including the jade collection and the Chinese vases, as well as a receipt to say he was taking them to the bank for safekeeping. He had warned her to keep both of them safely locked away if she had a jewellery box, or some other safe place. Rina had been surprised on Monday evening when the first thing her mother asked was, 'Have you brought the jade back here so we can keep it safely?'

'No Mr MacQuade took it away to the bank.' She saw that her mother was furious and instinct made her keep silent about the valuation certificate and the receipt. That evening she put both in an envelope and added a letter to say if anything should happen to her, the contents would belong to Mrs Margaret Greig to use as she wished. She sealed it with sealing wax and wrote her own name on the outside. On Tuesday morning when she rode over to Bonnybrae she gave the envelope to Maggie and asked her to keep it safely. It did not strike her as strange that she trusted her grandfather's illegitimate daughter more than her mother.

The tiny lambs were surviving and she loved the peace and contentment as she sat beside Jamie in the barn patiently coaxing each one to swallow the precious milk. The ewe's health was improving and her milk supply had increased but Jamie explained it would never be enough to rear both lambs without supplementing them from a bottle.

'You two are doing a good job there,' Jim said, coming into the barn. 'She is one of our best ewes and these two are both ewe lambs so if they survive you will both deserve a special reward.'

'I don't need a reward,' Rina said, glancing up at him. 'I love feeding them and helping them survive. It will be enough if I can see them skipping around the field when the weather gets warmer.'

'Ye're a good lassie, Rina. Nobody would believe ye were the laird's daughter, or that you had spent so much time at a finishing school for young ladies.' Rina smiled sadly.

'Even Grandfather knew that was a waste of time for me.'

Jamie understood how tense and agitated Rina felt as the weekend drew near with Lord Tannahill's visit. He was extra gentle and affectionate. He hated the thought of her belonging to anyone else, especially a man as old as her father. The thought made him shudder with revulsion, but he knew he could never do as she had asked, not even to save her from a marriage she dreaded. Maggie understood too. She had considered over and over how they could help. On Friday afternoon she said doubtfully, 'I could make a lunch at midday, here at Bonnybrae, Rina, if you think Lord Tannahill would not be offended?'

'You would do that? For my sake?' Rina asked eagerly, her eyes misting with tears.

'If you do want him to see that some of your friends are very ordinary folk . . .' Rina flew into her arms and hugged her.

'You're not ordinary. You're kind and generous. If Lord Tannahill doesn't enjoy riding, then I shall tell him he can stay at home and talk to Mother. He must see I have my own friends and interests,' she said desperately. 'Mr MacQuade promised to see if there is anything he can do to help. He has also invited us for a meal at midday on Sunday, after we have been to church. Mother doesn't know yet. She will not be pleased. She says she doesn't like lawyers but I think it is only Mr MacQuade. She wouldn't even meet my new friend, Mel.'

'It is difficult to know what anyone can do to help while you are so young and in your parents' care,' Maggie said uncertainly. 'Perhaps they do know what is best for your future, Rina?'

'Not if they force me into marriage,' Rina insisted, thrusting out her small jaw.

Jamie led Duke in from the paddock on Friday. He gave her a goodbye hug and would have kissed her cheek but she turned her head so their lips met. She clung to him. 'Oh Jamie,' she whispered brokenly, 'promise you will always be my friend, whatever happens.'

'You know I will, Rina.' His voice was gruff. 'Let him know what is in your heart. Tell him what is on your mind and of your ambitions and dreams. He doesn't know if you don't tell him. Now you'd better get home and change for dinner before he sees you.' He slapped Duke's rump as soon as she was safely on his back and Rina cantered away, but it was several minutes before she had blinked away her tears, clenched her teeth and set Duke to a gallop. She was still riding fast when they reached the drive into Stavondale and almost ran into a motor car which had arrived from the other direction. Duke had never seen a motor car at close quarters or heard an engine. He was inclined to buck and prance skittishly until Rina leaned forward and patted his neck and spoke to him in soothing tones, but her own heart was beating fast. Could the man in the motor car be Lord Tannahill? Who else could it be? She had intended to reach home well before he arrived and be changed and ladylike as her mother expected. Now there would be trouble before the weekend had even begun. When the car reached the turnoff for the stable yard it stopped just beyond the entrance and the driver got out. He walked towards the stables as Rina jumped lightly from Duke's back.

'Do you always ride so fast Miss Catherina Capel?' he asked, but there was amusement in his deep voice and a glimmer of admiration in his eyes.

'Not always so fast, no, Lord Tannahill, though Duke and I do enjoy a good gallop. We expected to be home before you arrived. Now I shall be in trouble.'

'In trouble? Surely not. I admired the way you controlled your horse. It is clear you enjoy riding. I like a good gallop myself, especially when following the hunt.'

'You don't spend all your time in London then, as my mother seems to think?'

'I get away whenever I can but I have affairs which often need my attention in the city and I try to take my seat regularly in the House of Lords to keep up to date.'

'I see.' Rina's tone was as stiff as her manner.

'Do you have a horse I could borrow? I would enjoy a ride out tomorrow. Perhaps you could show me around the estate and the countryside?' Rina's eyes widened. This was exactly what she had planned but had scarcely dared to hope for.

'You could borrow Devon, my father's horse. He doesn't get enough exercise so I'm sure Father wouldn't mind.' This suited her admirably but she knew her mother would object. 'I'm afraid my mother will be making other arrangements for your entertainment so you will have to make it clear what you would prefer,' she told him firmly.

'You think she will disapprove?' He wasn't sure whether Rina gave a reluctant smile or a grimace.

'I know she will, Lord Tannahill. I may as well be honest with you from the beginning. I am not the demure, well-behaved young lady my mother would have you believe and I am no use at pretending. She doesn't approve of me riding. She will certainly not be pleased if she knows you have seen me wearing breeches and riding astride.' She looked him in the eye defiantly. He saw she had spirit and he was glad. He hadn't the stomach for a simpering young Miss who was intent on pleasing both him and her mama.

'So how do you manage to avoid her seeing you like this?' he asked and there was no doubting the amusement curving his mouth. Rina's eyes widened when she saw his upper lip.

'You've shaved it off. How did you know I hated it?' her cheeks flushed scarlet when she realised what she had said. 'Y-your m-moustache I m-meant,' she stammered. 'I'm sorry. I didn't mean to be rude.'

'That's all right.' His eyes twinkled. 'I'm pleased I have obliged you, however unintentionally. Now tell me, how do you deceive your lady mother about your — er, costume? I am intrigued.'

'Grandfather never disapproved. He bought me my first pair of breeches and a jacket and I've always had a room of my own in his home where I changed. Mother locked up the house after he died. I couldn't get in but I have been using one of the boxes at the end of the stables. Ernest, the stable boy, knew but he would not have told anyone. Grandfather's lawyer came on Monday to value the contents of his home. He had a key and he has left it with me so I can get into my old room again now. I will be as quick as I can, but I do need to give Duke a good grooming before I turn him out to his paddock.'

'You look after him yourself?' Lord Tannahill raised his eyebrows in surprise.

'Of course I do. Grandfather said it was one of the first essentials if I wanted to ride and have a pony of my own. He taught me when I was three years old.' Her love and admiration for the old man shone in her eyes and Lord Tannahill wished he had met him. Perhaps he was one member of the Capel family he could have respected, and his granddaughter might be another. At least she seemed sincere and honest and not at all like her mother and her affectations.

'Now if you will excuse me. I'm afraid Mother is going to be very annoyed that I am not groomed myself, and dressed and waiting to greet you as she believes a young lady should.'

'In that case I could always help you groom your horse and wait until you change into respectable attire, then I can follow after a short interval.'

'Respectable? So you don't approve either,' she sighed. 'I suppose it is because you are as old as my parents and it is the way you think.' She didn't see Lord Tannahill wince. She was right of course. For the first time he wished he had been fifteen years younger. She was so delightfully young and fresh and honest.

'I didn't say I don't approve. I was simply assuming 'respectable' is what your mother would say.' True to his word he helped her groom Duke and she could see by the way he wielded the brush and the strength behind his arm that he was in the habit of grooming his own horses, at least some of the time. She approved of that. Afterward he followed her to the house. She hesitated before she unlocked the door.

'You want to come in while I change my clothes?' He saw the doubt and confusion in her expressive face.

'You are quite safe, Catherina,' he said gently. 'I have never forced myself on a woman yet. I have no intention of starting now.' Rina blushed.

'Thank you,' she said gruffly. While she changed Lord Tannahill strolled around the hall looking at family portraits and one or two oil paintings. As far as he could tell none of them were of exceptional value. Rina joined him, struggling to replace the pins in her hair as she ran down the wide staircase.

'That was quick.' He smiled, knowing most young women spent a long time on clothes and preening in front of their mirrors, especially if they were hoping to attract a man's attention. Clearly that was not Catherina's aim, he thought wryly. She was more concerned with avoiding her mother's anger than pleasing him with her appearance.

'You will need to lock the door again so I will wait in my car for a few minutes to give you time to placate your mama.'

'If you're sure? I know Grandfather's servants are completely trustworthy if I leave the door unlocked. In any case Mr MacQuade has removed the only items of value so they can be kept safely in the bank. Mother was not happy with him for doing that.' She frowned thoughtfully, then remembered she was keeping him waiting and she set off at a surprisingly fast run towards the wing of Stavondale Tower where her parents lived. He could not hide his smile. No one would believe she had spent the past eighteen months at a school for young ladies learning to be elegant and to please a gentleman at all costs. He suspected Miss Catherina Capel was a law unto herself in spite of her mother's assertions that she was ready for marriage.

Catherina almost collided with her mother but she did not stop to listen to her tirade. Instead she ran lightly up the stairs to her room to wash and change into the new dress already laid out on the bed. It had too many frills and too much lace but it had not been her choice. At least the deep blue suited her and the material fell almost to her feet like a waterfall of silk making her look slimmer. She considered the neckline was far too low but she collected the cream lace shawl which had been the last Christmas gift her grandfather had bought for her. Since he had never been far from his home for many months she wondered how he had obtained it, but it was too late to ask him now. She made her way slowly downstairs to find her mother effusively greeting Lord Tannahill. He raised his eyes to watch her descending the stairs and Rina thought she saw admiration in them. That was the last thing she wanted. She felt like pulling a childish face. Then he gave a very definite wink as her mother ushered him towards her and she had a sudden urge to laugh. Did he not realise it was her mother who was so eager for this marriage and she would prove the most reluctant bride any man could have if she was forced to marry him?

The staff at Stavondale had been cut to the minimum but her mother still clung to her own ladies' maid and her father still had his valet, though both were growing old so they had been exempt from war duties. During Lord Tannahill's visit Lady Capel had employed Victor, the gardener's youngest son, to act as footman, and Lucy, a niece of Mrs Bell, to wait at table. She was determined to keep up appearances and hide the fact that they could no longer afford the large staff she had once insisted on. Dinner was served in the main dining room but since there were only four of them several of the mahogany leaves had been removed from the long table and stored in their stand in the entrance hall. The smaller table made the meal more intimate and Rina was not sure she liked that, since it meant Lord Tannahill was seated directly opposite her. Lady Capel had already given Lucy a stern lecture about the importance of this particular guest and the service she was expecting but the maid was young and not very experienced at silver service, nor at serving on her own. Her hand shook like an aspen leaf as she tried to hold the soup bowls in one hand and ladle the soup with the other. It was fortunate there were only four of them and she succeeded without incident, other than a splash or two on the edge of the dishes. Rina felt sorry for Lucy when she saw her mother's stony face and gimlet eyes fixed on the girl. As she finished serving the soup Rina drew her close.

'Ask Mrs Bell to make sure the plates are hot and the tureens too before she sets them into their silver stands,' she said in a low voice. 'Bring them in on trays and set them on the table. We are perfectly able to serve ourselves.'

'Oh thank ye, Miss Rina,' Lucy whispered with noticeable relief.

'What did you say to the girl?' her mother demanded sharply as Lucy left the room.

'I told her we could serve ourselves if she brings in the dishes and sets them on the table.'

'You had no business to give instructions . . .'

'Mother,' Rina said patiently, but with a firmness which surprised Lady Capel into silence for a moment, 'anyone can see Lucy is as nervous as a kitten. It's no use pretending. She's not in the habit of serving at table. Would you rather end up with mashed potato in your lap, or gravy down Lord Tannahill's dinner jacket?' Her mother opened her mouth to retort but Lord Tannahill beat her to it.

'I much prefer to help myself, then I see what is on offer,' he said genially. 'It is good to see your daughter is considerate towards your staff, Lady Capel.' He turned to speak to his host without waiting for a reply and Lady Capel closed her mouth with a snap. 'Times are changing since the war. It's not so easy to replace the younger members of staff we lost when they were called to fight. I expect you are finding the same, Sir Roger?'

'You're right there. Many of them have seen a different side to life. They don't want to be servants.'

'Who can blame them? I hope my own daughter will grow up with some understanding of the difficulties other people face.'

'Ah yes, your daughter,' Lady Capel said. 'I suppose you will have been making plans to send her to boarding school in September?'

'I thought you said she was only six years old, Mother?' Rina said.

'She was six in February,' Lord Tannahill replied evenly but Rina saw his eyes were shadowed.

'It would be cruel to send such a young child away to school.' Rina looked him in the eye. She sensed her mother was glaring at her, willing her to be quiet, but Rina ignored her. 'Surely it's bad enough that she's lost her mama?'

'Boarding school will teach her to be independent,' Lady Capel stated with a quelling glare.

'And probably make her very unhappy,' Catherina persisted. 'She will think no one loves her. I was ten when you sent me away and I hated it. I tried to tell you, but neither of you listened. Grandfather was the only one who understood.' She threw a challenging glance at Lord Tannahill. 'Are you so hard and heartless you would send your own child away while she is still so young?'

'I can assure you I am neither hard nor heartless where Sylvia is concerned,' Lord Tannahill replied and there was a softening in his eyes. 'She is an adorable child but I do not see as much of her as I would like. She loves Nanny Bloom and I believe the feeling is mutual. She seems to be getting along very well with the young governess I employed recently too.'

'Then let her be happy while . . .'

'Catherina, will you be quiet!' her mother ordered. 'You don't know what you're talking about. You would not want another woman's child running around when you marry Lord Tannahill.'

'He has not asked me to marry him,' Rina said swiftly, her cheeks flushing with anger. Her mouth tightened. 'And I have told you, several times, I have no desire to marry anyone yet.'

'Catherina! Apologise to Lord Tannahill at once.'

'Why should I apologise for telling the truth?' She glanced across the table then back to her mother. 'You never listen to what I am telling you, Mama so I shall gladly leave the company.' She pushed back her chair 'Good night, Lord Tannahill. I hope you will not feel you have had a wasted journey.'

'Indeed I think my journey will have been very worthwhile. I look forward to riding out with you in the morning as we arranged?'

'If you're sure that is still what you want?'

'You — you're riding together tomorrow?' Rina saw relief in her mother's eyes, then she smiled like a cat with the cream. Rina sighed audibly.

'I hoped we could ride together if you don't mind me borrowing one of your horses?' Lord Tannahill said smoothly, looking at Sir Roger.

'Of course you may ride Roger's horse,' Lady Capel insisted before her husband could reply.

As Rina closed the door behind her she heard her mother making excuses for her behaviour and resuming her flirting and simpering. Didn't she realise how foolish she was being? Rina cringed inwardly. She was surprised Lord Tannahill still wanted to go riding with her. She could never have managed the arrangement if he had not already agreed to it, she realised. He had handled her mother skilfully.

The following morning Rina told Mrs Bell they would not be back for luncheon at midday but they would return in good time for dinner that evening. Lord Tannahill overheard her and his eyes narrowed thoughtfully. He was looking forward to a good ride but he had a feeling Miss Catherina Capel had planned her day before they even met. Was he being manipulated?

'Does this mean I am to starve until dinner tonight?' he asked, quirking an eyebrow at her?'

'Of course not. So long as you don't mind good plain fare you will be well fed.'

'I enjoy good food without so many trimmings that the meat is disguised. I had hoped you would show me around your father's estate. I don't know the area well but I assumed there were only small villages and no old coaching inns or other places where we might dine.' They were on their way to the stables and Rina turned to face him.

'Can we be absolutely honest with each other without offence?'

'Are you ever anything else but honest, Catherina?

'I like to think I am sincere at least. I am not good at pretence, Lord Tannahill, though I don't mean to be blunt or hurtful. I hated the sort of pretence they would have had us practise at the school for young ladies and the flirting and eye fluttering makes me feel quite sick.' She didn't say when she saw her mother doing it, but Lord Tannahill guessed that is what she meant. He had seen her cringe and he sympathised.

'Very well. I think my shoulders are broad enough to stand anything you may wish to say, so long as you don't plan to starve me of my lunch?' Rina smiled then and he glimpsed the youthful impishness.

'Then I must tell you plainly it is not personal when I say I do not want to be married yet. I would like to train to be a nurse and help people who are sick.'

'I see . . .' Lord Tannahill whistled. He had not expected that. 'What does Lady Capel think to that?'

'She thinks it is a silly whim and that it will pass. She is adamant that I should be married soon and she insists you are the man I must marry. I thought if you meet my friends, the people with whom I feel relaxed and comfortable, people who could never move in your circle, then you might decide I am not the sort of person you want for a wife anyway.' She raised her small chin defiantly. 'If ever I do marry I do not expect to give up my friends to suit a husband however many titles he may have.'

'I understand,' Lord Tannahill said quietly but she saw the amusement in his eyes and the curve of his mouth. 'So it is not the difference in our ages which is the only problem?'

'We-ell, you are almost as old as my father, although I admit you do not look it and you seem very lithe and fit. I think I could have enjoyed your company if you had been my uncle or a much older brother,' she said truthfully. He tried not to wince.

'I think you may be right about companionship. I find your mixture of mature wisdom and youthful honesty a refreshing change from the usual company I keep. While we are being frank may I ask if you understand the state of your father's affairs, Catherina? Or why your mama is so keen for you to marry me?'

'I don't know the details but I do understand there are death duties to pay and that my parents have not allowed for such things as they should have done. I believe the outlying farms are to be sold to raise the money. Grandfather might not have worried about that but he was concerned because he felt my parents spent too much time in London and one of his old friends hinted that my father had other debts from gambling. He always felt my mother wanted to move in circles beyond her reach too. Mother blamed Grandfather for keeping tight purse strings, as she called it. I think she thought my father was wealthier than he was and she has been bitter and disappointed with her life at Stavondale.'

'You seem to have a fair grasp of the situation.' He was surprised. 'Did your grandfather discuss these things with you?'

'He talked to me a lot during the past eighteen months. He was fairly sure my parents will sell Stavondale Tower so he left a house for me. I can take whatever I want from his wing to furnish it. He knew I would hate living in the city you see. I am also to get a small allowance. He knew I wanted to train as a nurse and that I would need money to do that for the first few years.' She looked up at him, her eyes pleading for understanding. 'He was afraid my parents might force me into marriage and he wanted me to know I have a choice, even though being a nurse will not be easy.'

'I see. Your grandfather was a wise man and he must have loved you very much.'

'Oh he did, just as I loved him more than anyone in the world,' she said with conviction.' The impish smile flashed briefly. 'Of course I know he was not perfect. He told me he did not always behave like a gentleman when he was a young man.'

'Did he indeed? I suppose none of us are perfect, especially in our youth. Are you going to tell me what great sins he committed?'

'I will tell you later when we return from our ride. Now we had better get going.'

'Don't you want to change into your breeches first?' he asked, amusement glinting in his eyes.

'Wouldn't you object to being seen with me dressed like a boy?' she asked doubtfully.

'Of course I wouldn't object if you feel more comfortable and if it makes you feel safer to ride astride. The main thing is that you enjoy riding, as I do myself. I am looking forward to it whatever costume you choose to wear.'

'In that case I do prefer my breeches and jacket. I will go and change now, but first I will ask Ernest to change the side saddle for my usual one.'

'I'll do that while I'm waiting.'

'You will? I thought most gentlemen needed lots of valets and footmen and grooms before they could set out for the day.' She gave him a merry smile.

'Not this gentleman, cheeky Miss.' He grinned as he made his way to the stable, wishing once more he was a young man in his twenties again.

They chatted companionably as they cantered along the narrow country roads. Few people had motor cars in this area, or even in the towns, but they did need to draw aside once or twice for a horse and cart.

'The tenants may not remember who I am,' Rina said. 'It is a long time since I accompanied Grandfather. He visited them all regularly, even though he employed an agent. He disapproved when my father sacked the agent. He has increased the rents recently so they may not welcome us.'

'Don't worry. If we are not welcome, we shall not stay.' They came to a long straight stretch of smooth track and Rina let Duke have his head and took off at a gallop. Lord Tannahill followed but he soon realised Devon was not as fit as he ought to be for a four-year-old and when Rina put her horse to jump over a hedge he wondered whether he dare follow. Fortunately Devon obeyed and they landed safely.

'This field belongs to one of the farms we're going to and Duke enjoys a jump or two.'

'It is not only Duke who enjoys the jump. I can see the exhilaration in your face. You come alive.'

When they arrived at the farmyard they both sprang lightly from their saddles and tied their mounts to the hitching post beside a water trough.

'Why Miss Catherina! My but it is good to see ye. It's a long time since ye were last here.'

'Good morning Mr Massie.' Rina smiled at his welcome. 'Are you keeping well? And Mrs Massie?'

'We are that, and all the better for seeing that smile o' yours. 'Tis like a ray of sunshine.' He looked enquiringly at her companion.

'This is Lord Tannahill, a friend of my parents. He does not know this area very well so we are taking a ride around some of the farms'. Mrs Massie came to the door, her plump face wreathed in smiles and invited them in for a cup of tea but Rina declined politely saying they needed to earn their refreshments first as this was the first farm they had called at.

'Are ye going round them all then?' Mr Massie asked.

'Oh no, just one or two today.'

'D' ye know who is taking over the outlying sheep farms yet? We heard they were for sale to cover your grandfather's death duties. He was a fine man, and a good landlord.'

'Thank you, Mr Massie. No, I have not heard who will be buying the farms. I don't think it's settled.'

'My brother-in-law is in one of them. He and his son are worried they might not be able to keep on the tenancy.' Before Rina could reply Lord Tannahill said, 'most landlords are only too happy to keep on decent tenants who pay their rent on time and do their best to make a good job of their farms.'

'I hope ye're right, milord. Bert and his laddie work hard.'

After a little more chat they took their leave and cantered down the farm track towards the public road but when they were out of sight of the farmhouse Lord Tannahill, who was in front, drew his horse to a halt and indicated Rina should do the same. He looked serious.

'What's wrong?' Rina asked. 'Did I say something to offend you?'

'No, not at all and they were obviously pleased to see you. It's just that there are things you ought to know.' He frowned. 'Things your parents should have told you before I came to visit. I had heard your father was intending selling his outlying farms and I made enquiries. I have seen the five farm steadings and the in-bye land. The rest is very steep but I think with some help they might prove to be good shooting. As soon as they heard I might be interested your parents invited me to visit and they, well it was your mother actually, offered me a package . . .'

'What sort of package?' Rina asked warily.

'The five farms and their daughter as my bride. In return for a damned high price, I might add.'

Rina stared in dismay. 'Y-you mean I am to be bought? I'm their sacrificial lamb!'

'O-oh, I wouldn't say that exactly.' His mouth curved at the corners as though suppressing a smile. He thought of at least two pretty young widows who did their best to attract him whenever he was in the same company, not to mention innumerable mothers with marriageable daughters.

'But you're saying I am part of a bargain package to get my parents out of debt?' The colour had drained from Rina's rosy cheeks. She began to tremble, but her eyes still sparked indignantly. 'Are you saying you will buy the land, but only if I consent to marry you?'

'I am not agreeing, or denying anything, at present, Catherina. I never rush into things without considering all the angles. However, it will be surprising if some of the existing tenants have not heard that I have looked at the farms. In my experience country folk are not long in adding two and two and making half a dozen.' Rina knew that was true. She chewed her lower lip and looked up at him, her eyes troubled now.

'If my parents loved me they could never trade me for money.' Her chin wobbled as she struggled to hold back tears.

'They would not be the first to marry off their daughters as a way of settling their debts,' he said gently, 'but times are changing. Already since the war many of the large estates are in financial trouble, some because their sons have been killed, some can't afford to hire staff to keep them in the style to which they were accustomed.' Rina didn't reply. She felt the spring sunshine had gone behind a cloud, never to reappear. Lord Tannahill didn't like to see her so downcast. He had been looking forward to her company and her lively wit.

'Don't look so subdued, Catherina. If any of the other tenants ask questions shall we say I am considering buying the farms but nothing has been decided yet? After all that is the truth at the moment.'

'Maybe it is but Mother will hold me responsible if you change your mind about buying the farms. It is — it's like blackmailing me into marriage.'

'Heaven forbid! Catherina you may consider me too old for marriage but I assure you I can take my pick of several young women who would be delighted to become Lady Tannahill. For them feelings do not enter into it. They want the money and position in society. That is what makes you so refreshingly different. When you do marry, your husband will be a fortunate man for I believe you will love him with all your heart and be loyal and faithful to the end of your days. Very few men are so fortunate. Now cheer up and let us ride on. Remember I am not an ogre. If I want the land enough I shall buy it with, or without, a pretty young bride as part of the package.'

'You will?' Rina asked eagerly.

'If I decide I really want it.' They rode on in silence.

'This is the next farm where I thought we might call,' Rina said at length. 'I used to love coming here with Grandfather, but Mr and Mrs Fletcher were getting old even then. I don't even know if they are still alive, but they did have a son to carry on. Grandfather thought he would make a good farmer.' Lord Tannahill was surprised and pleased at how much she knew and understood about the different tenants and their types of farming. They did not all keep cows to milk, except for a house cow for the family.

'Some of them are too far away from the railway station to get the milk to the train in time. It is important to get it into Glasgow early, before it can go sour, especially in the summer. A few of the wives used to make cheese and keep pigs to drink the whey but I think they could not get enough money for their cheese.'

It was young Mr Fletcher who came out of the barn to greet them when he heard the horses. He seemed delighted to see Rina.

76

'Edna, my wife, has just had a baby boy, Miss Catherina. He is three weeks old today. Will you come in and see her? She will be ever so pleased to meet you, and so will my father. It grieved him terribly when your grandfather died. It was only a month after my mother had passed on so we were all feeling sad.'

They followed him into the farmhouse where his wife was changing her baby son before settling him into his crib again. Mr Fletcher had been sitting in a wooden armchair by the fire but he rose stiffly to his feet, smiling jovially.

'Why, Miss Catherina what a delight it is to see ye lassie. Have you come to see my grandson — another young Fletcher to carry on the tenancy, or at least we hope he will.'

'I'm sure he will if he is like his father and grandfather,' Rina smiled. 'This is, er, Mr Tannahill from London, a friend of my parents.

'I'm pleased to meet you, sir.'

'This is Edna, my wife.' His son introduced a shy looking young woman.

'I'm very pleased to meet you, Edna,' Rina smiled her wide friendly smile and the young woman relaxed and smiled back at her. 'May I hold your baby? What is his name?'

'He's called Charles Reginald,' Mr Fletcher spoke up proudly. 'Charles after me and Reginald after the old laird.'

'My grandfather would have been pleased,' Rina told him.

'Aye he was a fine man.'

Rina declined the offer of refreshment but young Mr Fletcher accompanied them outside and showed them the first of the young lambs in one of the barns and a few other early lambing ewes housed indoors.

'I try to have a few lambs ready for the Easter market to get a higher price, but we can only spare one shed to bring them in. We have two pairs of horses again but it was a blow when the soldiers came and took away one of our mares and a fine young gelding we had just broken to the plough.'

'Yes,' Lord Tannahill nodded, 'the war affected the farmers badly, taking their horses and their men to fight without warning, then expecting them to keep the country from starving when the ships were sunk.' Rina thought he sounded a little bitter. 'They should have foreseen the ships would be a target bringing in the nation's food.'

'Politicians don't understand,' Mr Fletcher agreed. 'We keep the windows and doors repaired as best we can, Miss Catherina but we lost slates from the high roof above the stable loft in the storms the year before last. They're getting worse but we need a slater to go up there to repair them.'

'I will tell my father,' Rina promised. 'Or rather I shall keep reminding him. I'm sure he must be aware you need repairs to the roof. The rain will waste the hay in the loft above the stable.' She frowned and nodded. 'I will tell him the repairs are urgent.'

When they left the farm Lord Tannahill walked his horse beside hers. He smiled.

'You would make a good land agent, Catherina. You grandfather trained you well even though you must have been very young.'

'He always made a note of any repairs that were needing done. He used to say that proverb . . .'

'A stitch in time?' Lord Tannahill prompted with a smile.

'Yes, that's right. It seemed a strange thing to say when it was applied to buildings but he liked to keep everything in good repair.'

'A man after my own heart I think. I inspect my own tenants regularly and now that I have met you I shall teach Sylvia to ride without delay and take her with me whenever I can. That way I shall see more of her and she might grow up to be as knowledgeable and interesting as you are. Your grandfather has made a good job.'

'My mother would not agree,' Rina said ruefully. 'They often quarrelled about what I ought to do and how I should be dressed, but it was Grandfather who paid for my education, and Johnathan's, so sometimes he got his own way.'

'Your brother? Was he interested in the land? Did your grandfather take him round the farms?'

'Not as often as he took me.' She sighed. 'Johnathan had two very good friends before he went to boarding school and they stayed friends all the time, as well as a fourth boy they met at school. They often stayed in each other's homes, though not often with us. They all went to fight in the war.' She blinked away her tears. 'Only one of them returned. He is in a home for wounded soldiers. He lost an arm and a leg.'

'War is cruel. So many good men died, or were maimed,' Lord Tannahill agreed.

They accepted coffee and gingerbread at the next farm and Lord Tannahill gathered from the conversation that this had been Catherina's favourite stopping place. Mrs Hardie was a cheery middle-aged woman with two teenage sons and a daughter still at school and it was clear they were all pleased to see Catherina. This time she introduced him as Lord Tannahill. She had explained that she had introduced him as plain mister to the Fletchers because she thought his title might fluster Edna. Mr Hardie said they were needing some roof repairs too and Lord Tannahill wondered when Sir Roger had last inspected his farms. His mouth tightened. He hated to see waste or neglect. The five farms he had looked at with a view to buying had all been in good repair though so he had expected the rest of the Stavondale Estate would be the same.

'If ye were calling at old man Lorimer's, Miss Catherina, I'd give him a miss if I were you.'

'Oh, why is that? Is he ill?'

'No, but he always liked to complain even when your grandfather came round,' Mr Hardie explained. 'But it's a good while since we saw Sir Roger and we all need repairs. Most of us do the best we can but some things need an expert.'

'Yes, I can understand that,' Rina said with a little frown. It seemed her father had been neglecting things badly since her grandfather had left the estate under his care.

'Aye, well Lorimer never did much to help himself or keep the gates and fences in good repair. Now he's threatening to withhold his rent until Sir Roger does some repairs for him. Of course his farm neighbours the five that are to be sold ye see and Sir Roger has been keeping them in good repair to get a better price, but that makes old man Lorimer more sour than ever, and his son isna much better.'

'I see,' Catherina said, looking from the Hardies to Lord Tannahill with troubled eyes. 'In that case I think we shall not call today.'

Eventually they took their leave. Lord Tannahill saw Catherina's troubled expression.

'The repairs are not your responsibility, Catherina,' he said hoping to offer comfort. 'All the tenants we met have been happy to see you.'

'I know, and I know it is up to my father to see that repairs are carried out, but Mother does not make it easy. She grudges the money he spends on the farms and they often quarrel about it, just as she blamed Grandfather because he spent money maintaining his property.'

'Some women have no concept about running an estate, while others, like yourself, understand it is the rents from the farms which keep them. The more I see of you the more I think what an excellent wife and partner you would make.' She glanced at him sharply, then away again, seeing his teasing smile.

'This is a good stretch for a gallop.' Without waiting for a reply she gave Duke his head.

CHAPTER SIX

Rina drew to a halt when they reached the entrance to the Bonnybrae track. Lord Tannahill admired the way she considered her horse and treated him gently. Her grandfather had taught her well, at least in that respect and he resolved to teach his own daughter himself.

'This looks a fine house and in good repair,' he commented. 'Is it part of Stavondale Estate?'

'This is Braeside. It was a small farm and part of Grandfather's estate. It was run down when the tenants died so he added the land to the Sinclairs' tenancy at Bonnybrae which is further up. The house now belongs to Mr and Mrs Greig. They rebuilt it and put in a bathroom. It is lovely inside. Grandfather asked his lawyer to make sure no one, including my father, would have any claim on the house or the land on which it stands, except Mr and Mrs Greig.' She looked him in the eye and said solemnly. 'I told you Grandfather had not always behaved as a gentleman in his youth. Mrs Greig is his daughter.'

'What? Whew! I see . . .' Lord Tannahill whistled, his eye widening. There was nothing dramatic about Catherina's announcement, as there would have been with most women repeating gossip. 'Your grandfather told you this himself, did he?'

'Yes, but only when he was dying. He had never claimed her as his daughter you see. Mr Sinclair brought her up as his own daughter. She loved him dearly, and her brothers and sisters. My father refuses to believe it. He said Grandfather was raving mad. He would be furious if he knew I had told you, or that we were going to Bonnybrae for lunch.'

'Then it will be our secret.'

'I come here whenever I am free. Grandfather encouraged me to visit so I could report the progress when the house was being rebuilt. I was ten years old then. That was when I first met Jamie. He is my best friend. When I was at boarding school Matron would not allow us to write to boys who were not brothers so I addressed my letters to Aunt Maggie — that is Mrs Greig, and I enclosed Jamie's inside. He did the same to reply. I was so miserable. I don't know what I would have done if Aunt Maggie and Jamie had not sent me letters every week. I love the animals and they always told me what was going on. Grandfather knew. He liked to hear their news too. Later on, when he knew he was dying, he said if ever I needed a friend, someone I could trust, I should come to Aunt Maggie.'

'He said that, even though he barely knew her?'

'Yes, and he was right. I needed to contact Grandfather's lawyer but I dare not trust Mother not to open my letters, so I asked Mr MacQuade to write via Mrs Greig. He understood because he had asked for me to be present when he was reading Grandfather's will. My parents refused. Grandfather had told me he had done his best to give me a choice. He thought I would make a good nurse and he believed the war would bring changes and women would be more independent.'

'I think I agree with him there,' Lord Tannahill said slowly. 'Already women over thirty have been given the vote.'

'Yes, I know.' She grinned. 'Aunt Maggie was all in favour of that and she made sure she used hers. Anyway, I had told Mother I wanted to train as a nurse but she scoffed at the idea. She doesn't want me to have a choice. She wants me to marry a wealthy husband.'

'Yes, I see, and I think I understand why you feel resentful, but tell me, if Mrs Greig lives at Braeside, why are we going to the farm for lunch, and who is this Jamie?'

'Aunt Maggie worked at Bonnybrae all her life so she returns each day to cook a meal for her brother and Jamie, who is both her nephew and Uncle Joe's. He is at his factory during the week but he comes to the farm with Aunt Maggie at weekends so you will meet them all. Jamie's father is her brother too but he lives in Yorkshire. Aunt Maggie only found out the truth about her father when her mother was dying and revealed her guilty secret. So you see she has carried on looking after Bonnybrae and everyone connected with it. Mrs Edgar helps in the house but she is getting old now and not so fit.'

'And your best friend, Jamie?'

'We have been friends since the day he arrived when he was fourteen. He ran away because he was unhappy in Yorkshire. I don't know why exactly because he goes back to visit his family twice each year. He came up here to work for his Grandfather Sinclair, and his Uncle Jim. They are partners now.' She sighed. 'That is another story to do with my father increasing the rents.' She shuddered. 'I'm glad Jamie didn't go to fight in the war. He felt he ought to go when so many other young men were going, but two of the other workers had already been forced to go and the army had taken two of their best horses. His Uncle Jim said he couldn't manage the farm without him. Then my brother came home on leave and I brought him to talk to Jamie. Two of his brothers had already volunteered and one had been killed. Jonathan, Nat I called him, he told Jamie he would be foolish to go to fight. He told us how dreadful the conditions were in the trenches and he said the best thing Jamie, and other farmers, could do was to produce as much food as they could to feed the nation. He said the Germans were trying to starve us into submission by sinking the ships which were bringing in food. Our government had thought the British navy was invincible and they had taken too long before they realised what was happening.'

'I agree with him there.' Lord Tannahill's mouth tightened. 'Several of us did our best to inform the prime minister what was happening in the country with the shortage of men and horses and hay, but the government didn't want to listen to the House of Lords. Britain had allowed too much free trade. The resulting imports made the prices to British farmers variable and often impossibly low. Land was being neglected. Fewer and fewer acres were being ploughed for cereals. The Germans had protected their farmers from excessive free trade and they were also growing sugar beet. They had far more naval power than we had anticipated. A great many people were discontented with Mr Asquith as prime minister. The bad harvest of 1916, and the heavy losses of men and ships, brought us near to catastrophe. But I'm afraid I am boring you, Catherina. I'm so sorry. It is one of many subjects I feel strongly about.'

'I am not bored at all. Please do go on. Grandfather always talked to me about world affairs and things he had read in the newspapers. I learned far more about the world from him than I ever did at school. Tell me about the coalition? He seemed to approve of that.'

'Aah, well whatever his faults Lloyd George is a vigorous leader and he realised the importance of growing our own food, and the fact that men were needed to work the land and rear the animals. There was an acute shortage of potatoes at the 1916 harvest and the spring of 1917 was very late. The government brought in guaranteed prices to encourage farmers to plough up their land again and grow more cereals.'

'Ah yes, I know the prices are to be guaranteed until 1922 . . .' Her tone was almost bitter and Lord Tannahill was dismayed to see her small face crumple as though she might burst into tears.

'Are you all right, my dear?' he asked gently.

'Y-yes, I'm fine.' She blinked rapidly and swiped an angry hand across her eyes.

'I can see you are upset, Catherina, but why should the prices trouble you?'

'It was just . . . The last time Nat was home on leave he and Father had an awful quarrel. Father told him that things would be much easier and better for him when he came home from the war because the farmers were promised better prices for their produce and he was going to increase the farm rents considerably, even the hill farm rents.' Nat strongly disagreed.

'You can't do that, Father!' he said 'The whole point is to give our British farmers encouragement to produce more food to feed the nation. As it is there is a shortage of lime with no men to work the quarries, and a shortage of farm men and horses. The town dairies can't buy enough hay to feed their cattle so the milk is in short supply. Don't you think there are enough problems without greedy landlords claiming their money before the tenants have had a chance to make any? Don't you realise how desperate the situation is?' It was not like Nat to fly into a rage. Father was furious at being contradicted and called greedy. He — he swore at Nat . . . He said he needed the money as much as his tenants.

'"What for? To pay for repairs you never do?" Nat snarled at him. It was awful. Grandfather was with us. It was a rare mild day and we were sitting outside.

'"The laddie is right," Grandfather said very quietly. "This is not the time to be thinking about ourselves with so many men sacrificing their lives."

'"See Father, even Grandfather understands the situation from his armchair. It's time you had a good look round your estate and did something to help your tenants."

'"That's none of your business!" Father was so angry.

'"Then why the devil am I fighting for British freedom?" Nat shouted. "I shall never speak to you again if you increase the rents at a time like this. And if we do win this bloody war the government will probably go back to their old ways of buying in our food so they can sell all the manufactured goods abroad. Will you lower the rents again? I know damn well you will not!"'

'I can understand your brother being angry,' Lord Tannahill said soothingly.

'I know, so do I, b-but they parted in anger and he never came back.' She wiped away a stray tear, sniffed hard then spurred Duke to a brisk walk. 'You must be famished and Aunt Maggie will think we're never coming. She is a very good cook but she doesn't do things elaborately as Mother instructs cook to do when she considers we have a special guest. I hope it will be satisfactory,' she said, but her anxiety was for her beloved aunt, rather than her companion.

'I am certain it will be very good. You know, Catherina, I do visit my own tenants regularly, sometimes with my agent, and sometimes alone. I often share a meal with them. I am quite human, even if I did inherit a title.' He smiled.

'I suppose so,' Catherina acknowledged. She was surprised and embarrassed that she had talked to him so frankly, but he was a good listener.

Maggie greeted them warmly, although she was a little diffident with Lord Tannahill. Joe, on the other hand, had met many men, both workers and businessmen in his years at the factory. He was straight and honest and well respected and his confidence with strangers had grown. He led Lord Tannahill into the sitting room and introduced him to Jim and Jamie while Rina stayed behind, volunteering as she always did to help Maggie serve their meal.

'I set it in the dining room today,' Maggie said with a smile. 'I thought we should do our best to impress.'

'Oh my, it all looks lovely,' Rina exclaimed in delight. 'I didn't know you had so many beautiful things, but I'm sure we have put you to a lot of trouble.'

'It's nice to get everything out once in a while and this is as good an occasion as any. How are you getting on with his lordship?' she asked anxiously.

'He is a good companion and pleasant company. He is considerate too. I-I just wish he was my uncle or cousin, or something. I can't imagine being his wife.' She looked at Maggie with troubled eyes.

'Have you told him how you feel.'

'Yes, at least I think so. I did tell him he was almost as old as my father but he didn't seem to mind. He didn't get angry anyway. He is very easy to talk to — too easy in fact. I think I have talked too much.'

Eventually the men came through to the dining room and Rina was relieved to see they all seemed to be getting on and talking freely, except Jamie who was quieter than usual. Lord Tannahill noticed they all called her Rina and asked about this.

'All my friends call me Rina, and Nat and Grandfather did too. Mother and Father always call me Catherina and they insist the servants call me Miss Catherina.'

Maggie served up bowls of steaming ham-and-pea soup with crusty bread made that morning and curls of butter.'

'That was delicious,' Lord Tannahill said with relish when he had finished the last drop. 'I see you make your own butter?'

'Oh yes,' Maggie nodded, 'but only for our own household and the people who work at Bonnybrae. The prices are too low to make it worthwhile selling. Anyway, Jim and Jamie like to sell as much milk as they can to the buyer in Glasgow.'

'I will clear these dishes Aunt Maggie, while you bring in the next course.'

'You shouldn't be doing that today, Rina,' Maggie said in a low voice with a look at their guest.

'I always help. Why should today be any different?' She looked at Lord Tannahill and gave him a mischievous smile. 'You don't mind, do you my lord?'

'I don't mind at all, but if I did, I doubt if it would make any difference. I am getting used to the fact that Catherina goes her own way with or without approval.'

'You're right about that,' Joe said with a grin. 'We found her big smile and wide-eyed innocence hard to resist from the day she first called to see us. She was only ten years old. Sometimes it is hard to remember she is Miss Catherina Capel of Stavondale Tower. I . . . er, I reckon any man who aims to marry her will have to accept her the way she is or she will be like a precious flower that has been transplanted to foreign soil. Her personality will wither and die.' He looked Lord Tannahill in the eye.

'I think I agree with you Mr Greig, even though I have known her such a short time. I find her company refreshing and her honesty is a delight, especially compared to the ladies I usually meet.' Jamie scowled. It didn't sound as though anything would put him off wanting Rina for his wife.

Rina came back carrying a tray laden with hot plates and tureens of vegetables. Jamie stood up and smiled at her. 'You hold the tray, Rina. I'll lift everything on to the table.'

'Be careful, Jamie! The plates are very hot,' she said with concern. 'Use a spare napkin to hold them. Sit them in front of your Uncle Jim. Aunt Maggie is bringing the roast for him to carve.' It was roast pork with side dishes of stuffing and apple sauce, roast potatoes and rich brown gravy. Joe brought a jug of water and a flagon of cider and filled their glasses. Lord Tannahill watched with interest at the way they all helped and he envied the happy, easy atmosphere. He enjoyed the meal tremendously.

'I have always loved the crackling from the pork roast. That was wonderfully crisp and tasty. I have not had any like that since I was a boy when I used to creep down to the kitchens in secret. Cook knew how much I loved it so she used to tell one of the maids to let me know.'

'I hope you have saved room for some of Aunt Maggie's trifle,' Rina told him. 'She makes the best trifle in the world with lots of sherry and raspberries.'

'You will wait for me to help feed the two lambs, Jamie?' Rina said when the meal was finished. 'I must help Aunt Maggie clear and wash the dishes first.'

'Don't worry, I'll wait for you,' Jamie said, looking up with a grin. 'It's much easier with two of us. They're getting bigger and stronger now.'

'I wouldn't mind a walk round outside and round the lower ground. If you're agreeable?' Lord Tannahill asked Jim.

'I need to walk off some of that splendid meal. We have been to some of the other farms but we only saw the outside of the buildings and met the tenants.'

'That suits me,' Jim said. 'I have a cow calving so I'd like to take a look at her and make sure she's all right. Are you coming with us Joe?'

'If that's all right?' He looked at Lord Tannahill.

'Of course it is. I am pleased to meet you both and I'm interested to see if the farming up here is much different to the way my own tenants do things further south. I am amazed at Catherina's interest and her knowledge of the farms. She is not at all like her mother.'

'No, she's been keen on the animals since the first time she came and she's not afraid to get her hands dirty. She wouldn't be such a regular caller if she was like her mother I suppose,' Joe said.

'Or her father,' Jim added drily. 'He's not like Sir Reginald. He often had a ride around the farms, with or without his agent. He tried to keep things in good repair. He knew all his tenants and their families. We have Joe here to thank for our repairs.' He clapped his brother-in-law on the back.

'I enjoy working with my hands and I hate to see things being neglected,' Joe said simply. 'If I was any good at plumbing I would install a water closet in the farmhouse like the ones we have at Braeside.'

'Yes, most of my tenants have them now but I have two who refused. They can't believe the house will not smell like a cowshed. I expect Catherina will tell you I'm considering buying the five hill farms on the northern boundary of Stavondale Estate. I think they might make good shooting. Sir Roger will be selling them anyway to raise money for the death duties.' He didn't tell them Catherina had been offered as part of the deal by her mother. The more he saw of Lady Capel the less he liked her.

'If all the rumours prove true he might be selling the rest of the estate in a few years' time,' Jim said gloomily. 'He may not be the best of landlords but better the devil you know. I only hope Jamie gets a chance to farm. My word, look at the time! We must have taken longer than I thought walking round the fields. Maggie will have tea ready before we start the milking. I'll bring the horses into the stable. Will you tell her we're just coming, Joe? Lord Tannahill you'll probably find Rina is still with the lambs. She would take them home if she could. They're in the small shed next to the stable.'

Lord Tannahill had thoroughly enjoyed his walk and the conversation of two adult men with the same interests in the countryside as himself. They had answered his questions about other farms and tenants on the Stavondale Estate and given him things to think about in his dealings with Sir Roger. He walked thoughtfully towards the shed. He paused when he saw Jamie and Catherina sitting companionably together on a pile of straw, so clearly at ease and happy in each other's company, and both so young with their lives before them. He sighed, silently envying their youth and their obvious affection for each other. They had not heard him approach. One of the lambs lay sleeping with its head on Catherina's lap. A collie dog lay curled at Jamie's feet, while the other, obviously older lay on the straw beside him while he absently fondled her velvety ears.

'I know that, Jamie,' Catherina said wistfully, 'but he can't give me what I want most.'

'I know he could give you everything I can never hope to give you, Rina. I wanted to hate him but I have to admit he seems a decent fellow, even if he is a lord and as old as my father. He didn't look on us with disdain. In fact, he seemed at ease. I think he enjoyed his meal. Aunt Maggie will be relieved.'

'Who wouldn't enjoy Aunt Maggie's . . . ?' Lord Tannahill stepped back into the yard then made noisy footsteps before he entered the building. Rina broke off. They both looked up at him, a little flushed.

'I think it is time we took our leave, Catherina. I have had a splendid afternoon seeing the farm and the sheep.

You have a cowshed full of fine Ayrshire cattle waiting to be milked.'

'Oh but we can't go yet,' Catherina said. 'Aunt Maggie has baked fresh scones and shortbread for tea and it's the best shortbread you'll ever taste.' They stood up and walked, one on either side of him, back to the house. Catherina wondered whether he could have overheard them discussing him.

As they rode back to Stavondale Lord Tannahill told Catherina how much he had enjoyed his day.

'Mother is never usually interested enough to ask where I have been or what I have been doing but if she asks where we ate I shall be vague and say at one of the farms. I hope Father doesn't ask which one.'

'I can't see why it should matter. We had a most enjoyable meal and pleasant company.'

'Father will never forgive Uncle Joe for owning Braeside and for making such an excellent job of rebuilding it, even though he had no intention of doing anything with it himself. He doesn't want to admit that Aunt Maggie could be his half-sister but I'm sure that's why Grandfather made certain everything was legal. Aunt Maggie can never be put out of her home.'

'He has nothing to be ashamed of with Mrs Greig. She is a pretty woman still and an excellent cook.'

'We shall have to tell Mother where we are going for lunch tomorrow after the kirk. Or at least where I have arranged for us to go if you agree?'

'And where might that be?' he asked with a tolerant smile.

'Mr and Mrs MacQuade have invited us for lunch at one o' clock. Their daughter Melissa is my friend and we both want to train to be nurses.' He thought he detected defiance as though she was testing his reaction. 'Mel is finding out how we should go about it. I-I shall have to explain that my parents have offered me in marriage as part of a package of land for sale.' There was no doubting the bitterness in her tone this time. 'I don't think they ever loved me.' He drew his horse to a halt and turned to face her.

'Make no mistake about it, Catherina, most men would think themselves fortunate indeed to have a young and pretty bride with keen intelligence coupled with sincerity and a lively sense of humour. I am no different to other men in that, so I am probably being my own worst enemy in assisting you with your plans. However, you can leave tomorrow's arrangements to me. I will deal with your parents.'

'B-but you will still take me to the MacQuade's?' Rina asked uncertainly.

'Of course, since that is what you want. I shall simply tell them I wish to have you to myself so I am taking you out for lunch. Even your mama will not be foolish enough to ask where we are going, I think.' He smiled wryly. 'She seems more than happy to leave you in my company without a chaperone so I have no doubt her hopes of an imminent marriage will increase a hundredfold. If I am honest I do not like the way your parents, in particular your mother, have tried to manipulate both of us into marriage.'

'It will be a great relief if you can help me avoid a dispute over the MacQuades. I hate quarrels but I never lie to my parents. Mr MacQuade was Grandfather's lawyer you see and now he is my trustee. Father thinks he is interfering but he is only trying to see that I am treated fairly regarding the small legacy Grandfather was able to provide for me.' She shrugged and gave him a fleeting smile. 'I admit I don't always tell them things, but that is not the same as telling an untruth, is it?' She looked up at him, wide-eyed and innocent and he was reminded of Joe Greig's description of her. He shook his head and smiled wryly.

'I must be the most stupid man on earth not to snatch you up right now and carry you away.'

* * *

The following morning Lady Capel was at pains to introduce him to everyone she met at the local kirk as 'Lord Tannahill, a close friend of my daughter's.' He greeted everyone politely, even to the garrulous little man who was the gravedigger, but twice he caught the expression of embarrassment on Catherina's face. The first time he winked. The second time he gave a wry smile and swiftly made their excuses to leave, cutting short her mother's triumph.

Lunch at the MacQuades' was a little more formal than it had been the previous day at Bonnybrae. During the week Mrs MacQuade had a woman to help with laundry and bedrooms plus a general woman who came each weekday morning. Neither usually worked on Sunday's but Grace had agreed to come in to serve the meal in the main dining room and clear away afterwards as she did when Mr MacQuade invited clients to lunch. Mrs MacQuade was an excellent cook herself and they enjoyed a good meal. Afterwards Neil MacQuade and his son, Charles, lingered in the dining room with a bottle of port and Lord Tannahill got the impression the lawyer wanted an opportunity to speak to him without the ladies. He felt he could respect both MacQuade senior and his son and he hoped to find out a little more about the Stavondale Estate and how Catherina would be affected if she did not marry him. He was developing a growing distrust of her parents, especially her mother's scheming. It troubled him but he was a little surprised to find himself being inter-rogated, even though MacQuade was skilful in the way he directed the conversation.

'I can't imagine how this situation came about now that I have met you, Lord Tannahill,' Neil MacQuade said even-tually. 'I was prepared to do my best to make Rina a ward of court if her parents insisted that she must marry you against her will. Now we have met I doubt if you want an unwilling bride.'

'If you mean I could have a choice of women who want my title, or my money, or both, you would be right. Catherina is completely different. I am finding her a delight-ful young person who doesn't seem interested in either. I believe the only thing she craves is love. It is interesting now you mention making her a ward of court. Presumably you told Lady Capel that. Now I understand what she was

93

inferring this morning when she gave her irritating laugh and said we were not so very far from Gretna Green if I should feel inclined to force Catherina to do as we all desired. There is no way I would get involved in that sort of scandal, even if I was desperate for a bride, but as a matter of interest, would it be possible for you to have her made a ward of court when she is still in her parents' care?'

'Since we are being frank, I admit we have not looked into the legality of the situation yet. I hoped things could be resolved without resorting to such a strategy. That is the reason I wanted to meet you. I know Sir Reginald did not trust his daughter-in-law, or his own son for that matter, when it came to money. He has been proved correct, I'm sorry to say. Catherina is my client now and I mean to do the very best I can to protect her interests. Her happiness is important to me and my family. I thought she might decide she did want to marry you of her own free will.'

'It is something Catherina and I must discuss, preferably on the way back to Stavondale where we can be free from interruption. I have found Catherina interesting and delightful company this weekend. Few men in my situation would not be drawn to her, but I am astonished at the things I have learned myself from a girl so young. I am no longer sure I need a wife who might, or might not, provide me with a son. I have a small daughter already and when I return home I intend to be a much better parent than I have been so far. I shall take a leaf out of Sir Reginald's book. Catherina adored her grandfather and he obviously felt the same. I can tell you that I have made up my mind, whether or not Catherina becomes my wife, I shall stand by my offer to buy the outlying farms from Sir Roger. Will you be acting for him?'

'I doubt it,' MacQuade said ruefully. 'We do not see eye to eye.'

'I'm sorry to hear that. I think the business would have been conducted more smoothly.'

'I can tell you that every penny Sir Roger gets for the farms will be needed to settle the death duties. He had already drained the estate of the capital fund his father had accumulated for such things as taxes and repairs, though what he spent so much on I don't know, other than his wife's extravagant tastes.'

'I did wonder how they had achieved such grandeur at Stavondale Tower, at least in their part of it. The exterior is needing some maintenance I see. Sir Roger himself has some large gambling debts to settle and unless he can settle them soon I think he will be selling more than the outlying farms. I wouldn't like to think of Catherina suffering for her parents' folly. Can you ensure her future will be secure if she does not marry me?'

'She will have a small income from Manor Farm so long as I can prevent her parents draining it dry for their own ends. It should be enough to see her through her nurse's training if that is what she decides to do. She also own Stavondale Manor if she needs a home when Sir Roger sells Stavondale Tower. I'm fairly certain he will sell before long.'

'Catherina will not be wealthy then,' Lord Tannahill mused. 'Probably she will have enough to make her content if other aspects of her life give satisfaction.'

'Yes, I would say so,' MacQuade agreed. 'Charles and I will do our best to see that any money which comes into her trust fund is secure.'

'I am pleased to have had this opportunity to meet you and discuss things frankly. I think we both want Catherina's happiness.'

'It has been a pleasure meeting you, Lord Tannahill.'

As they drove slowly home through the leafy lanes Lord Tannahill gathered Catherina had spent most of the afternoon with Melissa discussing how they might start a nursing career.

'Can I ask you a question?' she asked anxiously.

'You can ask me anything, my dear, but I think we need to talk. I remember we passed a wood where the grass was wide enough to stop.' Eventually he drew the car to a halt and turned to face her. 'Now ask away and don't look so troubled.'

'I am troubled. You said I was part of the deal you made with my father — you would pay a good price for the outlying farms so long as I agreed to marry you. Does that mean you will not be buying the farms if I refuse?' He looked at her steadily for several seconds.

'If I said yes, would you marry me rather than see your parents in a debtor's court?'

'Are things as bad as that?' she asked hoarsely, her eyes wide, her face whitening. 'Grandfather feared there might be other debts. I couldn't bear to see them brought so low because I had refused your offer. Y-yes, I will marry you.'

CHAPTER SEVEN

Lord Tannahill took Rina's small face in both hands and looked deeply into her eyes, such trusting eyes. She reminded him of his beloved spaniel. He had been eleven when Stephie died but he had still wept in secret. He bent his head and kissed Rina gently on the lips. He increased the pressure enjoying the feel of her soft mouth. She neither withdrew nor responded. He knew she did not feel the slightest stirrings of the passion already tightening his gut. He sighed. He desired her but he would not take her under false pretences.

'I must be honest with you, Catherina. I know your father has other debts, beside death duties, but I don't know how bad things are. You can rest assured, my dear, I would never hold you to ransom, much as I would like you for my wife. I shall buy the farms at the price agreed, but I may take the opportunity to strike a different deal. As I told you the hill land will make good shooting but I would need a shooting lodge. I did not see any large houses in the area, other than Stavondale Tower.'

'I don't think there are any.'

'Mr MacQuade tells me you will have a house of your own and a small income if your parents sell Stavondale Tower. I would not have liked to see you homeless, any more than I would force you into a marriage you do not want. Now that I know you are provided for, I think it might suit your father to include Stavondale Tower in the deal.' His voice hardened. 'But I do not allow anyone to dictate a price. If the deal falls through, Catherina, you can be sure it is not your fault. It will be greed, possibly on your mother's part.'

'I understand.' She nodded. 'I-I'm sorry I can't be the wife you want,' she said in a small voice.

'Don't worry, Catherina. I have learned a lot in the short time I have spent in your company and I shall be proud of Sylvia if she grows up like you — so natural and considerate of your fellow men and women. I am pleased to have met you and if you changed your mind I would marry you tomorrow, but I think your heart is already given to Jamie Sinclair.'

'Jamie! Oh no. I-I mean Jamie would never marry me.'

'Why not? I believe he loves you, and I believe you love him, whether you realise it yet or not.'

'I-I . . . Maybe I do, but even if he could afford to take a wife, he thinks I'm out of his reach. He doesn't understand that I don't care about money, or living in a big house. I would be happy helping him with his animals.' She sighed heavily. 'Even if he was willing I couldn't marry him. Mother would be so furious she would insist that Father evict Jamie and his uncle from Bonnybrae. I could never risk that. Grandfather told me there had been Sinclair's in Bonnybrae for several generations and they were the best tenants on the estate.'

'I can believe that. They certainly make a good job and keep things tidy too. But some day Catherina, perhaps when you have worked as a nurse with ordinary men and women from various backgrounds, maybe then Jamie will realise he is the only one who can give you what you most desire — to be loved for yourself.'

'You're generous and very kind even though I don't deserve it.'

'My dear girl you do deserve happiness, but I suspect your mother will be angry when she hears there will be no wedding.

Allow me to take the blame. I shall tell her I have changed my mind. You know that is not the truth. Whatever reasons I give to convince her, remember it is only to deflect her wrath from you. Tomorrow I shall be gone but you will still be here.'

Lady Capel could barely wait until dinner was over that evening to ask if they had settled on a date for their wedding. She thought Catherina looked more serene than she had seen her since her grandfather's death and she noticed the smile she exchanged with Lord Tannahill as they took their places at table. Her hopes soared. When the last dishes were cleared from the table and the door to the kitchens closed, Lord Tannahill cleared his throat.

'As you know I shall be leaving tomorrow morning but I would like to say I have enjoyed my weekend, and especially the lively company of your daughter. I only wish I had been fifteen years younger.' He sighed theatrically. 'As you know when I offered to buy the five outlying farms it was at your suggestion that marriage to Catherina should be included. Now that we have met, and I have had time to consider, I have come to the conclusion that marriage is not for me, but . . .' Lady Capel gasped with shock. He held up his hand to continue but her face was almost purple with rage.

'What have you done? You stupid girl! You have spent all weekend alone with him. How can you have failed so badly? You're wayward and selfish. You know how much I longed for you to move to London so that your father and I could visit you often and get away from this — this mausoleum that is supposed to be the ancestral home.' She almost spat the words.

'One moment Lady Capel!' Lord Tannahill raised his voice to silence her. His tone was stern. 'You can move away from Stavondale Tower if you wish. If you will let me finish I was about to tell Sir Roger that I have a different proposition to make. I think it would be better if we adjourned to your own offices Roger so that we might have peace to discuss business.' Lady Capel opened her mouth to protest but he gave her such a quelling glare that she subsided. 'Before we go

Lady Capel, I would like to make one thing very clear. Even if I had married your daughter, we should not have spent so much time in London now the war is over. Also, I already have one mother-in-law who visits once a month to visit her granddaughter. She loves Sylvia very much. Unlike yourself she is a gentle person who does not enjoy the social round or city life. That is the way I prefer it. I would not have allowed you to visit for more than brief periods and you would have had to abide by the rules I set for my guests. You would not have enjoyed it as you seem to think. As for Catherina, you should be proud of your daughter. Being in her company has made me see my own shortcomings as a father to my own child. I know now I do not need a wife, or a son . . .'

'But the title . . . ?' Lady Capel said, and Rina almost felt sorry for her defeated look.

'The title is merely that, a name. I have two nephews. The eldest will be pleased to inherit the title, but my daughter will inherit my estate. I hope I can teach her to be as knowledgeable and caring towards my land and its tenants as Sir Reginald has taught Catherina to . . .'

'Sir Reginald!' Lady Capel shrieked. 'He is the root of all our problems. He ruined Catherina . . .'

'He loved Catherina, Lady Capel.' His voice was quiet but it had a thread of steel. 'He obviously loved her for herself and the captivating, intelligent child she must have been. I shall go home and teach my own child to ride her pony and accompany me whenever possible. I shall spend as much time with her as I can. I have learned a valuable lesson this weekend. We all need love, and a little tenderness.' He reached out his foot beneath the table and touched Catherina's toe. She acknowledged his glance with a slight nod.

'It has been a long day and I have a terrible headache,' she said, drawing a hand across her brow. 'If you will all excuse me I would like to go to bed now.' At the door she paused and looked back.

'I shall see you in the morning before you leave Lord Tannahill.'

'Very well.' He turned to her father. 'I think it is time you heard my alternative proposal, Roger?' Catherina heard the two men crossing the hall towards her father's study as she approached her bedroom. She undressed hurriedly and got into bed in case her mother should come to disturb her. In spite of Lord Tannahill's plain speaking and his plan to take the blame for there being no marriage she knew her mother would still hold her responsible for dashing her own hopes. Apart from frequent visits to London she had longed to have a titled son-in-law, even though her own family had never had any form of a title.

Rina was up early the following morning and she had just boiled up the porridge when Lord Tannahill, hearing movements, traced her into the kitchen.

'Are you cooking, Catherina?' he asked in surprise. She laughed, a warm, happy sound.

'There is nothing difficult about making porridge. Mrs Bell leaves the oatmeal steeping overnight so it is easy enough to set the porringer on to boil. She knows I am the only one who gets up early, and I enjoy making my own breakfast. Do you like porridge?'

'I do indeed, especially when it is served with a bowl of cream, a Scottish custom, I think?'

'I don't know. We didn't have porridge at the school for young ladies.' She pulled a face. 'It was probably considered too fattening. I will bring it through to the dining room if you . . .'

'Not at all. I see you intended eating here so I shall join you. It is warm and friendly in here. I always liked going to the kitchens when I was a boy and cook usually saved me some treat or other.' He grinned.

'Would you like bacon and egg to follow, or an omelette, or scrambled egg?'

'Can you cook all these things? Did they teach you to cook in Gloucestershire?'

'Oh no. Young ladies are supposed to have servants you know.' She wrinkled her nose at him. 'But I like to know how things are done myself. Whenever Aunt Maggie was cooking I asked her to show me and she always let me help. She bought me a book and a pen so I could write down the recipes. She keeps it for me at Braeside. I shall always have it when I need to cook myself. I think nurses need to be able to make simple dishes like beef tea and egg custard, but Aunt Maggie says working men need more substantial food than that. I can cook most things now but I could never get all the dishes ready together for a dinner as Aunt Maggie or Mrs Bell do. Aunt Maggie says that comes with practice.'

'I suppose she's right. If you're sure it will be no trouble I would like a plain omelette.'

'All right. It is better if it is eaten the moment it comes out of the pan. Then we can have coffee and toast. We have plenty of honey from our own bees. We do have marmalade but Mrs Bell hasn't made so much these past few years because we couldn't get oranges.'

'No, I suppose the ships couldn't get through to bring them. I'm amazed you understand such things. You surprise me more each time I talk with you Catherina. Perhaps I have made a mistake and I should be carrying you off for my wife.' His tone was teasing but Catherina went rigid. Then she turned to face him.

'You wouldn't go back on your word?'

'No.' The smile died from his face, but there was still a teasing gleam in his eyes. 'I never go back on my word, Catherina, but I think I shall regret it in this case and I did mean what I said, if you ever change your mind about marrying me.'

'Thank you,' she said in a low voice. She tipped a large fluffy omelette onto a hot plate and carried it across to him. He caught her wrist as she set it down.

'I thought we were friends now? True friends should be able to trust each other.'

'Yes, I think that's true,' she said after a few moments thought. 'I do trust my real friends. All of them call me Rina.'

'Yes, I have noticed. Then I shall call you Rina too. This omelette is excellent by the way.'

'I'm glad,' she said simply, bringing a silver toast rack to the table filled with crisp golden toast. 'Did you manage to reach a deal with my father last night?'

'Yes, I think so. We stayed up very late discussing the details. It remains for our respective lawyers to draw up the legal documents now. I have agreed to buy two more of the smaller, outlying farms. My plan is to join two neighbouring farms into one and use the spare house and buildings to house a game-keeper. The other two are farmed by a father and son and I think the son will be pleased to take on all the land. We shall rear pheasants and manage the bracken and heather and maybe get some grouse shooting in time. The changes will take place as soon as the documents are drawn up and signed. I told your father I thought things would go more smoothly with the MacQuades. I shall not stand for trickery or cheating over the boundaries. His tone hardened. 'I have offered a fair price and I expect a fair deal, or there will be no deal at all. I think he understands I mean that.'

'That is the way my grandfather expected to do business,' Rina nodded.

'There is another part to the deal but it will not take place for eleven months from the date of signing. I have arranged to buy Stavondale Tower to make into a shooting lodge but it will give your parents time to decide where they want to live.'

'But what about the farms?'

'I expect his agent will oversee them and report to him when he moves away.'

'Father has not employed a land agent for several years.'

'I don't expect he enjoys visiting his tenants either if they remind him of the repairs required. He should have enough capital left, after the death duties, to carry out repairs, unless he has a lot of other debts.'

Rina suspected her father would not pay any attention to his tenants' needs if he and her mother moved away. She felt slightly sick when she remembered the care her grandfather had taken. She wondered what would happen in the future.

Lord Tannahill would not be interested in buying the rest of the farms because he already had an estate in Warwickshire as well as a smaller estate in Kent, inherited from his mother's family. He had told her that himself.

'Don't look so troubled, Rina, my little friend,' he said breaking into her thoughts. 'If ever you are in trouble I hope you will come to me, or at least tell me, in case I can help. He drew a leather wallet from his inside pocket and took out an embossed card. He handed it to her. 'This will find me.' She looked at it.

'You have a telephone machine? Mr MacQuade has one in his office and one at his home.'

'Yes, but he is in the town where there are poles and wires, as there are for my London home.'

'Uncle Joe has one at his factory but he says it will be a while before the telephone poles come up the glen to Bonnybrae.'

'I'm afraid he's right but many things have changed during the long reign of Queen Victoria and I believe they will go on changing with the spread of electricity and motor cars and telephones.'

'And new hospitals,' Rina said with a smile. 'Mel was telling me her father had been talking to an architect client of his who has just designed a new home especially for the nurses. He is going to arrange an interview for us with the nurse superintendent. I have to write to tell her when I shall be free.'

'As you are now, my dear. Before I leave, would you like to show me the house Mr MacQuade called Stavondale Manor? I understand it will become your home if your parents move to the city.'

'Yes it will. I will clear our breakfast dishes away, then I will walk down with you. Afterwards I shall ride Duke to Bonnybrae to tell Aunt Maggie my news. She worries about me more than my parents.'

'I think your father does care, Rina, but he seems to have a lot on his mind and I got the impression he is a little disillusioned with life. He told me it had not been his idea to marry you off when you are still so young. In fact, he had had serious doubts about the arrangement because he knew the main thing your mother wanted was to be able to live in London whenever it suited her. Apparently he had tried to tell her I was not the sort of man to let her take advantage.'

'Oh, I'm glad you told me that. Mother will still blame me but at least I shall know Father is not blaming me too. He has been subdued and withdrawn recently, maybe due to Grandfather's death, or Nat's.'

'Probably a combination of both. Death is such a final thing. I suspect he doesn't enjoy quarrels with your mother either and she will have no one else to blame now your grandfather is dead.'

'Except me,' Rina said wryly. 'I hope we shall not need to wait long before we start nursing.'

'It will be hard work and long hours for little money in the beginning.'

'I know. I don't mind the work if we can help people but Mel says we only get one day off each month and I shall not be able to get home and back in the same day. I shall miss Duke terribly and he will miss me. I shall ask Mr Sinclair if I can take him to Bonnybrae so that Jamie can exercise him.'

'Can Jamie ride?'

'Yes. He loves his horses. He could ride Duke round the sheep. He is used to looking after the Clydesdales they use for ploughing and carting. Then there is Peggy who takes the milk to the station every day. She would be company for Duke.' Lord Tannahill smiled.

'I see you have everything planned, but how will you get to Bonnybrae then, and how do you get from the railway station? It must be two or three miles.'

'I walk if there is no one to meet me with the pony and trap.'

'I didn't realise Stavondale Manor was so big.' He said as they reached the house. 'It is in fine condition.'

'Yes. Grandfather built on this new part last year with the large kitchen and a small cloakroom. There is a bathroom and a bedroom above. He also added a small bathroom attached to the largest bedroom. I didn't know he was doing it all for me. When I was on holiday he kept asking me to check on the progress but he never saw it himself,' she added sadly.

'Will you be lonely on your own, Rina?'

'I don't mind my own company and Mrs MacCrindle will probably be in most days to check on things.' She chuckled. 'And to feed me up when I do get home. I shall furnish two of the rooms and two bedrooms then I shall store the rest of Grandfather's things in one of the empty rooms until I see whether I need them. Mr McGill, the farm manager, is going to send three of the men with farm carts to help me move things. I have to let him know when I'm ready. I shall get everything moved soon now I know Stavondale Tower will be sold eventually. I need to be organized before I start nursing.'

'Sometimes it is hard to believe you are so young, Rina.' He sighed. 'I hope you will meet Sylvia one day. I'm sure she would like you. She is still a little shy. I am considering taking her to my country house in Warwickshire and possibly asking her governess if she will give lessons to some of the estate children around her age. Do you think that is a good idea?'

'Oh yes. It will be good for her to have young friends, at least so long as you still see her and spend time with her as often as you can. I would have loved to do that instead of being sent to boarding school.'

'Then I shall look into it. I'm sure we shall meet again. Now I had better be on my way.' He bent and kissed her on both cheeks, then after a slight hesitation he kissed her mouth one more time.' His eyes twinkled. 'You're hard for an old man to resist, my dear, and you blush so delightfully.' He walked away with a jaunty step, definitely not an old man, she thought, but not for her. At the garden fence he turned. '*Au revoir*. Until we meet again,' he called.

* * *

106

Knowing his architect client, Mr Carruthers, was on good terms with the matron, or nursing superintendent, as he referred to her, Neil MacQuade had lost no time in asking him to make enquiries about nursing training for his daughter and her friend, but the news was not good when they met again.

'Miss Gilroy says your daughter and her friend will not be eligible to train in general nursing at the Glasgow Infirmary until they reach twenty-one, but they could gain valuable experience at smaller specialised hospitals nursing sick children, mentally ill patients or at the Fever Hospital, where she is in charge. The nurses' home we have been renovating is there. She agreed to see both the girls but she has serious doubts about your daughter's friend being suitable for nursing considering her background and the menial tasks nurses need to do. I'm sorry to say she is rather scathing about wealthy young ladies learning to be coquettes and attracting the attention of gentlemen.'

'Miss Capel is no coquette,' Neil MacQuade said with a frown. 'She has a warm, friendly personality, and a lovely smile. I think it would cheer sickly patients.'

Arrangements were made. Rina was to travel by train to Strathlinn, the small town where the MacQuades lived, then Mel's father would drive them both the four miles to the hospital for their interviews. It was on the outskirts of a large village called Belroon. There was no railway station, but it did have a horse-drawn bus twice a week which was more than either of the villages near Stavondale had so Rina did not consider it as strange as Mel, who was used to living in the town. Both girls were excited but Mel's face was pale and she was so nervous she began to tremble. Rina suggested she should go in first rather than get even more nervous. When she came out her face was beaming with pleasure and she nodded at Rina to let her know she had been accepted. Consequently Rina was unprepared for the disapproving expression on Matron Gilroy's stern face and the hostile manner in which she shot questions at her about her school and her home life. She looked sceptical when Rina said yes, she could cook a variety of plain dishes, and bake scones, a cake and shortbread.

Being innately truthful Rina added anxiously, 'I am not sure I could cook a three-course meal with meat and potatoes as well as two vegetables and gravy, and have everything ready together at the right time. I could practise if that is what you require me to do,' she offered eagerly. Since Miss Gilroy herself struggled with anything more than meat, potatoes and a vegetable at any one time. Her manner relaxed a little. 'Yes, I can make a bed,' Rina said. 'We had to make our own at boarding school.' Matron nodded. The girl appeared to be more practical than she had expected, given her background. She watched Rina carefully as she proceeded to describe some of the worst chores such as emptying bedpans, washing and sterilising sick bowls and sputum pots for patients with tuberculosis, if she should be transferred to that part of the hospital which was situated at the other end of the hospital grounds for the purpose of isolation and fresh air for patients.

'Are you fully aware what is meant by a hospital for infectious diseases, Miss Capel, with illnesses such as scarlet fever, typhoid, diphtheria and general infectious ailments? You may be asked to act as a relief nurse in one of the tuberculosis pavilions. Their beds are constantly full. Would this trouble you?'

'Oh no,' Rina replied promptly. 'I would like to learn about everything you do here. I enjoy working with animals and I would like it even more if I can help people get well, especially the children.'

'I see. Well, I hope your enthusiasm continues,' Miss Gilroy said drily. 'Do your family understand what kind of work you will be doing?' Rina had not dared mention to her mother that she would be going to a hospital with infectious diseases for an interview, much less aiming to work there.

'My mother does not approve. She thinks I want to be some sort of famous heroine like Florence Nightingale, or Edith Cavill, the brave lady who was shot by the Germans.'

Rina shuddered. 'I am not so brave. I just want to help people who are ill. Mother couldn't understand why I wanted to stay with Grandfather all night, or why I held him up to help him drink when he was dying.' Her young face showed her emotion at the memory and Miss Gilroy decided she had misjudged the girl if she was telling the truth.

'It will be no use asking for references from your school for young ladies,' she said wryly, 'so I think I must give you a month's trial. You understand you will be expected to attend talks and study for examinations in order to qualify for a certificate, especially if you intend to go on to general nursing when you are older. Your pay will be three pounds at the end of each month. You must live in the nurses' home where you will have a single room, illuminated by electric light.'

'Electric light?' Rina echoed in excitement. 'We do not have that where I live.'

'No doubt it will reach country areas eventually. As I was saying you will have board and lodging and uniform provided. Dresses must be no more than six inches above the ankle and you will be expected to keep your cap, cuffs, collar and apron spotlessly clean and starched at all times. You will wear black lisle stockings and black shoes. You will have one day off each month. Home Sister will make sure you understand her rules regarding the use of bathrooms, time for lights out, and doors locked at 10.30 p.m. You must obey the rules while you are living in the nurses' home. There is a recreation room and a separate room for nurses who are ill. Do you understand?'

'Yes, Miss Gil . . . Yes, Matron.'

'I shall expect both of you to report to me next Monday at seven in the morning so you will need to report to Home Sister on Sunday and settle in. Night nurses move to another, quieter, part of the home during their periods of night duty. These are from nine in the evening to eight in the morning, six nights per week for four weeks at a time. You will have two weeks' rest after each of your night duty periods. These occur four times a year.' Matron's stern manner had returned. 'There will be no favours asked or given and you and your friend cannot expect to work on the same shifts or wards just because you are friends. You will be sent where you are most needed. Is that clear, Miss Capel?'

'Yes. Thank you very much.' Her relief and delight were obvious.

* * *

Rina told her parents she would be starting her training to be a nurse the following Monday but her father seemed too distracted to pay attention and her mother responded with waspish comments. Saddened by their lack of interest Rina made her way to the door, intending to sort through some of her clothes in her bedroom.

'I expect you think everything is all right now your father has done another deal with Lord Tannahill but it isn't. There's nothing clever being a nurse. You'll be lucky if you can keep yourself in rags. You could have been a great help to us if you had married him.'

'Oh Mother,' Rina sighed. 'You're never satisfied about anything I do, or Father.'

'No, and I'll tell you why. There will be nothing left by the time the death duties are paid and he has bought a dingy little house in Edinburgh.'

'Father said you have already chosen a house. He says it's the size of a small mansion in one of the most expensive areas of the city,' Rina said defensively.

'And did your precious father tell you there will be nothing left to keep up any kind of style by the time he's settled his gambling debts?'

'Gambling debts?' Rina's face paled. 'But you have not been to London recently.'

'We haven't been to London because he couldn't pay his debts. Now your grandfather's death means more debts. He's playing for time but his creditors will not wait for ever. They would have been more patient if our only daughter had done what she was supposed to do and caught a big rich fish for a husband.' Rina didn't know whether her mother was exaggerating about their debts or not but when she looked at her bitter, discontented face she felt sick. There was no joy at Stavondale anymore.

The following day Rina rode over to Bonnybrae to report on her interview with Miss Gilroy. Maggie was always eager to hear how she had got on and she listened to every detail. When it came to the uniform Rina chuckled.

'I don't know what Matron Gilroy would think if she saw me in breeches.'

'It will be a long week's work, Rina. Are you sure it will not be too much for you, dear?' Maggie asked with concern. 'We shall all miss your visits.'

'I know. I shall miss not being able to see you all. Mother wants to move to Edinburgh as soon as she can and when Lord Tannahill takes over he means to make changes. So tomorrow I must take the things I want to keep from Grandfather's home.' Her voice broke for a moment but she added firmly, 'Mr McGill and his men are helping me move furniture and carpets into Stavondale Manor.

'I don't like to think of you on your own at Stavondale Manor, Rina when your parents move away. You know you will always be welcome to stay with Joe and me. We have plenty of rooms. You could make one of them your own so that you don't need to carry luggage every time you want to stay.'

'Dear Aunt Maggie. Grandfather was so right about you. You're the very best of friends. I would like to stay sometimes but I shall not be able to travel this far on my day off. There are no trains from Belroon where the hospital is and it is at least four miles to Strathlinn to get the train, then a three mile walk from the station to here. It would take me most of the day travelling to get here and back again before the doors are locked. The thought of not seeing you all for ages makes me sad. I shall miss Duke terribly too. Ernest, Grandfather's stable boy, is going to look for more work somewhere else. Do you think I could ask Jamie's uncle if I could bring Duke here? Maybe Jamie could exercise him riding round the sheep?'

'Jamie would enjoy that. He has bought himself one of those bicycles so it will not take him so long to go down to Locheagle to visit his Uncle Davy and Aunt Julie. He visits his Uncle Richard too of course but Davy was always a favourite. He and Emma, that's Jamie's mother, were always very close.'

'I hope you and Jamie will write to me too when I am away.' Rina said wistfully. 'Mother never writes and she's so bitter because I didn't marry Lord Tannahill. He understood. We parted as friends. He said he would bring his little daughter to visit sometime.'

'We all thought he seemed a very decent man, but I believe he realised he was too old for you. In later life the difference doesn't seem so great.'

'Hi Rina,' Jamie called through the kitchen window at Bonnybrae. 'Come and see my new bicycle.'

'But I'm helping Aunt Maggie prepare the dinner. Ride it past the window and I'll watch you.'

'You'd better go and see him, Rina,' Maggie chuckled. 'He's like a wee laddie with a new toy. It took him a while to learn to balance but he seems to have mastered it all right now.'

'It looks easy,' she said when she saw Jamie cycling round the yard with apparent ease.

'Come on then. I'll give you a go. I'll steady you until you get the hang of it.' Rina found it was not so easy as it looked but Jamie insisted she persevere while he held onto the seat. He let go, thinking she was managing well but as soon as she realised he was not holding her she began to wobble precariously and would have fallen had Jamie not run forward to catch her in his arms. For a moment they clung to each other, laughing, their faces almost touching. It seemed the most natural thing for Jamie to kiss her lips but he was unprepared for the intense yearning in Rina's response and the flare of desire she aroused in his gut. His arms tightened automatically, pressing her closer, then he remembered they were in full view of the kitchen window and he needed no reminder of the gulf between Miss Capel of Stavondale and himself, a lowly tenant farmer.

'Forgive me, Rina. I'm going to miss you dreadfully when you go away to your hospital. I pray you'll be safe there, and happy.'

'Oh Jamie,' Rina murmured softly and he knew she felt as he did. He sensed she was near to tears.

'Come on,' he said with forced cheerfulness. 'One more pedal round the yard to see if you're getting the hang of it.' She continued to wobble but before long he was able to release his hold and she continued her ride even if she was a bit shaky.

Jim had agreed Duke could stay at Bonnybrae while Rina was away so two days later she rode him over. Jamie had promised to ride his bicycle most of the way back with her.

'If we're lucky I may be able to give you a lift on the crossbar,' he grinned.

'So long as we don't both end up in the ditch,' Rina chuckled.

'Rina did you say your stable boy is looking for another job?' Jim asked as they gathered around the table for supper.

'Yes he is. His father was head horseman at Manor Farm but he died suddenly a month ago and Ernest needs to earn more money to help support his mother and two younger sisters. Mr McGill offered him work with Jed Taylor, the man who has taken his father's place. He was second horseman but he and Ernest never got on. That's why Grandfather gave him a job, but he was a young boy then and there is not enough for him to do now, especially when Duke will not be there, nor Father's horse.'

'How old is he? Would he want to work with heavy horses here do you think?'

'He's seventeen. He was always small for his age, no bigger than I am, but this last year he has grown almost as tall as Jamie, although he's still skinny. He often helped at

Manor Farm while his father was alive. I think that's why Jed resented him.'

'Mmm, that happens sometimes. Well if he wants work and he is willing to have a go at everything, including learning to milk, then ask him to come and see me. He would need to live in the bothy though, but Mrs Edgar and Maggie would feed him between them. The young fellow we used to have before the war lost a leg. Even if he wanted to come back here to work he's no use behind a plough now.'

'I will tell Ernest. I'm sure he would like to work at Bonnybrae,' Rina said.

As soon as the meal was over and Rina had helped Maggie wash the dishes, Jamie insisted they leave.

'It will be dark soon. I have a lamp for my bicycle but I don't know how well it works. Anyway, I want to be sure you get safely up the drive to Stavondale before it gets too dark when you're on your own.'

'It's a pity I haven't got a motor bike yet,' Joe said with a wide grin and a wink. 'I could have given our wee Rina a ride on the back of it.'

'Joe!' Maggie admonished. 'Stop teasing. You know I don't want you to get one of those horrible machines. You might fall off and get yourself killed.'

'Dear Maggie,' Joe smiled and stroked his wife's cheek gently. 'I promise I shall not do anything dangerous, but it would be good not to have a long walk at either end of the train journey every day,' he added seriously. 'I'm not getting any younger you know.'

'I know, I know,' Maggie said with remorse. 'I'm selfish but I couldn't bear to lose you.'

Ten minutes later Jamie hurtled along with Rina balancing on the cross bar of his bike.

'This is fun,' she said, laughing up at him. 'And it's a lot quicker than walking. Maybe I should save up for one to help me get to the railway station on my day off. Is Joe really thinking of buying a motor bike do you think? I have seen one or two in Strathlinn while I was visiting the MacQuades.'

'I think he would like one now that he has seen how fast an ordinary bike can go, but Aunt Maggie is very nervous about the idea and he doesn't want to hurt her or have her worrying. He walks several miles every day to and from the stations, as well as doing his day's work. He says he would go all the way on a motor bike in half the time.'

'Aunt Maggie worries because they love each other. Mother wouldn't care what my father did.'

'Don't be cynical, Rina,' Jamie said gently. 'It's not like you. I'm sure she wouldn't want anything to happen to him really. Maybe she will be happier when they go to live in Edinburgh.'

That happened even quicker than Rina had anticipated and she was glad she had already started her nurses' training so she didn't have to watch her old home being dismantled. She was truly thankful she had removed everything she wanted from her own room and from her grandfather's home. She had had a lot of help and advice from a tearful Mrs MacCrindle as well as from Mr McGill and his men, and she was grateful to them all.

CHAPTER EIGHT

Melissa and Rina were glad they had each other for company as they investigated their new accommodation in the nurses' home. All the bedrooms were identical with a built-in wardrobe and waxed wooden floors with a small bedside rug. They located the lavatories and the linen and blanket storerooms, but for Rina the electric light was a novelty.

'I shall be able to write my letters in the evenings even when the winter nights come again.'

'You will, so long as you remember lights have to be out by ten-thirty,' Mel reminded her with a smile. The floors in the corridors were also of waxed maple wood and the walls above the dado were distempered in pale green. Rina felt everything was fresh and clean but she knew her mother would have been scathing about the simplicity. The bathrooms had tiled dados and they were an improvement on the toilet facilities at Stavondale Tower, although not as good as the ones at Stavondale Manor which her grandfather had installed more recently, especially for her. Her eyes swam with unexpected tears at the thought of the old man she had loved so dearly. Mel suggested they should find their way to the dining room which was approached by an outside staircase made of concrete.

'Mr Carruthers, the architect, told father the whole renovation cost £2500,' Mel said, 'so we're probably lucky it has been done before we started. I do hope we shall like nursing,' she added nervously.

'I'm sure we shall, Mel,' Rina said, 'and I mean to work really hard at our studies. I feel I must prove I can do this, both to my parents and to Matron. I'm sure she thinks I'm an empty-headed coquette because I attended a school for young ladies. If only she knew how boring I found it.'

'I am sure you will prove them all wrong and you will do really well.'

'There is one thing which troubles me,' Rina confessed slowly. 'I'm not sure how I shall feel if any of the children die, and I know many children do die with the dreadful diphtheria and scarlet fever.'

The first week seemed long. It was hard work so both girls were thankful they could relax on their day off. The hospital grounds and surrounding countryside were pleasant but as time went on Rina felt more homesick for Bonnybrae and its occupants than she had ever felt for her own home and parents. When their days off coincided, she accompanied Mel to visit her parents at Strathlinn, walking the four miles except when their free time coincided with the horse-drawn bus. The MacQuades always welcomed her warmly. As the days lengthened and the sun shone many of the nurses were happy to share a game of tennis in the hospital grounds. They were encouraged to make the most of the fresh air and exercise. Both Mel and Rina had made other friends, and Rina particularly enjoyed walking into the countryside when she could.

She was always vigilant and she had been paying special attention to a pretty four-year-old girl who had been admitted with diphtheria. It was a terrible blow to her when the child died. Apart from being the first death she had witnessed it had seemed so tragic that someone so young and so pretty should die. She remembered Matron's advice when they first began, telling them they must not allow their emotions to become involved. That was easier said than done and Rina wept into her pillow that night. She found comfort in writing about it but it was to Jamie she expressed her sorrow. She had heard nothing from her parents since they left Stavondale.

On the sixth of June it was Jamie's twenty-second birthday and Rina wished she could have gone to Bonnybrae to help Maggie make a birthday tea and some of the butter toffee he still enjoyed, but in his weekly letter he told her he planned to visit his parents in Yorkshire. She wondered if he would see the girl Aunt Maggie had mentioned after one of his earlier visits to Yorkshire, but it was his dog who was his main concern, rather than a girlfriend.

'I'm worried about Jill,' he wrote, 'she is nine now. I knew she had aged after her last litter of pups but she seems worse since the lambing finished, almost as though she knows it will be her last. I expect when you see so many sick people Rina, you think I'm selfish to grieve about a dog, but Jill has been part of my life for so long and I know I shall miss her terribly, even though I have her daughter and two granddaughters.'

Rina replied by return.

'Dearest Jamie, I love Jill almost as much as you must do. I would never think you selfish because you care. It is one of the qualities I admire in you. You often tease me about meeting clever or handsome doctors but sometimes I feel they must be hardened to the suffering of other people. I know we are not supposed to get involved but some people care more than others and I'm pleased and proud you are a caring person. I shall pray that nothing happens to Jill while you are away, though I know she will miss you. I expect you will need to be back for the sheep shearing, and then the haymaking. I like my new life as a nurse but I miss you all, and the animals at Bonnybrae. How is Ernest settling in? Does he enjoy his work?'

'*Ernest is proving a fine young horseman,*' Jamie told her in his next letter.

He is a hard worker but he is patient with the horses. He is a bit slow at learning to milk — not as good as you yet!

He is also good at working the dogs to round up the sheep so that saves Uncle Jim's energy, especially since Mr Edgar has not been keeping so well. He and his wife are quite a bit older than Aunt Maggie. Uncle Jim thinks we should be looking out for a young couple to help with the milking and lend Aunt Maggie a hand in the house at Bonnybrae. We have a spare cottage now so we could hire a married couple. Most of the men still move at the term, May and November, but Uncle Jim dislikes going to hiring fares. He thinks it's degrading for men standing in line waiting to be chosen. Anyway, that's five months away.

It was Rina's eighteenth birthday on the twenty-sixth of June but they were so busy in the hospital she barely had time to remember. Later in the day she collected her post and found a beautiful birthday card from Maggie, Joe and Jim Sinclair. There was also an affectionate letter from Jamie, even though she had already received his usual weekly letter on Monday. Mrs MacCrindle sent a postcard with birthday greetings from herself, the McGills and all the workers at Manor Farm. There was nothing from her parents. It was as she had expected but she still felt a pang of regret. She knew her mother would never forgive her for not marrying Lord Tannahill.

There was no time to feel sorry for herself; they were all kept busy with an epidemic of whooping cough and the admission of several new young patients. She soothed and comforted the ones who cried for their mothers, who were only permitted to wave to them through the windows. Patiently she administered to their needs, and those of the older children, who seemed to be more severely affected. She was exhausted and relieved when her day off dawned on Saturday. She planned to have a leisurely morning and per-haps enjoy a game of tennis or a good walk in the fresh air in the afternoon. She was surprised when Home Sister sent for her about eleven-fifteen. She hurried down the stairs, hoping none of the other nurses had fallen ill and she was not needed to do an extra shift. There in the entrance hall stood Maggie.

'Aunt Maggie!' Rina flew into her arms, oblivious to the presence of Home Sister, whose usually stern demeanour relaxed. She even smiled as she watched the genuine affection and joy with which the two women greeted each other. She knew Rina regularly received letters, but as far as she could tell there appeared to be no communication between Lady Capel and her daughter. 'How did you get here?' Rina asked. 'It's such a difficult journey from Bonnybrae. But oh, I'm so pleased to see you.' She turned to Home Sister then. 'I'm so sorry, I didn't mean to interrupt your conversation. Would it be all right to show my aunt my room?'

'Very well,' Home Sister said.

'We must not be long,' Maggie said. 'Joe is waiting outside.'

'Uncle Joe has come too? How lovely. We'll not bother looking at my room then. I can't tell you how happy I am to see you.'

'Thank you for your assistance,' Maggie said to Home Sister with her friendly smile as she followed Rina outside.

'Well!' Rina gasped when she saw Joe standing beside a motor bike and side car. 'So this is how you got here?' She turned to look at Maggie. 'So he did get one after all! What does this mean, BSA?'

'It stands for Birmingham Small Arms which is a combination of companies,' Joe told her with a grin. 'They have been manufacturing guns for the army during the war but now they have gone back to making bicycles and motor bikes. I was not allowed to have one with only two wheels though,' he winked at Rina, 'but this will be even better now that I have persuaded Maggie to ride in it.'

'Today was the first time,' Maggie beamed. 'I sat in the wee pram at the side. I was scared out of my wits.' Joe threw back his head and laughed aloud.

'She was too. But she really wanted to see you again, Rina, so she soon got used to it, didn't you, dearest Maggie?'

'Yes, but I made him promise to drive very slowly, and he did, but not for long. I confess I enjoyed it though, seeing so much countryside and travelling so many miles. I have never been so far from Bonnybrae before. I wrote a letter to your lady, who looks after you in the nurses' home. We wanted to be sure you would be here and that this was your free day. She wrote back immediately and said she would make sure you were free. She says there is a pleasant wee tearoom in the village where we can get something to eat when Jamie comes.' She clapped a hand over her mouth. 'Oh I forgot. He wanted it to be a surprise. Rina you will have to pretend.'

'There's no need. Here he is now,' Joe chuckled. They all turned as Jamie pedalled towards them.

'Did you cycle all the way here?' Rina asked incredulously. 'That's not the bicycle you had before.'

'I rode on the back of Joe's motorbike as far as Strathlinn,' Jamie grinned. 'Aunt Maggie and Mr MacQuade arranged everything so we went to the MacQuades' home. This bicycle is for ladies and it is your birthday present from all of us, including Uncle Jim. I set off here straight away while these two sat enjoying coffee and scones with Mrs MacQuade,' he said pulling a face. 'I was nearly here by the time they caught up with me. Now I'm famished.'

'We thought it would let you explore the countryside a bit, Rina,' Joe said.

'Yes, we all know how you hate being cooped up,' Jamie grinned. 'Maybe you will be able to bike to the railway station and bring it with you on the train so you can cycle to Bonnybrae sometimes while the summer days are so long and light.'

'The bicycle bag on the back is a gift from the MacQuades. Inside it has a kit to mend any punctures in the tyres, and a spanner,' Maggie said. 'Jamie you must lower the seat again after riding it with your long legs. Mr MacQuade helped us organize everything with the bicycle shop in Strathlinn. The basket on the front is from Mrs MacCrindle. There is a tin in it with one of her fruit loaves. The lamp is from Mr and Mrs McGill.'

'How kind of everybody,' Rina said hoarsely, and blinked rapidly to dispel her tears. 'I never thought anyone would buy me a gift, especially nothing as fine as this.' Her mouth tightened. 'Mother and Father didn't remember it was my birthday.'

'Never mind dear,' Maggie comforted and gave her another hug. 'Shall we all walk to the tearoom now and see if we can get some of the delicious soup your lady nurse recommended?'

'Let me see if you can still ride a bicycle first,' Jamie said with a chuckle, 'in case I need to hold you all the way up the street.' Rina pulled a face at him as he found the spanner and lowered the seat for her. She managed after a wobbly start but she was soon cycling confidently down the street and back again.

'It's wonderful!' she called. 'I can't believe this is really mine. I don't know how I can ever thank you all.'

'It's a pleasure to see ye so happy, lassie,' Joe said gruffly.

'Can you wait while I take it round to the bicycle shed to keep it safe?'

'I'll come with you,' Jamie offered. 'You ride it and I'll run beside, in case you fall off,' he added with a teasing grin.

Rina parked her bicycle in the shed provided. There were three others there belonging to nurses. She turned to Jamie and threw her arms around his neck in gratitude. She intended to kiss his cheek but somehow their lips met in a long, lingering kiss which neither wanted to end. Jamie enjoyed the feel of her pressed closely against him and the passion with which she responded. Gently he drew back.

'You must forgive me, Rina,' he said gruffly, 'but I have missed you terribly. We all have, but Aunt Maggie would not approve of me kissing you like this.' Rina looked slightly hurt.

'But I thought she liked me.'

'Of course she does. She loves you like a daughter. That's why she expects me to remember you are still the daughter of our landlord, even if you are a nurse now.'

'Jamie . . . ?' Rina's tone was diffident. 'Have you, have you kissed any other girls like that?' He hesitated for a second.

'I — no, not exactly.' He thought of his visits to Yorkshire and the evenings spent with his distant cousins, Ronnie and Hannah Kerr, and their friends. Rina frowned.

'What does that mean? Did you kiss other girls like you kiss me?'

'No, never. It's just . . . there's a girl in Yorkshire who seems to like kissing me.'

'Oh, I see,' Rina said in a small voice.

'No, you don't see, Rina. I try to avoid being in her company if I can, but she's a friend of Hannah's so it's not so easy. She's not my type at all. You're worth a dozen of her.'

'Truly?' He nodded. 'I'm so glad.' Rina's smiles were restored. In his heart Jamie knew it was true, just as he knew Rina could never be for him.

They all strolled at a leisurely pace along the village street. It was quite long with houses mostly aligned on either side, interspersed with a post office, a bakers, a newsagent and sweet shop, a blacksmith's forge and a haberdashery shop. Farms and fields stretched out beyond the main street. Home Sister had told Maggie that the village tearoom was run by the daughter of one of the farmers who had lost her husband and needed to earn a living to support her two young children so hospital staff tried to help by recommending her to visitors. The food was excellent. Joe insisted on paying, saying it was his day out and his treat. They all ate the chicken and rice soup with new baked rolls and homemade butter, followed by a rich beef stew with carrots, onions and mushrooms and accompanied by new potatoes and garden peas. The young woman told them her brother cultivated the garden for her and he liked to have vegetables ready before anyone else in the village. They finished their meal with rhubarb pie and cream followed by a good cup of tea.

'Whew, I'm glad I don't have to cycle back to Strathlinn,' Jamie chuckled. 'I'm sure I'm several pounds heavier.' Another customer had overheard Rina telling them about her work at the hospital and when they were ready to leave she suggested they take a turning to the left and they would find a pleasant walk through the woods, leading to a wee burn.

'Just ye follow the burn, it brings ye out on the lane at the back o' the hospital. Some o' the women who work in the kitchen and the laundry come frae the next village so they use that path as a short cut.'

As they walked in twos Jamie told Rina that Mr MacQuade has promised to buy Mel a bicycle if Rina could persuade her to learn to ride. Maggie overheard.

'Mrs MacQuade said we must be sure to tell you Rina, that you will be very welcome to visit them, even if your day off is not the same as Melissa's. She says she loves young people around her. They are grateful for the way you have helped Mel make friends. Is she enjoying her work here?'

'Oh yes, and she is very good with the young patients.' Rina smiled. 'She also has a rather nice young doctor for a friend. I think he admires her calm, quiet manner. The other nurses like her too, now they realise she is a naturally quiet and thoughtful person and she doesn't gossip.' It was a lovely visit and Rina was sad to see them go but she knew Jamie had to be back in time for the milking. He laughed at her expression as she watched him climb on behind Joe.

'You look as worried as Aunt Maggie,' he chuckled, 'but I hold on tight.'

'We have all enjoyed our visit and seeing you, dear Rina,' Maggie said and gave her one more hug before she climbed into the little sidecar.

On the rare occasions when Rina's day off fell on a Sunday she made a point of cycling to Strathlinn and catching the train. The porters were all helpful about loading her bicycle and at the other end she lost no time in cycling the three miles to Bonnybrae. She knew Jim and Jamie would be busy at each end of the day attending to the animals and milking the cows but Sundays were the Sabbath day and no other work was done so it was the best time to visit, even though it meant missing the kirk, something her grandfather had been very strict about. Once or twice she visited on a Saturday and arrived in time to help Maggie with the cooking if Jamie was busy in the fields. Ernest seemed over-joyed to see her and thanked her for helping him get a job at Bonnybrae. He gave her all the news about Manor Farm and the tenants on the estate.

Towards the end of August Rina visited Bonnybrae knowing it might be the last time she would be free on Sundays while the evenings were still light. Ernest told her Lord Tannahill had been up to stay at Stavondale Tower and he was making changes. He and his daughter and her govern-ess were going to live in the wing which her grandfather had occupied and he was making the other wing into accommo-dation for shooting parties who might wish to come when he was not there himself. He was going to hire a couple to oversee the housekeeping and the gardens.

'He said if I saw you, Miss Rina, I was to say you would be very welcome to visit and he would show you around if he is there. He said he was sorry I had moved away because he hoped to keep a pony for his wee lassie and at least one of his own, but I told him I liked working here at Bonnybrae.'

'I'm glad you're happy, Ernest,' Rina said with a warm smile.

'Oh I am Miss, but I don't think everybody will be pleased with Lord Tannahill. He has already made changes to two of the farms nearest Craigs Hill. He is joining them together and The Forbes's son is going to run them both, but Doug Lamont from the other wee farm is walking out with Alice Forbes and they wanted to get married. Now Doug will be out of his farm. He doesna want to work for his brother-in-law. He asked Mr McGill but he has no jobs going and Alice doesn't want to live too far from her parents.'

'I remember Alice from when I went round with Grandfather. She is a few years older than I am but she loved the sheep and she milked their two house cows.'

'Aye, she's upset about it all, although she's glad for her brother and his wife because they have three children and it will be better when they have more acres.'

'Have you told Mr Sinclair about them, Ernest? Or if you know Doug you could tell him to try applying for a job at Bonnybrae. I'm sure Jamie's uncle mentioned wanting another man with a wife who would help with the milking. I think Alice would do that if it means she can marry Doug and have a home of their own.'

'D'ye think so Miss Rina?' Ernest's eyes brightened. 'I ken Doug. He was older than me and he stuck up for me because I was the littlest in my class and some o' the bigger lads kept bullying me. They stopped when Doug threatened them. Maybe I'll walk up there and tell him what you said.'

'Well it would be worth a try. After all, Bonnybrae would not be far from Alice's parents.'

It had become Jamie's custom to cycle back to the station with Rina and see her and her bicycle onto the train. Now that her parents no longer lived at Stavondale she didn't care if anyone noticed them. Her own outlook on life had broadened considerably since she had mixed with the other nurses. She gave Jamie a hug and kissed him goodbye as usual but in her heart she knew he would always feel he was at a disadvantage because she was the laird's daughter.

Time passed swiftly because both Mel and Rina were studying hard to take their first examinations along with the nurses who had started earlier. Matron Gilroy had sent for them and told them she had heard good reports of both their nursing and their studying. She said they had both had opportunities in education which the other nurses had not had and if they could take their preliminary examination, which was approved by the General Nursing Council of Scotland, at the same time as the others, and pass them, it would keep them all together and save the cost of bringing doctors for extra lectures. She recommended books and publications they should read as extras. Mel was nearly sick with worry at the pressure.

'We should be flattered Matron considers us able to do this, Mel,' Rina said gently. 'We can only do our best and if we don't pass the exams it doesn't mean we must leave nursing. We can try again.'

As it happened they both passed well enough to earn Matron's approval. Only one of the nurses failed and she left soon afterwards, telling them she was getting married and she was going to work in the laundry and have regular hours. Word soon leaked out that she was expecting a baby and she was marrying one of the young men who worked in the boiler room maintaining the hot water system.

Rina was pleased when Maggie wrote to tell her Doug Lamont and Alice Forbes had been to see Jim.

'*I was at Bonnybrae when they called,*' she wrote.

Alice was neatly dressed and had a spotlessly clean apron and cap beneath her cloak, which she said she had made herself. I think she will be a thrifty wife and a good worker, but you probably know that dearest Rina as I believe it was your suggestion that they should contact Jim. Alice said she would be happy to help me in the house if I needed her now that Mrs Edgar is less able. I confess I feel my own old bones sometimes these days. It would be good to know Jim and Jamie would have someone to look after them if I couldn't do it myself. Alice seemed keener to help with the milking than Doug but he is a keen shepherd and has plenty of experience at shearing and lambing. They are to start work at the November term so they're going to arrange their wedding. Alice would like to come to clean the cottage and distemper some of the rooms so that it is fresh and clean before they start work at Bonnybrae. I rather like them, Rina.

* * *

Rina was halfway through her second year of preliminary nursing when Jamie wrote to tell her Maggie had had a bad bout of influenza and the doctor had insisted she must stay in bed for a week and then take things easy for at least a couple of weeks to make a full recovery.

Mrs Edgar and Alice are looking after Uncle Jim and me. Alice has also been down to Braeside to take Maggie pans of soup as well as a stew so Uncle Joe is grateful to her. He stayed away from work for the first three days. His partner, Mr Courton, understood his anxiety because his own wife had recently suffered from a similar illness. He told Joe it had even made him consider selling the factory but she has made a good recovery so he wants to carry on for another year or two so long as Joe stays too, to share the responsibility.

Anyway Rina, you'll never believe this but Joe has persuaded Uncle Jim to install a bathroom upstairs at Bonnybrae and a hot water system with a sink and hot water in the kitchen, just like he did at Braeside. Uncle Jim was reluctant because Bonnybrae does not belong to us but Uncle Joe persuaded him that it would be a lot easier for Aunt Maggie if she didn't have to carry buckets of water to fill the boiler beside the fire, and boil kettles of hot water in addition. He said it would be more convenient for us too when we didn't need to use the tin bath every Friday night. Anyway they have agreed. Mr Courton is helping Joe get the bath and other things at wholesale price from a man he knows in Glasgow, but Uncle Jim insists on paying for it. I don't know if you have ever seen upstairs at Bonnybrae but there are four big bedrooms and another stair to a large attic. The bedroom above the kitchen is huge so Uncle Joe is going to make a wooden wall to divide it in two. One half will be directly over the kitchen so the plumbing will be easier. There will be a cold water tank in the attic as well as a small tank for the water closet, with a chain through the ceiling to flush the toilet. I don't suppose you want to know all this Rina but it is causing great excitement for Uncle Jim and me. We wonder how it will all work. Uncle Joe and Uncle Davy know a plumber from Locheagle who was at school with them so he is going to come next weekend if Uncle Joe and Uncle Davy do the labouring and woodwork. It should be finished before you come again. I know Aunt Maggie will be pleased because it always bothered her that you had to use the closet in the orchard when you were at Bonnybrae. Uncle Joe wishes we could have a telephone up here too but of course there are no poles for the telephone wires, or for electricity.

He didn't tell Rina Uncle Jim's concern was that her father would increase the rent again if he heard they had improved the house so much, but there was no land agent to inspect and Sir Roger himself had never been to see any of his tenants. Rina had made one brief visit to Edinburgh to see her parents but it had not been a joyful reunion, although her father had seemed pleased to see her. She confided in Maggie that he looked older since he left Stavondale and her mother had spent her time flirting with a man named Wardle, a widower, who was a frequent visitor. She had thought him loud and brash and not at all like a gentleman. He had a house in France and had made a lot of money during the war with the manufacture of guns. Now his company were making vans.

It was May 1920 and Rina was studying for her second year's examinations when they had to deal with an epidemic of diphtheria. It distressed Rina when young patients died. Those who survived were in the hospital for six weeks or longer so all the nurses were kept extremely busy. It made matters worse when three patients were admitted with typhoid fever. The doctors decreed that only nurses who had been vaccinated should nurse patients with typhoid. They knew how lethal the disease had been amongst some of the soldiers fighting abroad during the war. Neither Rina nor Mel had had the injections and it soon became apparent that this applied to several of the other nurses too. It was decided they should all be vaccinated, but they would be treated over a period since some nurses suffered more severe reactions than others and might be off sick for twenty-four hours or even longer in some cases.

Rina had always been healthy and when epidemics of childhood ailments affected her school she had usually made a quick recovery so it never occurred to her that she would react badly to the typhoid vaccination. She mentioned the program of vaccinations in her letter to Maggie. She enjoyed discovering anything to do with fevers and their treatments since she started work at the hospital so she had read about the man called Almwroth Edward Wright who had worked on, and discovered, a vaccine for typhoid. In 1896 the vaccine had been used to save the lives of many military men. Two of the other nurses, who happened to be vaccinated on the same day, by the same doctor, reacted badly, as did Rina. She had no idea where she was or who was caring for her during several days of delirium when her temperature became dangerously high. It was only later she learned Mel had not been allowed to visit her, even though she had recovered from her own vaccination with nothing more than a bad headache and twenty-four hours with a temperature and no appetite.

When Maggie did not receive Rina's usual weekly letter she began to worry. The days passed and still no letter. Maggie was convinced something must be wrong. She begged Joe to take her in his motor bike and side car to the hospital. Home Sister was kind and patient but she was adamant that Rina was not allowed any visitors.

'She would not know you, even if we permitted you to see her,' she explained, 'but the risk is too great. We hope the fever will break soon but I'm afraid it will leave Nurse Capel feeling very weak. She will need time to recover.'

'B-but you are sure she will recover?' Maggie persisted anxiously. Home Sister frowned. One nurse had died and they were all concerned about the condition of Rina and her colleague.

'We shall be able to tell you more in a few days,' she said trying to sound reassuring. 'It is unusual to suffer such a severe reaction but I assure you we are giving Nurse Capel the best nursing care we can.'

'Is there anything she needs, anything I can do for her?' Maggie pleaded. 'Will she be allowed to leave the hospital to convalesce?'

'She will need rest and good food for some time,' Home Sister said carefully.

'Please . . . will you write and let us know as soon as she recovers from the delirium? And when we may take her home?' Maggie scribbled down her address and handed it over.

'Is her home with you, Mrs Greig?' Sister asked with a note of surprise. 'I know she corresponds regularly with this address of course but . . .'

'I am her aunt. We will take great care of her until she is well again.' Maggie said firmly. 'My husband will collect her.'

'Very well. I shall keep you informed.'

Concern grew as Rina reached a crisis and it was then Home Sister and Matron Gilroy realised Rina had given Mrs Margaret Greig as her next of kin and they had no contact address for Sir Roger and Lady Capel in Edinburgh. It was a great relief all round when her temperature broke and her thrashing, restless limbs grew calmer. She drifted into a natural sleep at last. For two whole days she slept and sipped water but on the third day Home Sister sat beside her bed and took her hand.

'You have been very ill, Catherina. We have been very anxious about your extreme reaction to the typhoid vaccine. You will need a few weeks to recuperate fully and regain your strength but we do not have Lady Capel's address to contact her.' Rina drew her hand away and her eyes filled with tears, a sure sign of weakness in a young person who had proved herself to be strong and resilient and an excellent nurse.

'There would be no point in informing my mother,' she said at last. Even her voice was weak. 'She never wanted me to become a nurse.'

'I'm sorry to hear that my dear when you have done so well. But we really ought to inform your parents.' Rina closed her eyes wearily.

'Mother would not want me within a mile of her if she knew I had been ill, especially with a fever. She never nursed Jonathan and me when we were children. She said that was nanny's job.' Again her eyes misted with tears and she brushed them away.

'Your aunt came to visit you but we could not let her near the isolation ward while you were so ill.'

'My aunt?'

'Mrs Greig. You gave her as your next of kin. She said she was your aunt . . .' Sister said uncertainly.

'She is my aunt. My parents don't acknowledge her.' Rina smiled for the first time. 'Aunt Maggie is a lovely person. She wouldn't be afraid of anything.'

'She is very anxious about you. I promised to write her a letter and tell her as soon as you began to recover. She wants to look after you while you regain your strength but you know you are very welcome to stay here to convalesce.'

'I feel so tired. My legs . . . they're so wobbly when I try to stand.'

'Yes, it will take a day or two before you are able to walk to the bathroom, even though it is just across the corridor.'

'I would love to stay with Aunt Maggie.' She yawned. 'I'm sorry. If only I didn't feel so weary . . .'

'Time and good nourishment is what you need now child,' Home Sister said. Rina had never known her sound so kind or so human and her eyes swam with the infuriating tears. She brushed them away.

'I d-don't know wh-what's wrong with me.'

'It is natural to feel weak and tired after being so ill, Catherina. I will order an egg custard for your supper and I will write to your aunt tonight. Maybe by the weekend your uncle will be able to come and collect you.'

Joe and Jamie waited beside Sister's desk in the small reception hall. It was a shock to see Rina coming slowly and carefully down the stairs towards them. Even when she reached the bottom she came round by the wall instead of across the floor. Home Sister put her hand on the back of a waiting chair and Rina sank onto it gratefully. It was only then she looked up at them and smiled, but it was a travesty of the wide smile and dancing eyes they were used to. Joe felt a lump in his throat and his heart swelled with tenderness as though she was his daughter. Jamie was not so controlled. He moved to her side and knelt in front of her, taking her hands in his warm, strong fingers.

'What have they done to you my dearest Rina?' he asked in a husky voice.

'Young man we have given your cousin the best nursing care we can but she has been extremely ill and it will take her a few weeks to regain her strength. I should tell you she is insisting on taking these books with her but I have told her she must not exhaust herself with studying. She can always take it next year. Our main concern is that she should regain her stamina and her natural resistance to infection before she returns to work.'

'We shall take good care of her,' Joe said and smiled his thanks. Jamie did not wait for more instructions he lifted Rina in his strong young arms and held her close.

'I will carry her out. She feels frail enough for a wind to blow her away.' Although it was a warm day, Rina was dressed in her winter coat and hat. Joe had parked the motor bike as near to the door as he could but he had not realised Rina would be so weak and pale. He hurried in front of them to open the door of the little side car and lift out the shawl and a wool rug which Maggie had sent, along with strict instruction to Jamie to wrap her up well. Jamie was still too shocked by Rina's appearance to do anything but obey and he folded the shawl into a triangle and draped it gently over Rina's head and shoulders.

'Aunt Maggie said we should fasten it tightly around your chest so it will not blow away or let you get a draft as we travel.'

'Snuggle down low lassie and the screen will shield you from most of the wind,' Joe said, handing Jamie the woollen rug. He tucked it around Rina as patiently as any mother, Joe thought and in that moment he knew his nephew would never love any other woman the way he loved Rina. He sighed heavily, wishing there was not such a gap between their families. Yet Home Sister said Rina had given Maggie's name as her next of kin. She had been deeply touched and shed a few tears about that.

Rina couldn't believe it when she opened her eyes and the engine was silent.

'Are we home already?' she asked. 'Surely I can't have slept the whole way to Braeside?' Over her head Joe and Maggie exchanged glances. Their hearts were full with both joy and sadness to hear Rina thought of this as home. What sort of a person could Lady Capel be when her own daughter did not turn to her after being so ill.

'We're home all right,' Jamie grinned down at her, 'And Aunt Maggie can't wait to look after you.' He lifted her in his arms. Rina made no protest, a sure sign she felt too weak to trust her own legs, Joe thought. 'Shall I take her straight through to the sitting room?'

'Yes, please do,' Maggie said, trying to hide her dismay at the sight of Rina's thin pale face. She had always had rounded rosy cheeks. 'Jim and Ernest helped me bring the bed downstairs and the fire is keeping the room nice and cosy.'

'Oh dear,' Rina said. 'I don't want to cause so much extra work. Maybe you should take me to Stavondale Manor, Uncle Joe? Mrs MacCrindle would . . .'

'No! Rina, my dear it is a pleasure to care for you, but I feel so sad to see you so weak and ill. We wouldn't want you to go anywhere else but here.'

'See,' Jamie said triumphantly and cradled her even closer to his chest. 'This is where you belong. Will you open the door please Aunt Maggie and I'll carry her straight through?'

'Oh, this is lovely,' Rina said, her voice quivering with emotion as she saw the blazing fire and the cosy room.

'Shall I lay you on the bed, Rina? Or do you feel like sitting up in a chair for a while?' Jamie asked tenderly.

'I would like to sit in the chair, please,' Rina said but her eyes filmed with the tears she seemed unable to control. 'I must make an effort to get fit again.' She lowered her eyelids for a moment and she felt sure Jamie had brushed his mouth gently across them as he leaned down to sit her carefully in the chair beside the fire. Maggie bit her lower lip as she watched them. She had always known Jamie felt a great affection for Rina, as she did herself, but she was convinced now that he loved her as a man loves the woman he wants for his life's companion and friend. Joe caught her troubled look and shook his head imperceptibly. They had the deepest affection for both Jamie and Rina but there were too many obstacles in their path to lead to happiness.

CHAPTER NINE

Rina did little but sleep for the first few days she was at Braeside, but Maggie knew it was probably the best thing she could do to regain her strength. She made small portions of nourishing, easily digested food to tempt her appetite.

'I can't tell you how grateful I am,' Rina said. 'I know they would have let me stay at the hospital to convalesce but I love being at Braeside. I must pay for my keep though.' Maggie brushed that aside.

'Joe and I are pleased you have chosen to come to us my dear. We are so happy here, thanks to your grandfather, and it gives us pleasure whenever you visit us.'

Slowly Rina's health improved. Each day she walked in the garden, then eventually around the yard and the piggeries as her strength increased and her muscles strengthened. Each evening Jamie came to see her, even if it was only for half an hour if he and Jim and Doug Lamont were working late. She looked forward to his visits more than she cared to admit, even to herself. Alice called to see her and shyly thanked her for the part she had played in helping them find a place with Mr Sinclair at Bonnybrae.

'Aunt Maggie tells me she doesn't know how they would have managed without you, Alice,' Rina smiled. 'I'm sure that must be true while she has been spending so much time looking after me.' Alice was surprised to hear Rina calling Mrs Greig Aunt Maggie and she wondered if it was true that Sir Roger Capel was really Mrs Greig's half-sister as rumours implied.

'Come to think of it,' she said later to Doug, her husband, 'why would Miss Rina come to Braeside to be nursed. You can tell Mrs Greig thinks the world of her, almost as though Rina was her daughter.'

'I've noticed Jamie Sinclair goes down to the Greig's every night since Miss Rina's been staying.'

'Well, Mrs Greig is his father's sister and his mother is Mr Greig's sister, you couldn't get much closer relationship than that,' Alice pointed out.

'I know, but he doesna go down to see them every evening when Miss Rina is not there, and he doesna get washed and changed to see them either.'

'I hope he doesna get hurt then,' Alice frowned. 'I like Master Jamie. I reckon he's a kind and decent young fellow but Ma says he was born out o' wedlock. Even if that's not true I can't see Sir Roger and Lady Capel allowing their daughter to marry one o' their tenants.'

The weather turned warmer. Each morning Rina helped Maggie prepare vegetables for their dinner or they walked together up to Bonnybrae and made the meal there with Jim and Jamie. The first few times they went up to the farm Rina was glad to sit down as soon as they arrived but each day she felt her strength returning and her spirits rose. In the afternoon's she began to sit out in the garden and study for the approaching second-year nursing examination. Maggie fretted over her.

'Joe said your Home Sister told you not to worry about the exam, Rina. Are you sure you should be studying before you're properly recovered?'

'Dear Aunt Maggie,' Rina said with a warm smile, 'you have looked after me so well I am almost better now and I'm beginning to feel a fraud, even though Matron said I must not return until I've built up my stamina again and some resistance to diseases. Anyway, I don't want to postpone my exam until next year and I feel ready to study now. I was thinking of having a ride on Duke. If I ride a little while for a few afternoons to get toughened up I thought I could ride over to Stavondale Manor and see Mrs MacCrindle. I feel guilty not telling her I'm staying here but that house is too big for me on my own. I rarely stay there but she keeps it clean and aired all the time.'

'Don't worry lassie. I wrote her a note to say you were ill and staying with us. Joe took it himself and answered all her questions. She was anxious about you of course so Joe said he would take you to see her before you went back to work at the hospital.'

'Oh thank you. I'm so glad. She looked after Grandfather faithfully, especially at the end.' Her voice choked a little at the memory. 'She was always kind to me.'

'I'm sure you deserved it, Rina.' Maggie sighed. She had such a sweet nature but she didn't realise how heart-warming it was to those around her.

Rina returned to work in good time to take her second-year examinations. She had regained some weight but her dresses were too wide so she tightened her belt and drew them in. She had been dismayed and upset to hear that one of her fellow nurses had died and the young doctor who had administered their vaccinations had left the hospital fearing he must have given the wrong dose. He blamed himself.

'Surely that is not true?' she said to Mel. 'Others suffered a fever for several days, even if they were not as bad as we were.'

'No one else blamed him but he said he felt responsible. He was dreadfully upset when Nurse Wright died but she was always a frail wee thing. Maybe she didn't have as much stamina.'

Rina was deadly tired after the first week and, although she longed to return to Braeside on her day off she spent the time resting and catching up on sleep. Most of all she missed the evenings when Jamie had come down to Braeside to see her. As her strength returned he had asked her to walk with him to the garden gate each evening and he always kissed her cheek before they parted, but on her last evening before she returned to the hospital he drew her into his arms and held her close. She could feel his heart beating as she clung to him.

'Have you any idea how much I'm going to miss you, Rina?' he asked huskily.

'I shall miss you too Jamie, but I will come back when it's my day off.'

'I wish you didn't have to return to the hospital at all but I know it is not my place to say that when I have nothing to offer a girl like you, my dearest.'

'Oh Jamie,' her arms tightened around him. 'I am just the same as any other girl.'

'No, you're not. You're special, and you're extra special to me.' He had kissed her then, a long passionate kiss and she had felt the desire in him as he pressed her closer. She longed for his kiss to go on for ever, but he had broken away quickly with a whispered, 'Goodnight my love.' The memory of his last kiss had sustained her through her working day and long evenings but she ached for the feel of his strong arms around her again.

She passed her examinations with flying colours and both Matron and Home Sister were pleased, and said it was plain to see she had not wasted her time even though she was convalescing.

She returned to Braeside whenever she had a day off but Jamie was often busy, sheep shearing then making hay. Too soon it was harvest time with everyone struggling to gather up the sheaves of corn and bring them into the barns or stacks. The days grew shorter. As third-year nurses Rina and Mel were given more responsibilities, especially when there was a serious outbreak of diphtheria. Most of the patients were in hospital for six weeks or longer. Some of their patients died, and these were usually younger ones. There was an atmosphere of sadness throughout their little hospital. As the epidemic subsided regular time off was resumed. If the weather was reasonable and there was no snow Rina and Mel cycled to Strathlinn to visit Mel's parents if their time off coincided. Mrs MacQuade always had a hearty meal waiting for them and she seemed to take a genuine interest in hearing about their work. Most of all she liked to hear about Doctor Meadows. It was now accepted amongst the hospital staff that he and Mel were a couple. Mel and Rina had planned from the beginning that when they had completed their training at the Fever Hospital and attained their twenty-first birthdays they would move on to one of the larger training hospitals in Glasgow to start General Nursing Training to become State Registered Nurses. It was no secret that Doctor Meadows intended to move to the same hospital as Mel if it could be arranged so that he could continue his own training. As time went by Rina knew in her heart that she was not looking forward to moving to the city. The new cinemas, the theatre, and the dances held no great attraction for her in comparison to the time she could spend at Bonnybrae, especially if she could spend the time with Jamie. She looked forward to his weekly letters even more than Maggie's news, welcome though it was.

The final examinations were drawing nearer when Rina received a most unexpected letter. It was forwarded by Neil MacQuade from her father. She had never known him to write to her, even when she was at boarding school and longed for any link with home. He was planning to stay with her overnight at Stavondale Manor if she would write soon to let him know when she would be free. She sighed heavily. Neither of her parents understood the first thing about the world of work. After a lot of thought she reluctantly discussed her problem with Home Sister who suggested she exchanged shifts so that she could finish during the afternoon and travel home that evening to stay with her father, then travel back to work at the end of her usual free day. Fortunately, Mel was on the opposite shift to her and she was happy to change. She knew how rarely Rina heard anything from either of her parents and she mentioned this to her father on her own free day. Neil MacQuade frowned at the news of Sir Roger's visit.

'He has never managed to clear his gambling debts. I hope he doesn't try to persuade Rina to sell Stavondale Manor. It is a fine house since her grandfather made alterations. If you get an opportunity, Melissa, perhaps you could suggest she consults me before she does anything.'

Rina cycled up the drive from the station later in the evening after finishing her day on the wards. Mrs MacCrindle was in the garden picking fresh mint for the lamb she was preparing for their evening meal.

'Has my father arrived yet, Mrs Mac?' Rina asked.

'Aye, he has, Miss Rina. He came this morning and he's been wandering around like a lost soul waiting for ye. He has been round every room in the house. He says he had never looked round the house before when the manager lived in it. He did say what a fine job Sir Reginald has made of it. I made him some lunch but he didn't eat much then he went round the farm.' She frowned. 'If I didn't know how eager he and Lady Capel were to move to Edinburgh I'd have said he was homesick for his old home.'

'I see.' Rina wondered if that was why her father had come to visit her. She couldn't think of any other reason. As they ate their evening meal together Rina noticed her father did not eat with his usual relish. He had always had a healthy appetite and enjoyed good food and Mrs Mac was an excellent cook. Even their conversation was polite and stilted, but as Rina recalled, she had never had real conversations with either of her parents. They had issued instructions or asked questions and she had answered dutifully. Her grandfather, on the other hand, had talked to her as a person even when she was quite young. He remarked on anything and everything about the people and places they encountered on their rides around the estate, and when they had eaten together he had often recounted stories of his youth, or the latest news of the district.

Her father was subdued and preoccupied, toying with his meat as though it was unfamiliar.

'What have you done with Duke?' he asked out of the blue. Rina looked up in surprise.

'I don't get much time for riding when I'm working at the hospital. Ernest has gone to work as horseman at Bonnybrae so I sent Duke there too and Ernest or Jamie Sinclair exercise him for me.'

'I see. You are a lot thinner than you used to be. The MacCrindle woman says you have been ill?'

'I was. I had a fever but I am quite recovered. You can tell Mother there is no need to worry you will not be carrying home any diseases.' Her voice was flat.

'Your mother doesn't know I'm here. I told her I had some business to attend to.'

'I see.' Rina waited but he didn't enlighten her as to the kind of business and she wondered if it was to do with the tenants on the estate. 'You're not increasing the rents again, are you, Father?'

'No. Shall we move into your sitting room to drink our coffee?'

'All right. I have a bottle of whisky. Would you like a drink?' Without waiting for an answer, she brought her grandfather's silver tray with a crystal decanter and matching whisky glass and set it on the small table beside him. He helped himself.

'Don't you want anything?'

'I never liked whisky. I never liked wine much either. I always took a few sips but only to please Mother.' After a couple of glasses of whisky her father appeared brighter and he became more talkative.

'Your mother has always liked her wine.' He frowned. 'She wants me to take her to France. Have you met her new friend, Wardle? Eric Wardle?'

'Yes, he was there for a meal when I visited you in Edinburgh.'

'So you didn't like him either?' He looked up at her and for a fleeting second he reminded her of her grandfather, the way his eyes held a glint of understanding.

'I didn't say that.'

'You didn't need to, Catherina. The tone of your voice said it for you. Your face always expressed your feelings as a wee girl. I always knew when you were not pleased,' he mused. They were silent for a while, then he went on, 'Wardle has bought a chateau in France and a vineyard. He has invited us to visit but it is Helen he wants. She is eager to go.'

'But you're not keen to visit, Father?' Rina wondered if this was what he had come to tell her, or to sort out in his own mind. He was certainly not his decisive self.

'I can't stick the fellow! I don't know what your mother sees in him — except he has money of course. That seems to have grown more important to Helen than anything else,' he added, his tone bitter.

'He might have money but he didn't have manners,' Rina said more frankly than she would have done had she not felt her father was looking for some support. 'In fact, he was not even polite at table.'

'You're right there! He can't keep his hands off her either, but she doesn't seem to mind him pawing her, even in public. It's sickening to see them.'

'I don't understand, Father. Mother was always so strict about good manners and etiquette and behaving like a lady. I wasted two years at that school for young ladies and it was Mother who insisted.'

'I know, but she had set her heart on you marrying a titled gentleman and taking her into London society. It is where she always longed to be but we were only ever country gentlemen. Now all that seems to matter is having money to squander on pleasure. I've been a great disappointment to her, Catherina.' Rina didn't know how to respond to this so she changed the subject. She was deadly tired after a busy day at work, then cycling to the railway station, then home. When she tried to smother a second yawn her father decided they should both have an early night.

'I will walk to the station with you after lunch tomorrow. My train back to Edinburgh leaves about twenty minutes after yours.'

'All right. We had better set off in good time then because I take my bicycle with me. I need it to get back to the nurses' home from the station.' Rina noticed her father didn't seem to have his usual appetite for breakfast, nor at lunchtime. She was sure from his preoccupation he had something on his mind but whatever it was, he seemed unable to tell her, even though she gave him every opportunity.

She was well known to the railway staff by now and she always gave them a grateful smile when they stowed her bicycle safely in the luggage van. Neither of her parents had ever been demonstrative so she was surprised when she turned to say goodbye, Sir Roger pulled her into his arms and hugged her tightly.

'Forgive me Catherina,' he said huskily. 'I've been a poor father to you.'

'Oh Father . . .' Rina protested shakily.

'It's true. Now it's too late. Try not to judge me too harshly.' He kissed her cheek as she edged nearer to the open door of the railway carriage. 'And Catherina, when you marry choose the man you love and who loves you in return. Don't be like your mother. We were never in love. We were considered a "suitable match". Forgive me,' he repeated quickly and kissed her cheek again as she got on the train. He seemed reluctant to let her go, Rina thought as the doors of the carriages were slammed shut. She saw him standing on the platform, watching her train depart until they were lost from sight.

All the way back Rina pondered on her father's strange behaviour, and the things he had said. She mentioned her bewilderment in her letter to Jamie. As she finished she wrote:

It was good to see Father but I still cannot fathom the reason for his visit. I'm sure there was something he wanted to tell me. I missed my usual day at Braeside and your company cycling back to the station with me, especially as I shall not see you next week. You will be travelling to Yorkshire to see your family, and after that I shall be unable to visit again

until my exams are over. These are the final ones as a fever
nurse and the most important so I must do my best. I look
forward to your letters, dearest Jamie.
      All my love, Rina.

Jamie hugged the letter to his breast as he always did these days. He wondered if Rina really meant she loved him. She was so affectionate with people. He knew she finished her letters to Aunt Maggie and Uncle Joe "with love", but he liked to tell himself she meant a different kind of love for him.

A few days before Rina's exams were due to start Neil MacQuade received a letter from Sir Roger Capel. There was another letter enclosed for Rina. He asked for it to be forwarded to her as he had forgotten to ask for her address at the hospital. MacQuade swore under his breath. Rina had lived at the Belroon Fever Hospital for nearly three years. What sort of father was he that he had never asked for her address in all that time? But he gasped with shock as he read his own letter and he swore audibly. His son, Charles, who was also a partner in the firm, had just entered the room. He raised his eyebrows in surprise. He had rarely heard his father swear, and certainly not over a letter.

'Bad news, Father?' he asked casually.

'Hellish news!' Neil MacQuade looked up at his son. 'Not for us, but it's certainly bad news for Melissa's friend, Rina Capel, and for the tenants of the Stavondale Estate. Sir Roger Capel is selling the remaining farms and cottages on the estate and, you'll never believe the rat could do this!' He looked up at Charles. 'He has negotiated a private deal for the sale of Manor Farm and he wants us to handle the legal matters. He admits he knew his father intended Manor Farm should be transferred to Catherina in its entirety when she reached her twenty-fifth birthday.' He pushed a hand distractedly through his sandy hair.

'Good God! You mean he is cheating his own daughter out of her birth right? Can he do that?'

'Unfortunately he can until it is legally in her name. He knows she gets the trading profit from the farm business — not that she has ever used much of it, except for the upkeep of Stavondale Manor. As her trustee I put the surplus in the bank for her, but it will not last forever with a house the size of Stavondale Manor.' He pushed a hand through his thinning sandy hair. 'He can do as he pleases, as things stand at the present time. Catherina is not yet twenty-one. I tried to warn Sir Reginald at the time, but he knew her parents were not to be trusted. He thought he had given her security by making sure she had a home when he gave her a fine house and income for its upkeep and the promise of a farm of her own. What good will Stavondale Manor be without an income to run the bloody house? She can't afford it on a nurse's pay!'

'No I see that,' Charles said thoughtfully. 'She's a sweet girl. Is there anything we can do to help?'

'I don't think so. I had a feeling in my bones that something like this would happen. Sir Roger has never been able to keep his wife satisfied with money. The house they bought in Edinburgh cost too much.'

'I heard via some friends that Lady Capel has spent a fortune in addition, furnishing it and decorating it to her own taste,' Charles reflected.

'I expect it's true. Sir Roger says his need is greater than Catherina's and he hopes she will forgive him in time. I expect he has written to tell her what a treacherous louse he is in the letter he has written to her.' He tapped the sealed envelope. 'I shall have to send it on but she is starting her final exams in a day or two. I think I will send it to the Home Sister and tell her it is likely to contain unwelcome news. I'll suggest she holds on to it until Rina has finished her exams. What do you think?'

'I don't see any harm in delaying the letter for a few days. It's better than upsetting her.'

Home Sister agreed with his suggestion and sent him a short note by return post saying the examinations would finish on Monday and she would withhold the letter to Catherina over the weekend. She added that she had high hopes for both

Melissa and Catherina. They had worked hard and deserved success.

On Friday evening both Rina and Mel felt fairly satisfied with the exams they had taken so far.

'Just Monday's to come,' Mel said with relief, then if we're lucky we shall have passed our State Fever Examination. I am looking forward to moving on to a larger hospital and a wider variety of nursing, especially now I know Frank will be working at the same hospital.' Rina was silent. She didn't feel the same enthusiasm for moving to the city hospital as Mel did, although she had had a successful interview and been granted a place.

* * *

On Sunday morning a tired and hungry Lord Tannahill drove into the small town of Strathlinn and asked directions to the MacQuades' home. Although he had been there once before with Rina he could not remember the various turnings. He was thoroughly exhausted after driving through the night from his estate in the south and feeling sick with worry. He had come in response to a telegram from his nephew telling him there had been a tragic accident and summoning him to Stavondale urgently.

CHAPTER TEN

The MacQuades were astonished to find Lord Tannahill looking so distraught, on their doorstep on a Sunday morning. Mary MacQuade was unfazed by titles when she saw a man in a state of shock. She was sensible and motherly and she drew him into her home and left him with her husband while she went to make a cup of tea. He paced the room as he explained that his nephew Rupert had been staying at Stavondale for a few days with Mark Blackford, a close friend.

'Mark has not done much shooting. They wanted some practise before joining any of the shooting parties when the grouse shooting begins. The two of them had been shooting rabbits in the field behind Stavondale Tower earlier in the day. They had been quite successful so they moved on to the woods in the early evening, intending to shoot pigeons.' Lord Tannahill bit his lower lip but he went on. 'Rupert says they were not aware of anyone else staying at Stavondale Tower but he and Mark were staying in the West Tower which I keep for my private use.' He swallowed and drew a long breath. 'Neither of them had seen the man around. Mark had taken aim and was just pulling the trigger when the man appeared from behind a tree and walked in front of him.

Rupert says it was impossible to avoid him. He was carrying a rifle of his own. He appeared to step out deliberately. Both young men are dreadfully upset. I don't believe they would be careless . . .'

'Do they know who he is? The man's identity?' Neil MacQuade interrupted quietly but firmly.

'Of course! That's why I'm here.' Lord Tannahill wiped his forehead.

'Sit down before you fall down,' Neil MacQuade insisted. 'So, you know the man's name?'

'Of course I know it,' Lord Tannahill repeated impatiently, 'but Rupert and Mark had never met Sir Roger Capel before. As far as we know he had no reason to be there.'

'Oh my God. Sir Roger is dead?'

'Yes, he's dead. They asked McGill to bring the doctor as fast as he could. He was an elderly man and he knew the Capels. Apparently Sir Roger recognised him and he managed to gasp a few words — something like "ask her to forgive . . ." There was nothing the doctor could do. He called on the local policeman. He had questioned Rupert and Mark before I arrived. Rina — Miss Catherina — will have to be told, but I don't know where to find her.' Neil MacQuade was relieved to see his wife returning with a large pot of tea and some freshly made bacon and egg sandwiches.

'I suspect you have not eaten yet this morning, Lord Tannahill, and you look like a man in shock to me.' She poured a cup of tea and handed it to him while her husband drew up a small table. 'Tea is supposed to calm the nerves so please drink up. Eat something if you can. You will feel much better.' Neil waited until his wife had poured tea for all of them then he bade her sit down and prepare herself for bad news.

'Rina's father has been killed in a shooting accident.'

'Sir Roger? Oh no!'

'I'm afraid it's true. Lord Tannahill has come to tell her but I think it may be better if you and I drive over to the hospital and tell her in person. If you don't mind?' he asked, turning to their guest. 'We have got to know Rina well since she and my daughter became friends and started nursing together.'

'I would be very grateful if you would do that.' Lord Tannahill sighed heavily. 'Please tell her I am convinced my nephew and his friend are telling the truth and the accident truly was unavoidable. I will make arrangements for the funeral, if you think she will approve?'

'I think Rina will be too shocked to object.'

'I'm sure she will be very grateful, Lord Tannahill,' Mrs MacQuade assured him, 'but what about her mother, Lady Capel? Presumably Sir Roger will be buried at Stavondale in the family grave?'

'I will send a telegram to Lady Capel myself,' Lord Tannahill said, compressing his lips and frowning. 'If the gossip is true I doubt if she will be a grief-stricken widow for long, although I'm sure she will act the part. It is Rina I am concerned about. Please tell her I will pay for all the arrangements.'

'We will drive to the hospital without delay,' Neil MacQuade promised. 'There is no reason why you should deal with the funeral, or pay for it, Lord Tannahill. The responsibility should be Lady Capel's, but I think Rina may be relieved to know the arrangements are in your hands. I can't imagine Lady Capel being much use — except perhaps at stirring up trouble for the young man.'

'Exactly.' Lord Tannahill said grimly, his mouth tight. 'So please try to assure Rina it is for their sake I wish to pay. I hope it may give them a little relief.'

'I'm sure Lady Capel will have no objection to you paying,' Neil MacQuade said drily.

'I'm sure she will not. I'm not doing it for her sake.' Lord Tannahill said. 'This is not the time to discuss business but I heard from Sir Roger earlier this week. He offered to sell Manor Farm to me. We had discussed it some time ago, before I knew anything of his father's intention for Rina to inherit it.'

'As you say this is not a good time for business,' Neil MacQuade agreed, 'but we also had a letter saying he was selling it privately so if you hadn't bought it someone else would have got it. The whole estate is to be sold. The tenants who can raise the money will have an opportunity to buy their farms but I doubt if many of them will manage it. Sir Roger was heavily in debt so we are to wind up his affairs. I wonder . . . ?' He frowned thoughtfully. 'It's an unworthy thought, but for a moment I wondered whether Sir Roger did step in front of the gun deliberately.'

'I suppose it's possible if things are very bad. It is a blessing Rina's grandfather made sure she has a home of her own that he couldn't touch,' Lord Tannahill said with compassion.

'Stavondale Manor you mean? I'm afraid it will cost too much to maintain a house that size once she is deprived of any income from Manor Farm.'

'I hadn't thought of that. I will contact you at a more appropriate time to discuss such matters though. I cannot tell you how sorry I am that Rina has been left in such circumstances.'

'If you don't mind me saying so, Lord Tannahill, you look exhausted. I know you have driven a long way, but when you have had a rest I wonder if you could go to Bonnybrae and tell them the news. Rina is much closer to Mrs Greig than her own mother. We shall offer what comfort we can of course but I have a feeling this will turn her world upside down. She will need all the reassurance we can give her. All the tenants, including the Sinclairs, would receive letters on Friday telling them their farms are to be sold. They may have taken the news badly but it is not Rina's fault.'

'I am always amazed how fast news travels in the countryside, but I will visit the Sinclairs to make sure they know about Sir Roger. They are a fine family. I don't believe they will blame Rina for anything. I'm convinced Jamie Sinclair is in love with her but I suspect he thinks she is beyond his reach.' He turned to thank Mrs MacQuade for her hospitality before he took his leave.

'What a lovely man he is,' she said. 'It is a shame he is so much older than Rina.'

'If Mel is right Rina's heart is already given to someone else.'

'Well the poor girl is going to need all the love she can get now.'

'Even you, my dear, can't arrange people's lives to suit, but I'm glad you'll be coming with me. I think I will telephone the hospital before we set out. Rina will probably be on duty but I could tell Home Sister the reason for our visit and ask her to give Rina the letter from her father before we arrive. It may contain something of importance. I had not considered that.'

'Poor child. This is the worst possible time to receive bad news. Would you mind, Neil, if I ask her to come home with us until she can come to terms with her loss?'

'Of course I don't mind, my dear.'

He was surprised at Home Sister's reaction when he got through to her on the telephone.

'But Nurse Capel is taking her final examination tomorrow!' she exclaimed in dismay. 'Such news could not have come at a worse time.' She paused, apparently summoning her thoughts. 'She must be told of course. Yes, I will give her the letter you sent. I didn't get the impression she is close to her family. Neither of her parents ever visited her, even when she was so seriously ill. As far as I'm aware they never wrote to her either. Presumably Lady Capel will be arranging the funeral so I think it will be better if Catherina stays here and takes her examination tomorrow as planned. Afterwards she will have time to absorb the full implication of the news.'

'My wife and I had not considered it in that light,' Neil MacQuade said with a frown. 'We would like to see her and give her the news face to face, if you don't mind?' Home Sister did mind but it was a difficult dilemma. She liked the MacQuades and she knew Catherina regarded them as good friends.

'Very well. I will arrange for another nurse to take over her shift. She should be free by the time you get here.' Instead of arranging for Rina to be relived of her duties immediately Home Sister went to discuss the situation with Matron. Both women had made nursing their life and few things could be more important in their opinion. They agreed that Rina must be told the news of her father's death but if possible she should be persuaded to take her final examination tomorrow before leaving to attend to personal matters. They had great expectations for Nurse Capel excelling in her final examinations. The hospital could be proud of her.

When Neil and Mary MacQuade arrived at the Fever Hospital they found Rina standing in Home Sister's office, still in her nurses' uniform, finishing reading the letter from her father. Her face was pale. She looked stunned. Her eyes were dark with shock when she looked up at the MacQuades.

'How could my father do this, and without warning? Without notice to any of his tenants? What will they do at Bonnybrae? They will never want to speak to me again,' she said in an anguished voice. 'What will become of them?'

'Does your father mention that he is also selling Manor Farm, Rina?' Neil MacQuade asked quietly.

'Oh yes. He asks me to forgive him. Twice. But that is unimportant beside what he is doing to his tenants, especially to the people who mean more to me than anyone else in the world!' She looked distraught and Mary MacQuade swallowed hard. She looked at her husband and for once she realised he was uncertain how to handle the situation and break the news of Sir Roger's death.

'Rina my dear, I am afraid we have come with worse news. Your father died yesterday in a shooting accident. Lord Tannahill came to tell us this morning . . .'

'A shooting accident.' Rina repeated and sank onto the chair behind her. Home Sister hurried to her side. 'He has killed himself and it is all my fault.' Rina's voice was almost a wail of distress. 'I knew he was not himself! I knew he was unhappy when he came to see me. Why, oh why didn't I suspect he would do something like this? He kept asking me to forgive him. He says it again in his letter! I should have known. What sort of nurse can I be when I don't see how desperate my own father is?'

'Rina! Your father was shot. It was an accident. He didn't kill himself.' Mary MacQuade moved across the room and knelt before her, gripping her shoulders. 'Look at me Rina. This is not your fault. Not in any way. You can't blame yourself.'

'Oh but I do,' Rina said in a low voice, giving her kindly friend a pitying look when she didn't understand. 'He wanted to talk. He wanted to tell me something. I tried — I tried to — to encourage him but he seemed unable to confide in me.' She buried her face in her hands.

'Rina dear! Your father was killed by a friend of Lord Tannahill's nephew. He and Rupert were practising shooting at pigeons in the woods at Stavondale Tower when your father stepped out. It was an accident. The young man, Mark, is dreadfully shocked and upset. He told Lord Tannahill he will never lift another gun as long as he lives.' Rina shook her head from side to side as though in denial.

'Why was my father at Stavondale? He had not arranged to come. He knew I would not be at Stavondale Manor. Had he brought his own gun with him?'

'I, er . . .' Mary MacQuade looked at her husband for help.

'Yes Rina, your father was carrying his gun,' Neil MacQuade answered firmly. 'Why do you ask?'

'I believe now that he meant to take his own life,' Rina said in little more than a whisper. 'He was so down in spirits when he came to see me. He — he said, he and Mother . . .' She broke off, stifling a sob. 'He couldn't have known anyone else would be shooting there.' Home Sister had excused herself and now she returned carrying a tray of tea and some sweet biscuits.

'I think we all need a cup of strong tea,' she announced briskly and proceeded to pour a cup for them all. Then she took charge of the conversation, steering it the way she wanted it to go.

'If I understood correctly, Mr MacQuade, you say the funeral arrangements are being taken care of by Lord Tannahill?'

'Yes, that's correct,' Neil MacQuade agreed. 'The funeral will be from Stavondale Tower and Sir Roger Capel will be buried beside his parents in the family grave. Lord Tannahill wanted to do this and he is arranging for refreshments to be served after the service at Stavondale too.' Rina opened her mouth to protest but Neil went on quickly. 'Lord Tannahill hopes it will help in a small way to assuage the guilt and remorse his nephew, and his friend, are feeling. They know they can never compensate for your loss, Rina. As I said, young Mark is distraught about the whole thing. I doubt if he will rest easy until he has spoken to you and asked your forgiveness.'

'He doesn't need to ask for it. I don't consider him responsible,' Rina replied.

'There, then you see Catherina,' Home Sister said, 'the arrangements will be taken care of. I understand your mother is staying in Edinburgh. Do you intend to join her there?'

'No. I doubt if she will want me there,' Rina said almost harshly.

'In that case,' Sister continued firmly, 'I think you would be better to stay here where you have company, and take your final examination tomorrow as planned. I know Melissa will be a great comfort to you while you are with us. You can travel home on Tuesday. It is better that you should not be alone at such a time.' She shot Mrs MacQuade a quelling glance. 'It is better to be occupied.'

Rina considered this. Home Sister's personality was compelling and Rina complied with her suggestion. She thanked the MacQuades for coming to bring the news in person and for their kindness and offer of hospitality.

News soon spread through the small hospital. It was a close-knit community and Rina was popular with all her work colleagues. She was always pleasant and helpful, and they rallied round with companionship, words of sympathy and anything they could think of which might bring comfort. Rina had very few moments alone until she went to bed that night. Only then did she re-read the letter from her father and take in the fact that he was dead, but the news which distressed her most was that Bonnybrae was to be sold along with the other farms on the estate. Would they be able to keep the tenancy and their home with a new landlord? Would he increase the rents yet again? Could they survive or would Jamie return to his family in Yorkshire, and what would happen to his Uncle Jim? She offered another silent prayer that her grandfather had had the foresight to give Aunt Maggie and Uncle Joe security in their own home. She was sure they must consider her, and her family, responsible for their misfortune, as would the rest of the tenants. Her heart ached for them all, and for the memory of her grandfather who had cared about them and their welfare. Exhausted though she was, her emotions were in a turmoil. She could not sleep. All night she tossed and turned and when she drifted into sleep she was haunted by images of her father's unhappy face when they had said goodbye on the station platform. In her heart she was convinced he had intended to end his own life. Had he walked in front of the young man deliberately to save him using his own gun, to save him taking that last final decision to pull the trigger himself? Why else had he returned to Stavondale and why bring his gun? Even when he lived there he had rarely gone shooting in recent years. She should have known he was deeply troubled. She should have tried harder to get him to confide in her. Maybe she could have helped in some way. She would certainly have warned Jamie of his intention to sell the farms. He and his uncle would never believe she had not known how bad things were. Even now she did not fully understand why her father had so many debts.

When Home Sister glimpsed Rina's pale, drawn face and the dark circles beneath her eyes, indicating she had barely slept, she knew in her heart she had made a mistake in persuading the girl to stay and attempt the most important examination she had undertaken so far in her nursing career.

Rina felt her head was stuffed with cotton wool and she longed for a good gallop on Duke, her beloved pony. Even a cycle ride in the fresh air might have helped. She had no appetite for food and she followed the other nurses listlessly into the examination room. Over and over her mind went, reliving the day she had spent with her father, wondering what she could have done, what she should have said. Her brain didn't seem able to take in the questions in front of her, even less to concentrate on answering them. She knew she couldn't possibly do justice to her tutors and the doctors who had given their time to deliver lectures. What did the examination matter when the life of her dearest friend, Jamie, would be turned upside down, and the lives of his family too, people who had been so kind and welcomed her whenever she needed a friend. Jamie was more than a friend. He was the man she loved and he would think she had betrayed him. She pushed back her chair and left the room. She had to get away.

She made a small parcel of her shoes and the clothes she really needed and strapped them to her bicycle. She left everything else. She felt unable to contemplate her future. Although she appreciated the kindness of the MacQuades she needed to be alone. She cycled to the railway station and caught the first train which would take her near to Stavondale. When she alighted one of the porters came to help her retrieve her bicycle but the stationmaster came out of his office and took her hand, expressing his sympathy at the death of her father. He was clearly sincere and for the first time Rina felt the prick of tears behind her eyelids. She wondered what he would think when he heard her father had died in debt, or if he knew Sir Roger had intended to take his own life, if the young man had not accidentally done it for him. Once away from the station she pedalled hard, feeling the need of the cool air in her face, driving away the lethargy of her sleepless night.

Mrs MacCrindle was standing at her kitchen window when she saw Rina riding her bicycle up to Stavondale Manor. She had not expected her to return, and certainly not alone. She hurried along the drive to the house and in through the back door, startling Rina.

157

'Oh Miss Rina. I was not expecting you. Will ye be staying? Is your mother coming for company?'

'Hello Mrs MacCrindle. I didn't know what my plans were so I'm sorry I couldn't let you know. I'm supposed to be taking an examination today b-but I couldn't concentrate. I had to get away. I need time to think. No, Mother will certainly not be coming here.' Her tone hardened unconsciously.

'Oh lassie, ye canna stay here all on your own at a time like this.' Rina looked at the elderly woman she had known all her life, the woman who had ministered to her grandfather with such care and her chin wobbled as she struggled to control her emotions. Seconds later she was in Mrs Mac's arms.

'There, there now, lassie. It is a sad time, and so soon after your father's visit.'

'That's what troubles me,' Rina said, her voice shaking. 'I sensed he had a reason for coming. I was sure he wanted to tell me something but — but he never hinted he was in so much trouble.'

'In trouble, Miss Rina? Surely he just wanted to see ye, his only bairn . . .'

'No, he had something on his mind. I know he had. Perhaps he was going to tell me he was selling the rest of the Stavondale Estate. He must have known that would upset his tenants. But — but I'm sure it was more than that and I ought to have helped him. What sort of nurse am I when I didn't help him?'

'But Miss Rina . . . I-I dinna understand, lassie. His death was not your fault. It was an accident. That poor young man is worrying himself to death about it. Lord Tannahill says he can't get it out of his head and he can't sleep for thinking about it.'

'I'm sure it was not his fault,' Rina said in a muffled voice. Mrs Mac held Rina away from her and peered into her pale face.

'I reckon you didn't sleep much either and I don't suppose you have eaten any dinner. Now Miss Rina you know your grandfather would not approve of that. I have some good soup cooling on my hob. I'll go and bring it across for ye with a loaf of my newly baked bread. Everything will seem — well it will not seem quite so bad when you have something inside ye.' She hurried away but it seemed to Rina she was back with the soup in no time at all.

'I don't like to think of you sleeping in this big house all alone,' Mrs Mac said anxiously. 'It's not good for ye to brood on things all by yourself. Are you sure you wouldna be better staying with Mr and Mrs Greig like ye did when ye were so ill?'

'I shouldn't think the Greigs, or anyone else from Bonnybrae, will ever want to see me again if they have heard what my father has done to them.' Rina said in a low voice, speaking her thoughts aloud. Mrs Mac set a bowl of steaming vegetable broth in front of her with the bread, a pat of butter and a large wedge of cheese.

'Ye must eat up lassie,' she urged anxiously. 'Mrs McGill churned the butter and she has started making cheese again now that Lord Tannahill comes to stay at Stavondale with his wee lassie.' Rina didn't think she could swallow anything but with Mrs Mac standing by she knew she had to try. She surprised herself by finishing all the soup as well as drinking two cups of tea.

'You were right Mrs Mac, I do feel better now that I have eaten, but please don't worry about me. I had to get away from my friends at the hospital. I needed to be alone. I have to think and I need to know what arrangements Lord Tannahill has made for the funeral. I don't think many people will attend.'

'Of course they will, Miss Rina. Sir Roger was the laird!'

'A laird who has sold their homes and their livelihoods without warning,' Rina said harshly.

'Lord Tannahill says someone else will buy the estate and the tenants will probably go on renting their farms as they did before. He is more concerned about you, Miss Rina. He told Mr McGill he will be buying Manor Farm himself but he says it should never have been sold. He says your grandfather intended it as your inheritance when you reached twenty-five. But he says someone else would buy it if he didn't. The McGills are going to continue working for him as they do for you, Miss. Will you be going to live with your mother now, Miss Rina?'

'No,' Rina said with more vehemence than she realised. 'I don't know what I shall do,' she added wearily. 'I shall have to sell this house but that is the least of my concerns. But you must not worry, Mrs Mac. Mr MacQuade told me Grandfather made sure your cottage is safe for your lifetime. Even Father could not get his hands on that to sell.'

'Sir Reginald was a good man,' Mrs Mac reflected softly. 'I shall always be grateful to him and you will always be welcome in my wee house. Now,' she said more briskly, 'I'll be back with something for your evening meal.' She patted Rina's shoulder as she went out.

She met Mr McGill before she reached her own cottage and she told him she was concerned about Miss Catherina staying in that big house all alone at such a time.

'Something's troubling her sorely,' she said, 'and I don't think it's worrying about her own future. She is more concerned about the tenants and how they will manage.'

'Who can tell what the future holds? They might be better off with a new landlord,' McGill said sagely. 'There's been nothing done by way of repairs since Sir Reginald died, and Sir Roger has raised the rents twice. Of course we canna say that to Miss Catherina.'

'Well I don't know, I'm sure,' Mrs McCrindle said, pleating and re-pleating her white apron in agitation. 'I don't understand such things, but I wish I knew how to comfort the lassie. She seems to blame herself for her father's death. I don't understand it. Her grandfather would turn in his grave if he knew his own son had squandered her small inheritance as well as his own.'

'Squandered? Aye well I suppose that's the way of it.' McGill agreed. 'Rumours are that he gambled to try and make his fortune to keep his wife in the finery she craved but gambling is a fool's game. He should have stood firm against Lady Capel. I expect she'll be coming to the funeral. Will she stay here, at Stavondale Manor, with Miss Catherina?'

'I don't think Miss Rina wants her here. Lady Capel was never a normal mother. The only person she loved was herself,' she added with unaccustomed scorn.

McGill passed on the news of Rina's arrival at Stavondale Manor to Lord Tannahill when he met him riding back to the stables. He looked surprised.

'Mrs Mac has known her since she was a wee bairn and she's worried about her staying on her own at a time like this, but Miss Catherina says she needed to get away by herself to think.'

'I'm glad you told me, McGill,' Lord Tannahill said, 'not that anyone will change Miss Catherina's mind if she's made it up to stay there, but meeting her might help young Mark. He's still suffering from shock. He had never seen a dead person before and he's convinced he ought to have been able to avoid shooting a grown man, but Rupert says nobody could have missed him. They had no warning. He appeared from behind a tree as Mark was raising the gun to fire.'

'Aye, but it's a nasty experience to shoot another human being. We canna blame the laddie for being upset.'

'Well it might help him if Catherina will see him. I'm sure she is too sensible to believe Mark shot her father deliberately.'

'She's not a vindictive lassie. She'll understand. I'm not so sure about Lady Capel though. I heard she was often spiteful with her maids.'

'Lady Capel . . .' Lord Tannahill repeated, frowning. His first impression when he telephoned her from the police station in town had been that she was relieved at the news of her husband's death. Her immediate comment had been "Well at least I shall not have to put up with his moods anymore". Surely he must have misunderstood her reaction.

* * *

Rina finished eating the chicken casserole Mrs Mac had brought for her dinner that evening.

'You're very kind, Mrs Mac, but I can't eat another morsel.'

'I'll put the apple pie and cream in the pantry, then Miss Rina. Ye might fancy a bit later on and . . .' A firm knocking at the front door interrupted her. 'Now who can that be?' she asked irritably.

'Whoever it is tell them I'm not in,' Rina urged hurriedly, but Lord Tannahill was stepping inside the moment Mrs Mac opened the door and he was accompanied by a pale faced young man who looked as terrified as a rabbit confronting a weasel.

'I-I don't think Miss Catherina is up to seeing anyone tonight, my lord,' Mrs Mac said uncertainly.

'We shall not disturb her for long,' Lord Tannahill reassured her with his pleasant smile, 'but it is important I speak to her if I'm ever going to give this young man an escape from his demons.' He knew Mrs Mac had just come from the kitchen and he guessed Rina was still in there, especially when it was the cosiest room in the big empty house. He stepped quickly through with an unhappy Mark at his heels. Rina looked up at the intrusion. She sighed but she summoned a smile for Mrs Mac.

'Thank you for bringing my dinner,' she said. 'I will see Lord Tannahill out shortly.'

'Very well, Miss Catherina. The fires are set in both sitting rooms. Shall I put a light to the one in the small parlour?'

'No thanks, not tonight, Mrs Mac. I don't think Lord Tannahill will be staying long and I need an early night.' Lord Tannahill gave a rueful smile and nodded when Mrs Mac raised her eyebrows questioningly in his direction.

'We shall not keep Miss Capel long, Mrs MacCrindle, so don't worry. I hoped it might help Mark a little if he could meet her. He blames himself entirely for Sir Roger's death.'

'Oh no, you must not feel like that,' Rina said, rising instantly and taking both the young man's hands in hers. She looked up at his pale face and saw the dark circles beneath his anxious blue eyes. She knew he and Rupert must be well into their teens but at the moment he looked like a troubled fourteen-year-old.

'I-I should have lowered my gun, or raised it or . . . I truly didn't mean to-to k-kill a-a person.' He shuddered at the memory. Rina squeezed his hands and gave him the comforting smile she had given so many sick patients, but she saw the sheen of tears in his eyes and tactfully lowered her gaze from his face.

'Of course you didn't mean to kill anyone. Please sit over here next to me.' She drew him towards one of the two wooden armchairs near the kitchen range. The fire burned cheerily and Lord Tannahill gave a sigh of relief as he settled himself quietly on the long settle beneath the window. He had been sure he could rely on Rina, in spite of her own troubles, and here she was soothing the young man who was only a couple of years younger than herself. She turned towards Mark, her expression serious.

'My father had not arranged to come down to Stavondale for shooting so no one would expect to see him there. After all the shooting season has not begun, so I don't know why he was in the wood, or why he had his gun with him.' Remembering how preoccupied, how down in spirits her father had been she was convinced in her own heart that he had intended to shoot himself. 'He was not his usual self when he came down to stay with me. I'm sure he had something on his mind. I blame myself for — for not taking more time, for not persuading him to confide in me, for . . . Oh I don't know. I just know I should have helped him in some way. So please do not blame yourself, Mark.' She saw the relief in the youth's earnest gaze.

'Oh Miss Capel, it is a relief to hear you do not blame me. Honestly I try so hard to be careful with my gun.' He glanced across at Lord Tannahill. 'Rupert and his father tried to tell me it was an accident but I was sure you must hold me responsible.'

'Of course I don't.' Rina smiled gently and patted his hand. 'So now you can go and tell Rupert your conscience is clear.'

'Thank you, thank you so much for understanding.' He stood up. 'I feel as though a load has been lifted from me.'

'Yes, you go along and share your relief with Rupert, my boy. He has been worried about you.'

Rina was surprised when Lord Tannahill made no move to accompany Mark. He remained seated while Mark almost skipped out of the house in his eagerness to share his relief.

'Thank you, Rina,' Lord Tannahill said with quiet sincerity. 'I knew you would not hold Mark responsible but you reassured him so beautifully. I can see now you must make a splendid nurse, calm and reassuring to those who are ill or anxious.'

'Mmm, I'm not so sure about that anymore. I was supposed to take my last examination today but I could not concentrate to read the questions, even less form the answers. I walked out and left.'

'I see. Do the MacQuades know you have come here, or that you're staying alone? They assured me you were welcome to stay with them until the funeral. And what about Mr and Mrs Greig? I can't believe Jamie would be happy if he knew you were here on your own at such a time.'

'Jamie . . .' The name sounded almost like a wail of despair and Rina's face crumpled. Lord Tannahill rose from his seat then and came towards her, but with a supreme effort Rina controlled the tears which had sprung to her eyes. 'I doubt if Jamie, or any of the tenants, will ever want to see a member of my family again,' she said in a choked voice. 'Father gave them no warning he planned to sell the estate and their homes, the livelihoods of all his tenants. Jamie and his uncle will never believe I didn't know what was about to happen. I knew he was troubled about something but I had no idea things were so bad. I meant what I said to Mark. I believe Father must have been wandering around the woods aimlessly. He was so preoccupied when he came to see me. I should have tried harder to help him.'

'Please don't blame yourself, Rina. As for the Sinclairs, they will be as worried about you, as you are about them.

164

I would never have offered to buy Manor Farm if your father's hand had not been forced about selling the whole estate, including Manor Farm. I believe his creditors had looked into everything he owned, or could turn into money. Someone else would have bought it, just as someone will buy the rest of the farms. You do know that while I own Stavondale Tower you are welcome to come at any time, to stay, or to ride over the land.'

'Thank you,' Rina said in a choked voice. 'What did you mean about Father's hand being forced?'

'You don't know? He didn't mention . . . ? But no, I don't suppose it was easy for him to tell his only daughter he was selling her inheritance. What will you do now? Will you live here or will you go to stay with your mother in Edinburgh?'

'I shall definitely not stay with Mother. As for this house it has never been my home, or felt that it could be. I have barely stayed here so it will be no hardship to part with it. You avoided my question.'

'Did I? Which question?'

'Don't avoid the issue, please. Why was Father forced to sell? Why couldn't he warn the tenants?'

'I'm afraid . . .' Lord Tannahill drew a deep breath but Rina fixed her eyes on his face and he knew there was no prevaricating. 'I'm afraid your father had gambled often when he and your mother went to London, even before your grandfather died. He always managed to settle his debts then, or partially settle anyway. Since your grandfather died and your parents moved to Edinburgh I understand he — he gambled more recklessly. I'm sure most gamblers truly believe they will make their fortune one day but that never happened. As far as I understand the situation, his creditors had become impatient. Threatening. There are rumours your Father would be harmed — and possibly you too, unless he sold everything.'

'B-but how? I don't understand . . .' Rina's face had been pale before, now it was deathly white and her dark eyes looked huge as she stared at him. He sighed heavily.

'People like that have ways of sifting out information about a man, and his family, in fact anything which could hurt him. They don't do the dirty work themselves but they would pay others to do it. I can imagine how bad your father felt about selling Manor Farm when he knew your grandfather had intended you should inherit it outright eventually. Maybe he came to warn you. I'm sure he must have been very troubled when he came to visit you.'

'He was. I knew he was but I-I couldn't get him to confide in me.'

'You must not blame yourself, Rina. There is nothing you could have done to help, my dear.'

'Perhaps not, but I should have tried harder.' Rina said in a low voice.

'You look exhausted. I will leave you now. I suggest you take a little brandy to help you sleep.'

'I'll think about it,' she murmured and gave him a wan smile.

'Oh my dear Rina, if only there was something I could do to help. You do know that the offer of marriage still stands? I would very much like you to be my wife.' Rina had to blink hard to dispel tears. His voice was very gentle.

'Thank you. You're very kind, and I know you mean it, but I would be marrying you for all the wrong reasons. I could not love you as a wife should.' She frowned remembering her father's last words when he said goodbye at the railway station. 'It is very strange. The last thing my father said to me when we parted was, "when you marry choose the man you love and who loves you in return. Don't be like your mother. We were never in love. We were considered a suitable match". He sounded so defeated and unhappy.' The tears came freely now. She was powerless to stop them.

'Oh my dear, Rina.' Lord Tannahill drew her gently into his arms and stroked her hair, letting her shed the healing tears which she had bottled up too often and too long in her young life. She welcomed the strength of his arms and the warmth of his body and so she laid her head against his chest.

Shortly, as he had guessed she would, she straightened and brushed away the tears with an impatient hand. He drew a clean white handkerchief from his pocket and handed it to her with a wry smile.

'Thank you,' she huskily. 'I'm sorry for crying all over your waistcoat. I must be more tired than I thought.'

'I'm sure you must feel shattered,' he said gently. 'I'll see myself out but don't forget to drink a drop of brandy.' Rina nodded and summoned a brave little smile, but she knew she would not drink anything stronger than hot milk. She doubted if there was any brandy in the house.

CHAPTER ELEVEN

The following morning Lord Tannahill was pleased to see both his nephew and Mark, had slept better and were in a more cheerful frame of mind, which was just as well because Douglas Blackford had decided to support his son and join them for the funeral. Meanwhile he wanted to repay Rina for her help with Mark. He considered taking a ride over to Braeside to find out if Mrs Greig was aware Rina was staying at Stavondale Manor on her own. On his way to the stables he changed his mind and decided to drive there in his car. If Mrs Greig wanted to call on Rina he could drive her here.

Maggie was surprised and a little flustered when Lord Tannahill arrived at her door but his manner was so easy and pleasant she soon forgot her awe of him. She was dismayed to hear that Rina had returned from the hospital and was staying at Stavondale Manor alone.

'We thought she must be staying with the MacQuades. She ought not to be alone when she's upset.'

'She blames herself. She thinks her father needed help when he came to visit her but he gave her no hint of the trouble he was in. Even if he had, she could not have helped him. I don't like to think of her brooding alone in that large house but her main concern appears to be for the tenants, particularly Jamie and your brother. She thinks they will blame her for not warning them. I think they will all have heard from Mr MacQuade about the estate being for sale before she knew herself. Neil MacQuade didn't want her to have bad news in the middle of her final examinations so he asked Home Sister to delay giving her a letter from her father, but news of her father's death could not be withheld. Yesterday she was too distraught to attempt the examination. She said she could not concentrate. She had not slept the previous night. Her mind would be in a turmoil.'

'Oh my poor lamb,' Maggie murmured, and sank onto a chair. 'Why didn't she come here?'

'She said she needed to be alone to think. She is genuinely concerned for all her grandfather's tenants, but I believe she loves Jamie. He is her main concern. The tenants may fare better with a new laird but I could not say that to Rina.'

'Did she tell you she loves Jamie?' Maggie asked curiously. 'Joe and I have thought for a long time their childhood affection has developed into love, but Jamie has always known Rina is beyond his reach. Apart from a lack of money and being a mere tenant, he has another skeleton from his past. He was born before my brother married his mother. Emma came as a maid when she left school. Our mother was bitterly opposed to their marriage but they are very happy. Emma has made William a wonderful wife and she's a good mother to her children. Jamie was fine until he met his grandmother. She — she called him a bastard.'

'Whew!' Lord Tannahill drew a sharp breath. 'That was cruel.'

'Yes. He has never forgotten. The trouble is, even if Rina did want to marry him, all the old gossip would probably be resurrected. The only excuse I can offer for our mother is that she was an invalid by then and her mind was not always clear. Just before she died she confessed the man I had loved as my father, was not the man who sired me. It was a dreadful shock.'

'That is when you learned your real father was Sir Reginald Capel?'

169

'Yes. He told Rina when he was dying so we know it is the truth. Maybe we all need to confess our sins before we can die in peace,' Maggie added drily. 'He did make sure Joe and I would have the security of our own home, here at Braeside, and we're grateful to him for that.'

'Yes, Rina talked frankly about Sir Reginald Capel and how he encouraged her to visit you. It must have been a comfort to him to know she regarded you as her friend, especially when her own parents seem incapable of showing her the affection we all need at some stage in our lives.'

'Joe and I are very glad he did encourage Rina to come. She has a lovely nature and we have both grown to love her like our own daughter.'

'I am glad, for Rina's sake. You will not have heard that Sir Roger has sold Manor Farm as well as his own inheritance? It was to have been Rina's when she reached twenty-five. Stavondale Manor is too big to maintain without income from the farm so she will need to sell it. I doubt if her father considered that.'

'Oh dear, the poor child. What a lot of trouble she is having.'

'I don't think she is too sad about selling the house. She says it has never felt like home and she has hardly stayed there. Mr MacQuade will make sure she gets the best price for it. I told him I would be interested in buying it if Rina does decide to sell. I have a good young gamekeeper with six children, including two sets of twins. He is ready for more responsibility to earn more money and a larger house.'

'I see,' Maggie said doubtfully. 'Does Rina know this?'

'Not yet. I assured her she is welcome to stay at Stavondale whenever she wants, and to ride over the land. In fact . . .' he gave a wry smile, 'I told her I would still like to marry her. She would want for nothing then — or at least nothing that money could buy. Unfortunately, in Rina's case it can't buy the one thing she craves — to love and to be loved. She refused of course.'

'I see. I am so sorry,' Maggie said gently, 'I know you would treat her kindly and take care of her.'

'Anyway,' Lord Tannahill said briskly, 'changing the subject. As you see I came in my car in case you wanted a lift to Stavondale Manor to see Rina. I will give you both a lift back when you have had a chance to talk to her, if you can persuade her to come to stay here with you. She does seem very troubled. She thinks no one will attend the funeral after the way her father has treated his tenants.'

'Of course they will attend! After all he is — he was the laird. Besides I'm sure they will attend for Rina's sake. She was popular with them all when she was young. Is Lady Capel coming to stay with her?'

'No. I stay in the smaller west wing of Stavondale Tower but I offered her a night's accommodation in the east wing when I offered to arrange the funeral. She seized both offers. She didn't mention Rina. She said she would be bringing a friend with her for support at such a distressing time.' His tone had not changed and yet Maggie sensed his contempt. 'I got the impression Rina doesn't want her mother at Stavondale Manor anyway. You are more of a mother to her in every respect.'

'Then I will accept your offer of a lift. I don't like to think of Rina being all alone.'

* * *

Two hours after he had dropped her at Stavondale Manor, Lord Tannahill saw Maggie walking up the drive alone and carrying a large parcel.

'Rina not coming with you?' he asked in surprise.

'No, I'm afraid I couldn't persuade her, but she has let me have the black coat she wore to her grandfather's funeral. It swamped her small figure then and she lost such a lot of weight when she was ill. She has never quite regained it. She was a bit reluctant to try on her clothes but she has agreed I can shorten the coat and take in the seams.'

'Will you have it finished in time? The funeral is the day after tomorrow.'

'Oh yes. Joe will bring me back with it in good time. I'm worried about Rina though. She blames herself for not helping her father.' Maggie hesitated. 'Perhaps I should not be saying this. She only told me because she says he was my half-brother and that makes us part of his family so it is not quite so disloyal to discuss her fears. She believes he returned to Stavondale to shoot himself. She says he was very low in spirits when he came to see her. She blames herself for not persuading him to discuss his anxiety. He did tell her he and his wife had never been in love and now all Lady Capel thinks about is Wardle. Apparently he has bought a chateau with a vineyard. He wants her to go with him to France. Rina met him once and she says he has no breeding or manners so it can only be his money which attracts her mother. I have never heard her speak with such bitterness or openly criticise her mother.'

'I noticed she values loyalty. Sir Roger must have been unhappy to confide in her about Wardle.'

'If he has done everything to please his wife, including spending their only child's inheritance, and then she turns to someone else because he has more to give, he must have felt disheartened.'

'I agree with you, Mrs Greig. I feel some sympathy for the man myself. Surely the friend Lady Capel is bringing for support will not be the man Wardle when he is responsible for Sir Roger's despondency — at least in part? Even she would not be so insensitive.'

'I hope not. Apparently Rina cannot tolerate him.'

'If he is the friend we must make sure Rina has company during the funeral and afterwards,' Lord Tannahill said, his mouth setting with determination.

'You're a good man,' Maggie said softly. 'I am sorry Rina cannot grant you what you desire, and yet I know it will break my nephew's heart whoever she marries.'

'Then you must do all you can to smooth the path of true love for the pair of them,' Lord Tannahill said with a whimsical smile. 'Now I will drive you home and let you get on with your sewing. I'm sorry I dragged you here to no purpose.'

'Oh but I'm glad you brought me. I am not happy to leave Rina on her own, but we did speak frankly and I think it may have helped her to confide in me. There was nothing I could say to ease her mind about the plight of her father's tenants though.'

'Things may turn out better than any of them expect. I understand they are all to be given the opportunity to purchase their respective farms.'

'Yes, that's true. Jim, my brother, had a very nice letter from Mr MacQuade encouraging him to consider it. He said he would use his influence and do all he could if he needed a loan from the bank.'

'And has your brother considered?'

'Oh yes, but he and Jamie could only raise about half the money he thinks will be needed. Joe has offered to loan them the rest, or to stand guarantor at the bank, if they can negotiate a loan, but Jim will not hear of that. He thinks Joe would be taking too much of a risk.'

'You may tell him I would be willing to stand guarantor for him myself if it is necessary,' Lord Tannahill said calmly. 'When there is land as security it would not be a risk for me. In any case I can see for myself that Bonnybrae is one of the best run farms on the estate. Your brother is a good farmer and he has trained Jamie well. I would have no hesitation.'

'It is very kind of you to offer, Lord Tannahill,' Maggie said sincerely. 'I will tell Jim and Jamie but we have never owed money to anyone so I doubt if they will accept. Our parents were very strict about such things. Jim tells me farming has prospered since the war with the government guaranteeing prices for our meat and milk and cereals, but the guarantees are due to be removed next year. Before he died my father quoted the Bible several times, telling Jim to accumulate his wealth during the seven fat years because he was sure that seven lean years would follow as soon as the government had rebuilt the ships and food could be imported again.

Jim has followed his advice. He has money in the bank, but he believes my father was right and lean times are ahead.'

'Your father was a wise man. I agree with him. Things will not always be as good as they are now but the hardworking men who understand their land and their animals and have done their best to improve during the good years, will still survive, and remember, as owners they would have no rents to pay.' He drew the car to a halt at the gate of Braeside. Maggie turned to him with a smile.

'I don't know why you are so kind to us but maybe there will be a way to repay you one day. Thank you for taking me to see Rina. We shall all be at the funeral.'

As usual when Joe was working during the week Maggie made her way up to Bonnybrae to prepare a hot meal for Jim and Jamie. Sometimes she felt she was too tired for the daily routine but she always ate her own meal with her brother and nephew and she enjoyed their chat and whatever news was circulating amongst the farmers. She told them about Lord Tannahill taking her to see Rina at Stavondale Manor.

'Surely the lassie isna staying there on her own?' Jim said.

'She is. The house is big enough for two homes, or more. She feels guilty because her father is selling all the farms without warning any of the tenants. She thinks she could, and should, have helped him when he visited her.'

'Yes, when she wrote to me after his visit she was feeling very frustrated,' Jamie said. 'She was sure there were things he wanted to say to her. She thought he was very unhappy living in Edinburgh.'

'I expect he wanted to tell her he was selling Manor Farm, which should have been her inheritance apparently.' Maggie said grimly. 'She will not be able to afford to keep Stavondale Manor now, not that she seems worried about that. She says it has never felt like home. In fact, she sounded so forlorn. She said it's not bricks and mortar or fancy furnishings which made a house into a home, it's the people living in it.'

'Well I'd say she knows all about that,' Jim said. 'She has lived in style at Stavondale Tower but she still seemed happier coming to you and Joe at Braeside, Maggie.'

'I always thought she enjoyed staying with us,' Maggie said slowly, 'but I couldn't persuade her to come back with me. I think she is dreading the funeral and facing the tenants, although she doubts if any of them will be there — and then she's afraid her mother might bring that man she has met, the one who has bought a chateau in France.'

'Rina can't stand him,' Jamie said, 'and there aren't many people she really dislikes.'

'That's true,' Maggie agreed. She paused, frowning, gathering her thoughts. 'Rina hates disloyalty but what is really troubling her is she thinks her father came back to Stavondale intending to take his own life. She is convinced that is why he was carrying his gun. I hope you will not repeat this. She told me just before I left her. She says I am the only family she has now because I am his sister, or at least half-sister.'

'There's no need to repeat it,' Jim said grimly. 'Miss Rina is not the only one speculating. There's been some talk at the railway station about him coming back here carrying his gun. After they knew about the sale of the estate and his gambling debts several people think it was his only way out.'

'Oh no!' Maggie groaned. 'I tried to tell Rina he would never do that but I couldn't convince her, or give her comfort. Even if it was what he wanted it would take a great deal of courage to kill himself.'

'That's probably why he let someone do it for him when he saw the opportunity,' Jim said.

* * *

It was well after eight o'clock that evening before Doug Lamont and Jamie finished piling the rows of hay into small heaps or haycocks to help it to dry. Earlier they had left Jim to finish off the milking and take the cows back to their field.

All afternoon Jamie's thoughts had been with Rina. He hurried from the field, stripping off his shirt to give himself a hasty swill at the pump outside the back door, almost pulling off his dusty trousers as he ran to his room to change. He grabbed his cycle and pedalled down the road to Stavondale Manor.

Rina was surprised to see him and she did her best to tidy her curly hair but there was nothing she could do to hide the fact that she had been crying.

'I-I didn't expect to see you, Jamie,' she said in a small voice, holding the door wide for him to enter.

'Oh Rina . . .' All Jamie's well-rehearsed words flew out of his head. His heart ached at the sight of her pale face and reddened eyes. He opened his arms but he didn't need to draw her into them. She almost flung herself against his broad hard chest and nestled her head against the curly ginger hairs where he had left his shirt unbuttoned almost to the waist in his hurry to see her. He held her close and stroked her hair with a tender hand, murmuring soothing words against the crown of her head, but the feel of her soft body pressed so trustingly against his own was more than his will-power could stand. Gently he put a finger beneath her chin and tilted her face to his. He hadn't meant to kiss her but her mouth was tantalisingly close. He couldn't resist brushing her lips with his own. It had the effect of a lighted match on dry straw. Rina flung her arms around his neck and pressed closer, parting her lips in an invitation impossible to resist, in spite of the circumstances. Jamie knew Rina was at her most vulnerable and he must not take advantage, however tempted he might be. She needed comfort and love and she trusted him implicitly but it took all his resolve to lift his head and halt the tide of passion surging between them.

'Dearest Rina,' he whispered hoarsely, 'I'm glad I came but I don't like to see you so upset, especially when you are here alone. You must come back with me to Braeside. You know how much we want you there. Aunt Maggie keeps your bed and your room ready all the time.' He stepped back but he drew her with him to sit together on the long oak settle.

'I'm surprised anyone wants me after the trouble my family has caused.'

'Hush, don't say that. Anyway, you're not responsible for the actions of your family.'

'That's what Aunt Maggie said.' Rina caught back a dry sob. 'There will be even more for people to criticise about my family after the funeral,' she muttered with a trace of bitterness. Jamie kept his arm around her shoulders, trying to offer comfort and reassurance as she went on, 'Lord Tannahill came to see me again this afternoon. The postman brought him a letter from my mother. She is bringing that dreadful man with her to my father's funeral.' Rina shuddered. 'Everyone will see they are together already and my father is not even in his grave yet.'

'Surely most people will regard the man as a friend of both your parents.'

'They won't when they see him with her. It is ages since I visited them in Edinburgh and he couldn't keep his hands off my mother then. What was worse she giggled like a schoolgirl and gave the impression she enjoyed him — him pawing her.' Rina almost spat the last few words. 'Lord Tannahill came to tell me so that I would not get such a shock if she told me at the funeral.'

'Told you what, Rina?' Jamie asked puzzled.

'She has sold the Edinburgh house! He must have helped her do it, even before my father died. Father told me Wardle had invited them to his chateau in France. He didn't want to go. He never mentioned selling his house in Edinburgh though.' The tears began to trickle down her cheeks again. Jamie knew his handkerchief would be dusty so he reached for the towel hanging beside the range and gently dried her cheeks, drawing her onto his knee as he did so, cradling her in his arm like a child to comfort her.

'No one else down here will know their business, and even if they do, they will not blame you.'

'But she's my mother, even though she never loved us, Nat and me, like a normal mother would. She is going to live in France with that horrible man. They must have been planning it before — before . . . They have packed what they want to keep and it is to be sent ahead. They're leaving straight away, the day after Father's funeral. Even Lord Tannahill sounded shocked. He thinks they must be getting the money for the house out of the country before Father's creditors claim it.'

'Surely your mother didn't need to tell him all that in a letter.'

'He thinks she did it because no one can argue with a letter. She asked him to tell me so that I shall not cause a scene in public,' she added, her lip curling in scorn. She leaned away from him and looked into his face. 'Aunt Maggie will be shocked too when she hears this latest scandal, so I shall not blame you, Jamie, if you leave now and have no more to do with me, or my wretched family.' Her voice wavered in spite of her brave words. Jamie silenced her with a kiss.

'That was to stop you talking nonsense,' he said huskily when at length he lifted his head. 'Surely you know by now, Rina, I love you beyond all reason. Nothing your family can say or do will ever stop me loving you.' Rina stared up into his sunburned face, her eyes widening.

'Can you really mean that, Jamie?' she breathed. 'In spite of everything? You're not saying that to — to comfort me when everything else in my world seems to be falling apart?'

'Of course I mean it, Rina. I've loved you for a long time, but there has always been an unbridgeable gap between my life and yours. Even now, loving you as I do, it doesn't change anything,' he said bleakly. 'I have nothing to offer, not even a house of our own to live in. I have only just learned that Uncle Jim has been putting money in the bank for me every month since I came to Bonnybrae to work. Grandfather didn't believe in paying wages to his family you see, but he helped them all get stock and horses and what they needed to start in farms of their own. Uncle Jim says he saved the money for me in case I ever wanted to return to Yorkshire. Now he knows my life is here he is considering whether we should use his savings and mine to buy Bonnybrae. It was Mr MacQuade who suggested it when he wrote to tell us what was happening to the estate. The trouble is we would need to borrow some of the money from the bank. That worries Uncle Jim because he has never owed anyone a penny in his life. It bothers me because I shall never be able to afford to keep a wife or marry the woman I love. And I do truly love you, Rina. I hope you will always remember that, wherever you are.

'Oh Jamie,' she whispered his name, her lips soft and warm against his cheek. 'I loved you before and I love you even more now. I know I shall have to return to the hospital and continue earning my living as a nurse, but now that I know we love each other, nothing will seem as bad as it did a few minutes ago.' Her dark eyes shone with love and her lips curved in the loveliest of smiles. 'I'm sure we shall find a way. So long as we love each other I'll wait for you forever.'

'Dearest Rina.' Jamie bent his head in a long kiss, reluctant to part from her.

'This is meant to be a time of sadness,' Rina said, 'but I can't help the fountain of joy inside me.'

'Then you will cycle back with me to Braeside tonight, Rina? I can't bear to leave you here alone.'

'All right,' she agreed meekly. 'I must pack a few things to take with me and we should tell Lord Tannahill and Mrs Mac I shall not be here. They both keep looking in to make sure I'm all right.'

'I'll go and tell them then while you pack what you need. We'll strap some of your things to my bike if you can make two parcels.'

'Aunt Maggie already has my coat and hat for the funeral, but I must pack my black skirt.' She shuddered. 'I-I'm, dreading the funeral,' she said in a choked voice. Jamie immediately put his arm around her again and hugged her close.

'If it is seeing your mother again which distresses you, Rina, then you only have to tell us. Uncle Joe and Uncle Jim will be with us and I promise not to leave your side. I know the women will wait at Stavondale Tower after the service but Aunt Maggie will protect you like a mother hen with one chick if she knows that's what you want, but you need to tell her. She's the last person to come between you and your mother otherwise.' Rina's elfin face looked so woebegone he ended up giving her another long kiss.

The long summer day was fading fast as they cycled together up the track to Braeside. Maggie welcomed Rina with open arms and a sigh of relief. Joe pulled himself out of his armchair and hugged her in a warm embrace.

'We're so pleased you've come, lassie. This is not a time to grieve alone,' he said gruffly and Rina knew Braeside, with Joe and Maggie Greig, was the nearest she had ever felt to coming home.

The following morning as they worked side by side in the hayfield Doug Lamont grinned at Jamie.

'So how did ye find Miss Rina last night?'

'How do you know I saw her?'

'Where else would a man be going but to see the love of his life, dashing off hell for leather, half drowning himself to wash away the day's sweat and pedalling down the road as though he was powered by an engine.' Doug chuckled, but then added soberly and with concern, 'How is Miss Rina taking her father's death? I don't suppose Lady Capel has brought her much comfort?'

'No, she has not. Rina has not heard from her. I persuaded her to come back with me to Braeside last night so at least she will have company. She is not looking forward to seeing her mother at the funeral. She is bringing a friend with her and Rina doesn't like him. I have promised I will be at her side as protection if that's what she wants. I must remember and ask Aunt Maggie to stay with her when the women are waiting on their own while we're at the burial.'

When Doug went to his own cottage at midday Alice asked him if he had heard how Miss Rina was so he told her what Jamie had said.

'You'd have thought her mother would have come back straight away to be with her,' Alice said angrily, 'but my mother always said Lady Capel should never have been blessed with children because she always left them in someone else's care.' Later that afternoon Alice's mother came down to see her and share a chat over a cup of tea. Alice naturally passed on what Doug had told her.

'I'm glad ye mentioned it lassie,' Mrs Forbes said. 'Ye never quite know with the gentry whether ye're being too forward or not, especially with Lady Capel. She looked down her nose at all of us — poor tenants. Now that I know Miss Catherina would welcome our company I shall be sure to speak with her, whether her lady mother is there or not. She was always a lovely wee lassie with the brightest smile and the loveliest manners.' The two women moved onto other topics but that evening Mrs Forbes mentioned her visit and the funeral to Doug's mother. In turn she told two of her friends when they met on the way to the local kirk for the funeral, and so news went around as it usually did. They would all attend the tea which Lord Tannahill was providing at Stavondale Tower for the mourners. In any case most of them were curious to see inside and any changes he had made.

Lord Tannahill and Neil MacQuade had consulted each other and decided they would both drive to Bonnybrae to provide transport for Rina and the Sinclairs to and from the funeral, so saving Jim driving them in the pony and cart.

Rina was pale but composed and Maggie had skilfully taken in the seams of her black coat so that she now looked slim and smart rather than swamped in black as she had at her grandfather's funeral. She had even altered her felt hat so that it did not fall over her eyes, not that Rina's mind was on the way she looked as she took her seat with Jamie and Maggie in Lord Tannahill's car, while Jim and Joe travelled with Mr and Mrs MacQuade. Melissa was working at the hospital but she had sent Rina a letter to say how sorry she was she couldn't be with her for the funeral. Rina sat straight-backed and tense, but when she slipped her hand into Jamie's where it lay on the seat between them he squeezed her fingers and gave her a reassuring smile.

'We shall be at your side,' he whispered. Maggie had been apprehensive when Jamie said they were to sit with Rina in the front pew at the kirk.

'We can't sit in the laird's pew!' she said aghast.

'Please Aunt Maggie, I need you beside me so much today,' Rina pleaded. 'We can all sit in one of the front pews and my mother and her — her friend can sit in the other one.' Maggie agreed for Rina's sake but she was uneasy and she was aware of the angry glare which Lady Capel shot in their direction when she saw her daughter seated between Jamie and herself with Jim and Joe. After the service it was noticeable that people were so keen to offer their condolences to Rina while almost ignoring Lady Capel and the big man at her side. It was the same at Stavondale when they gathered for the food. The wives of most of the tenants hovered around Rina and Maggie while they waited for the men to return from the graveside. Lady Capel's mouth tightened as she watched them. Rina had avoided her eyes and made it clear she had no wish to make conversation. Later when the men returned, Wardle noticed what was displeasing his lady.

'Why is she the centre of attention?' he demanded, his voice a shade too loud.

'Miss Rina is very popular with the tenants and their wives,' Lord Tannahill informed him mildly.

'She acts like a bloody princess,' Wardle said. He turned to Lady Capel 'You're his widow. It's you they should be fussing over. They should show some respect. They're a bloody disgrace.' Tactfully Lord Tannahill ushered them towards the food and an assortment of drinks, but he turned his head and winked at Jim and Joe who were standing with Jamie's other uncles on the edge of the circle of women and were bound to have overheard. There was plenty of food and most of the mourners were content to linger and chat to each other while filling their plates for a second or third time. Rina was deadly tired. She longed to leave but she knew they would have to wait for Lord Tannahill to drive them back to Braeside, and as the host he could not leave yet. Fortunately Mrs MacQuade had noticed her white face and the tension in her eyes.

'You have been so brave, Rina,' she said gently. 'It has been a stressful time for you. Shall I ask Neil to drive you and Mrs Greig home now? Lord Tannahill can drive the men home later.'

'Oh yes please, if you think that would be alright,' Rina said gratefully.

'Could you squeeze me in as well, Mrs MacQuade?' Jamie asked. 'I need to get back and change my clothes. The cows will be coming in for milking soon. It's not often Uncle Jim and I are both away.'

'That is a good excuse for leaving young man,' Mrs MacQuade said with a smile.

'It will be a bit of squeeze,' Neil MacQuade said, 'but I'm sure you two youngsters will not mind.'

'We don't,' Rina smiled, then she clasped Jamie's hand and turned to Mrs MacQuade. 'I should say goodbye to Mother. Please rescue us if we're more than two minutes. You will come with me Jamie?' she pleaded, her small hand clenching his like a lifeline.

'Of course,' he agreed calmly, but he didn't feel calm. Lady Capel saw them approaching and hissed through her teeth at her companion.

'She's coming to speak to me now she's spoken to everyone else.'

'We are leaving now,' Rina said. 'I came to say goodbye.' Jamie noticed she did not address Lady Capel as Mother, or offer a cheek to kiss as she always did with Aunt Maggie.

'So you remembered you have a mother? And who is this person, clinging to your side like a limpet? Is he your bodyguard, or a fortune hunter afraid to let you out of his sight?' she suggested with a sneer. Jamie tensed. Rina stiffened. She stared at her mother. She did not try to hide her distaste.

'You would know more about fortune hunting than either of us will ever know. I hear you have sold what should have been my home, had I wanted a home with you. You have made sure I have no fortune to hunt, but I can only thank you for that. Jamie is the man I love and now that we're both paupers he can assure me of his love with sincerity and without fear of being misjudged by people like you, whose only god is money.'

'Don't you dare speak to your lady mother like that,' Eric Wardle boomed and gripped her upper arm so fiercely she winced.

'Take your hand off her,' Jamie ordered. His voice was low but the menacing glitter in his blue eyes held a warning the big man could not ignore. He released his grip, his hand flapping to his side.

'Don't come crying for my help when your pitiable tenant loses his farm and leaves you with a house full of children to feed,' Lady Capel jeered nastily. Jamie opened his mouth to speak but Rina hastily squeezed his fingers so he pursed his lips to keep silent.

'My father never had the opportunity to give you a house full of children and I know you never wanted me. He gambled his life away trying to give you everything you wanted. He told me you never loved each other. Now you have met a man with a fortune to squander and you are fleeing to France to hoard the money my father provided to give you the luxurious townhouse you craved. Well good luck to both of you, but when you are old and ill don't come asking me to nurse you because I never want to see you again. Goodbye.' She turned away. Jamie had never heard Rina speak so coldly, or with so much dignity as she did then, but he felt her trembling at his side and put his arm around her shoulders, guiding her outside to the car. Mrs MacQuade followed. She had been shocked by Lady Capel's cold mockery of her only daughter. Even when they were in the car Rina could not stop trembling.

'I should not have spoken like that,' she whispered hoarsely. 'She is my mother but she has no reason to criticise

Jamie. She made me so angry.' Jamie put his arm around her for all she was squeezed between Maggie and himself but it was Mrs MacQuade who spoke.

'If my daughter spoke to me like that I would know I had failed dismally as a mother, or that I had done something very wicked. I don't think you should blame yourself, Catherina. Your mother clearly wants to get away to France and away from the people she has known. I should not criticise because she is your mother but we know you well enough to know you have been a good daughter.'

'I have tried to be,' Rina said softly. 'I really tried. I have never argued or criticised before. She looked shocked.'

'Maybe that was the trouble, lassie,' Neil MacQuade spoke up, 'Maybe your father never refused her anything, or criticised either. I know your grandfather tried to guide her into less frivolous ways and she resented him for that.'

'I think you should put today right out of your mind, my dear,' Mrs MacQuade said. 'You were very brave and courageous and it was clear to me that all those people, who have known you all your life, love and respect you. Try to remember that.' Jamie squeezed her shoulder to show he agreed.

'Mrs MacQuade is right, Rina,' Maggie said quietly. 'We all know you have a sweet nature and a kind heart. They have treated you abominably but it's your mother's loss, selling his home, running away to France with that man, and before your father is cold in his grave.'

'You're all very kind,' Rina said wearily. 'I shall have to pick up the threads of my life again now the funeral is over. I need to write to Matron to see if I still have a job.'

'I'm sure you will have a job,' Mrs MacQuade assured her. Melissa says they're missing you badly and they're short-staffed but Home Sister told her you have had a big ordeal and she thought you should take a holiday after the funeral.'

'I see.'

'Meanwhile Rina,' Jamie said, 'I know the day has been a strain but it might help you forget it if you change into your old clothes and come and help me bring in the cows.' He smiled at her, his blue eyes sparkling with challenge as he added, 'I expect you have forgotten how to milk but we have some young calves to feed. What about it?'

'Yes, I'd like to do that. Do you mind Aunt Maggie?'

'Of course I don't mind lassie, and Jamie could be right. The fresh air will do you good but I suspect he wants your company. You show him — once you've learned to milk you never forget.'

'Did you hear that, Jamie? If you choose some quiet cows I would like to try milking again. Then I will feed the baby calves. I'll join you as soon as I have changed.'

Before they parted Mr MacQuade asked Rina if he could make an appointment for her to come in to his office on Monday morning. She agreed to catch the early train with Uncle Joe.

'I have got this correct? You do intend to sell Stavondale Manor now you will no longer have any income from the farm?'

'I shall have no option, but I rarely stayed there.'

'You could always buy a small house nearer the hospital, unless you plan to move to the city for more training, like Melissa?' Neil MacQuade suggested.

'I could.' She turned to smile at Maggie. 'But Braeside feels more like home than anywhere else has ever been, so long as you and Uncle Joe are not tired of having me to stay?'

'Oh Rina, we both love having you here for as long as you want. And I could see last night that you and Jamie had reached some kind of happy resolution so you will not want to be too far apart I think?'

'Yes, we did resolve some of our problems. We may have to wait for years before we can marry but now that we know we love each other that is all that matters.'

'You may not need to wait so many years,' Neil MacQuade said. 'First we need to discuss your affairs and the sale of Stavondale Manor. Lord Tannahill offered to store some of the furnishings for you. He has plenty of space apparently. He has also offered to buy the house himself but he was telling me today he knows someone who is interested in buying the estate if he could get a decent house to go with it. I believe the man was present at your father's funeral today. Do you know who he might be?'

'No, I didn't recognise some of the men there.' She shivered. 'I wondered if two of them might be the men who forced my father to sell everything.'

'It is possible, but these things take time so they will have to wait. There could be some competition for Stavondale Manor though and that will be in your favour, my dear Rina.'

Jamie was leaning against the fence waiting for Rina. It was a little later than usual and the cows seemed to know because they were beginning to amble towards the gate. Jamie had his elderly collie bitch with him.

'I thought you said Jill was too old to work now?' Rina said as she bent to pat the dog's silky head and fondle her ears.

'She is too old for rounding up sheep on the hill, but she is a canny wee dog with the cows. She lets them know she's there and which way they should be going and they obey, but she never chases them. That would never do with milk cows when their udders are heavy with milk. Running can waste the muscle that holds the udder firm. Sorry,' he grinned and drew her closer to plant a kiss on her upturned face. 'You don't want a lecture.'

'Oh but I like to know about such things,' Rina assured him quickly. She felt guilty because she was so happy to have his arm around her, today of all days. They rounded up the cows together. She had seen Doug Lamont in the dairy, assembling the milk cooler and milk churns and gathering up the milking pails. 'I would like to try milking again so long as you make sure I have the quietest cows.'

'I will choose the good ones, if you're sure, Rina?'

'I am. I enjoyed it when your Uncle Jim taught me what to do but that is ages ago now.' She sighed. I shall have to write to the hospital soon. I might get the train there after I have seen Mr MacQuade on Monday. It would be easier to speak to Matron face to face, then I shall know if she is very displeased with me for walking out of the examination room.'

'Will you be very disappointed if you can't move on to the Glasgow hospital with your friend Melissa?' Jamie asked gently.

'I think they would take me anyway but it would have been an advantage to have passed the State Fever Exam. I lay awake for a long time last night. Now that I know you love me, as I love you, I'm not sure I want to move to the city. I would be further away and we wouldn't be able to see each other often.'

'I thought of that too, my love, but I wouldn't want to hold you back if you have set your heart on becoming a State Registered Nurse, or whatever you called it. As a matter of fact, I couldn't sleep either so I wrote a letter to my mother and to my sister Meg to tell them I'm in love with the most wonderful girl in the world.' He grinned and stopped to pull her more closely into his arms while he kissed her thoroughly. When at last he released her Rina noticed some of the cows and stopped to stand and stare at them.

'They must wonder whatever we're doing,' she said and her happy laughter filled Jamie with joy. 'It always amazes me how they know which stall is theirs in the byre, and how quietly they stand while you fasten the chain around their neck.'

'The older cows show new heifers what to do and they soon turn them out if a heifer tries to take the stall of an older cow. I'm glad you're interested in everything, Rina. We shall be so happy together some day,' he promised. 'If only we can decide the best way to proceed over Bonnybrae. Sometimes I wonder if we should continue renting from the new landlord, whoever he turns out to be. Maybe I'd be able to afford to marry you sooner then.'

'Mr MacQuade might have heard more about the man who wants to buy the estate by Monday.'

'Maybe, but he told Uncle Jim we might never get the chance to purchase Bonnybrae again. He thinks we ought to buy. He seems sure he can help us get a bank loan and he said if we repaid the same amount back as we pay in rent we should manage to pay it back all right. Uncle Jim is not convinced about that. Prices may not be so good after the guarantees finish. He wants me to go with him when Mr MacQuade makes us an appointment at the bank. He thinks I might have questions to ask that he has not considered.' They ushered the last of the cows through the gate and Rina said softly.

'Let's just be happy for now. We can think about money later.'

'You're right,' Jamie said with a happy grin. 'Doug, I've brought another helper tonight.'

'Hello Miss Rina. Do you know how to milk a cow then?' he asked in surprise.

'I did. I hope I can remember.'

'Alice said she would come up to help tonight, Jamie. We thought it might be late before you and Mr Sinclair got back from the funeral.'

'Uncle Jim is not back yet. We got a lift with Mr MacQuade in his car.'

'Alice has always liked milking. She enjoys the company since we came to Bonnybrae.'

It was a very happy atmosphere in the byre that evening with Doug and Alice teasing each other and sometimes chaffing Jamie about being in love. They were not yet sure if they should be so familiar with Rina. They still remembered her as the granddaughter of the old laird, but they were surprised and impressed at the way she got on with the milking after she had regained her confidence with the first cow. Jim was astonished to find they had almost finished when he appeared in the doorway, still in his suit and black tie.

'My goodness me. I don't think you young folks need me at all,' he grinned. 'I expected we would be very late finished tonight. I'd better change my clothes and see what's left for me to do. Thank you for helping Alice, and I see you have not forgotten how to milk, Rina.'

'No I enjoy doing it. It is a lot more restful than hurrying around the wards on your feet all day.'

'Do you really mean that, Miss Rina?' Alice asked.

'Oh yes, I wouldn't say it otherwise.' Her expression grew solemn. She looked up at Jim. 'I do like helping people who are sick but it is so very sad if they die, especially the children. When we have had a fever epidemic like diphtheria and several die it is terribly discouraging.'

'Yes, it must be,' Jim said thoughtfully. 'We don't think of the problems other people encounter with their work.' He recalled this conversation later.

* * *

On Monday morning Rina was up early. Joe offered her a ride on his motor bike but he grinned knowingly when Rina chose to go with Jamie in the pony and trap taking the milk to the train.

'I'm going to make sure Jamie remembers to take my bicycle so that I shall have it for my return.'

'Oh yes, I'll believe you both,' Joe teased, 'but don't be stopping on the way for a wee cuddle and miss the milk train or Jim will have something to say.'

'We'll not do that,' Jamie assured him but it didn't stop him keeping one arm around Rina and holding the reins with his other hand, or stealing a kiss before they reached the station.

'Peggy would almost know the way blindfold anyway,' Jamie chuckled, 'so I'm not going to miss an opportunity while we are alone. I love you so much, Rina.'

Rina was in good time for her appointment with Neil MacQuade and they discussed the sale of the Manor House and when it could be available for occupation.

'I feel obliged to sell it to Lord Tannahill if he wants it. He has been so kind and he went to great expense to arrange Father's funeral and I don't believe Mother even thanked him. He will be storing some of my pictures and pieces of furniture too.'

'He is a businessman, Rina. He would not want special treatment and as your trustee I must get the best deal I can for you. Besides I can't help thinking the house is too fine for a gamekeeper with a large family of children. His wife would probably be much happier if Lord Tannahill built her a cosier house with plenty of bedrooms and a modern bathroom. It wouldn't cost him as much as buying the Manor House either.'

'I suppose that's true. Have you heard who the man is who might be interested in the estate?'

'Yes, I have.' He smiled. 'I admit I was curious so I drove over to Stavondale Tower to see if Lord Tannahill could tell me more. It turns out the man is staying with him while he has a look around the area. His name is Sir Douglas Blackford, father of the young man who shot your father.'

'Mark? Oh Gosh. He was very distressed at the funeral.'

'Yes, it would be an ordeal for him, but he said the locals had all been friendly and some seemed sympathetic. Apparently he is the youngest of three sons so his father is not as wealthy as some landowners. Since Lord Tannahill has bought some of the hill farms for his shooting, and he hopes Mr Sinclair will decide to buy Bonnybrae, the Stavondale Estate is far smaller than in your grandfather's time but it will be more affordable. I can understand they would want a suitable residence as well as land. Would you be able to show Sir Douglas and his son around the Manor House while they are up here?'

'Of course. I hope Lord Tannahill will not be offended.'

'He seems the sort of man who enjoys helping other people, and young Mark and his nephew are good friends.' They discussed a few other matters relating to her trust, including the two Chinese vases, the jade collection and the carved ivory figures which she had inherited from her grandfather, and which Neil MacQuade had put in the bank for safe keeping.

'If you take my advice I think you should leave them there. If ever the situation arises when you are in real need they will provide a small nest egg. As far as the proceeds from the Manor House are concerned you may be able to persuade Mr Sinclair to swallow his pride and let you help if he and Jamie decide to buy Bonnybrae, especially if you and Jamie are going to marry eventually.' Rina's eyes lit up.

'I never thought of that. It would be wonderful if I could persuade them to let me help. Maybe Jamie and I would be able to marry sooner.'

'You really do love the laddie, don't you?' Neil said with a smile. 'Tread carefully. I don't know him well but I can tell Jim Sinclair has more than his share of pride and independence. Are you retuning to Bonnybrae now?' he asked, drawing his gold watch from his breast pocket, 'or have you time for coffee with my wife?'

'I thought I would take the train to Belroon and visit the hospital to see Matron in person.'

'That's a good idea. I will be in touch as soon as I have any news and I'll ask Sir Douglas Blackford to contact you about seeing round the Manor House.'

Matron greeted Rina in a friendly manner and expressed her sympathy.

'I am sure we can get you accepted to train for your general nursing certificates with Nurse MacQuade. I confess, Nurse Capel, I had grave doubts about taking you on in the beginning. I believed you would be too much of a lady after being used to servants, but you have proved yourself a hardworking and caring nurse with an exemplary bedside manner.'

'Thank you Matron. I am not sure I want to move to the city hospital to do my general nursing.'

'No, Home Sister tells me you enjoy exploring the countryside and also going to see your family whenever you get the opportunity. You have been faced with a big ordeal so I suggest you take a fortnight's leave. Take time to come to terms with everything. However, if you wish to stay on here we would be delighted. I have mentioned you to the board and told them you are ready for more responsibility. If you return, and agree, you will be paid an extra five shillings per month and you will help to train the younger nurses. I am sure from your past records you will be able to teach them that compassion and diligent care are sometimes all we can offer to patients who are very sick. These are qualities which come naturally to you Nurse Capel, but I am sure you will have noticed some nurses get frustrated or impatient, while others get depressed. Neither helps the patient.'

'Thank you, Matron.' Rina gave the older woman the beaming smile which had earned her so many friends as a child. She needed her work more than ever now, but she knew she wanted to stay near to Jamie and Bonnybrae so they could meet whenever they were both free. She gave herself a mental hug and her heart sang "Jamie loves me and I love him".

She was in time to catch the mid-afternoon train back. She collected her bicycle from the porter and set off for Bonnybrae, her heart lighter than it had been for a long time in spite of her recent bereavement. As she drew nearer to the entrance to Stavondale she decided to make a detour and call on Lord Tannahill. She was pleased to find him at home, along with Rupert and Mark and a man she had not met before, although she knew he had been at her father's funeral. Lord Tannahill introduced him as Mark's father.

'Would you like some tea while we talk, Rina? We were just about to have some.'

'Oh yes please, I would, now that you mention it.' She smiled at him and not for the first time he wished he had been able to persuade her to marry him. 'I had an appointment with Mr MacQuade and afterwards I continued on the train to Belroon to see Matron at the hospital. I am to take a fortnight's leave and after that I must let her know if I wish to continue working at the Fever Hospital.'

'And of course you will,' Lord Tannahill smiled ruefully, 'in order to be nearer Jamie Sinclair?'

'Probably.' Rina blushed. 'As I was passing the road end I thought I should call to discuss the sale of the Manor House. Mr MacQuade says you are both interested in buying it,' she glanced apologetically towards Sir Douglas Blackford, then back to Lord Tannahill. 'You have been kind to me in so many ways, not least your latest generosity in organizing and paying for my father's funeral. I do appreciate everything you have done and if you want to buy the Manor I think you should have it.' Lord Tannahill opened his mouth to interrupt but Rina held up her hand. 'I know, I know Mr MacQuade said that is not good business and having competition would get me the best price, but I value your friendship.'

'Thank you, my dear Rina. Douglas and I have been friends for many years and we have discussed it. Of course,' he grinned, 'I shall see he pays at least as much as I would have offered, and maybe a little more since he wants it for young Mark here, and I would have used it for my gamekeeper. He is trying to persuade me I should be better building a larger cottage nearer to the shooting where my man can rear the pheasants.'

'I'm sure your gamekeeper's wife will appreciate a house nearer to her husband's work,' Sir Douglas said with a smile. 'In fact I think she would be uncomfortable in a house as grand as the Manor.'

'You could be right about that,' Lord Tannahill conceded, 'but they need plenty of room to house their ever-growing family.'

'In that case when would you like to see round the Manor House, Sir Douglas?' Rina asked.

'There's no time like the present, Miss Capel, if it is convenient to you to show us now. Naturally Mark wants to see his future home too.'

'In that case, Rina, you must eat another of these scones,' Lord Tannahill said, passing her the plate of fruit scones. 'I remember you have a very healthy appetite,' he grinned.

'Mmm, they are delicious and I have not eaten since breakfast.' She sank her strong little teeth into the scone with obvious enjoyment. Lord Tannahill winked at Mark.

'Take my advice young man and never have anything to do with women who play with their food and don't know how to enjoy it. Though I must say, Rina, you have never regained your former weight since you were so ill with the fever. Mrs Greig was dreadfully worried that we were going to lose you.'

'I am fully recovered now but Aunt Maggie is always trying to feed me up.'

'Has Mr Sinclair decided whether to buy his farm or not?'

'I don't know. I think he and Jamie are a bit anxious about the future when the government stop the guaranteed prices. They are afraid the ships will bring in food cheaper than British farmers can produce it.'

'They are probably right,' Lord Tannahill agreed seriously. 'There is a lot of unemployment in the country since the war too so naturally people are desperate for food at the cheapest prices, but land is a great asset. No one can produce more of that and the Sinclairs would not be paying rent every six months if they do buy. Of course each man knows his own business best and it is their decision.'

All four men accompanied her to the Manor House to look around. Both Sir Douglas Blackford and Lord Tannahill made a thorough inspection. Thanks to Mrs Mac everything was clean and tidy.

'It is a mansion house! It's far more splendid than I realised now I see it all,' Lord Tannahill remarked, 'but of course I have only seen a small part before. Your grandfather really did intend you to have the kind of home to which you were accustomed, Rina. I am sorry things are turning out so badly.'

'It is almost twice as big as it used to be when it was the land agent's house. Grandfather raised the roof and built a third floor. He imagined it would be needed for servants I think, but I didn't know he was doing it for me. He built on the extra wing at the side too but it takes more than a large house and fine furnishings to make a home. I have barely stayed here for more than a few days at a time so it will not break my heart to sell it, but I shall always be grateful that Grandfather did the best he could for me.'

'Yes, I'm sure you will remember him with great affection.'

'I really appreciate you storing the furniture for me. It will be a long time before I have a home to furnish.' Rina didn't realise she sounded so downcast. Lord Tannahill silently vowed to use his influence if he could help her.

'You were right, Douglas,' he said turning to his friend. 'My gamekeeper and his wife would never have been comfortable here after their tiny cottage. It will be a magnificent home for Mark. You will need to offer a good price,' he added with a grin.

'With you watching over my shoulder I expect I shall,' Sir Douglas said wryly. He turned to Rina. 'I am most impressed Miss Capel. This will make a splendid home for Mark and his wife, when he finds someone suitable, and the estate will be a good start for him. Do you agree Mark?'

'Yes, Father. The people here have all been friendly in spite of the dreadful accident.' He turned to Rina. 'It is something I shall never forget and I cannot thank you enough for being so decent about everything. Miss Capel never uttered one word of recrimination, Father.'

'So I understand, my boy.' He smiled at Rina. 'We are all very grateful to you Miss Capel.'

'That means they'll add a hundred or two to the price they offer,' Lord Tannahill suggested with a wink at Rina.

'Don't forget I have three sons to launch on the world. None of them are fighting men with a yearning to join the army. They all enjoy the land and the countryside.'

'Speaking of finding a suitable wife,' Rina said thoughtfully, 'almost the last things my father said to me was that he and my mother had been considered a "suitable match" but they had never loved each other and his marriage had not been a happy one. Perhaps the same should apply to your sons, sir.'

'Maybe your father was wise, but it is a good life when the woman you love is also suited to your lifestyle. My wife and I are happy and I hope our sons will be as fortunate as we are.'

'You have been luckier than most men in that respect, Douglas,' Lord Tannahill said quietly.

'Indeed I have, just as you were so unfortunate to lose your wife so tragically.'

* * *

When Rina got back to Braeside she told Maggie how her appointment with Mr MacQuade had gone and about her talk with Matron Gilroy at the hospital.

'I don't want to move to the city. I would hardly ever see Jamie and I do love him you know. So I have accepted Matron's offer of promotion and I shall continue working at the Fever Hospital, but she says I should take two weeks break before I start again.'

'Matron sounds very understanding,' Maggie said, 'and we all like to see you whenever you're free, Rina dear. Jamie will be happy to hear you are not moving further away.'

'I called at Stavondale Tower on my way home. It is Mark's father, Sir Douglas Blackford, who wants to buy the rest of the estate. It is for Mark so he will also offer a good price for the Manor House but he would like to settle things fairly soon. While I am free from work I must clear out my possessions. He agreed to buy some of the bigger items of furniture, so that is a relief.'

'We will all help you if you want us Rina, but I don't want to be a nuisance.'

'Oh, Aunt Maggie I would be grateful for your help.' Rina hugged her. 'You could never be a nuisance. Jamie's uncle might consider me a nuisance though if I tell him about Mr MacQuade's advice.'

'I'm sure Jim would never think that, Rina? What did Mr MacQuade say?'

'He said because I seem to love Jamie so much, and because we hope to be married someday, it would be a better investment if I offered the money from the Stavondale Manor to Mr Sinclair and Jamie to buy the farm. He meant instead of me buying, or building, a house near the hospital, as he first suggested. He said he believes Mr Sinclair is honourable and hardworking otherwise, as my trustee, he would not recommend such a step, but he believes he is proud and independent so I should not be hurt if he refuses.'

'I see. I expect Mr MacQuade is used to assessing a man's qualities. He's certainly right about Jim. Sometimes he's too proud and independent. He has refused Joe's help. Lord Tannahill also offered him a loan but he refused to consider it. I'll speak to Jim myself though and tell him what you say, Rina. It would give him time to consider before you mention it. If he does refuse at least he will not be so brusque.'

'Thank you. I was not looking forward to telling him myself,' Rina said with a smile. 'Mr MacQuade asked Lord Tannahill's opinion about a fair valuation for Bonnybrae. He told him it was by far the best farm on the estate but a lot of that was due to the hard work and good farming practice by the Sinclair family over the generations and he didn't see why they should have to pay for their own diligence. He has suggested Mr MacQuade should work out an average price per acre for the rest of the estate, then charge the same for Bonnybrae to keep the valuation down but avoid any dispute with the creditors. He said the money will only be going to men who don't deserve it, men who know nothing about hard work and are only interested in recouping their gambling debts. He thinks they don't deserve other people's hard-earned money. Apparently he is annoyed they will be getting so much, especially when they have demanded the sale of Manor Farm as well. Mr MacQuade says he will do his best to drive a hard bargain with the lawyers of my father's creditors after hearing Lord Tannahill's views. If he can negotiate a reasonable price it would be more of an advantage to Mr Sinclair to take the opportunity now to buy Bonnybrae.'

* * *

Rina spent a busy two weeks sorting out Stavondale Manor ready for sale and helping Jamie with various tasks at

Bonnybrae. Inevitably the time quickly came for her to return to her work at the Fever Hospital. It seemed a long two weeks before she had a full day free when she could see Jamie again and she missed him terribly in spite of his loving letters. She promised to try to catch the last train after she finished her shift on Saturday so they would have the rest of the evening together and more time on Sunday. She knew it would be a rush to cycle to the station in time but Jamie had promised to meet the train at the other end in the hope she was on it. It would be getting dark but they both had cycle lamps and late summer evenings were never as bad as the cold pitch black of winter. She could barely wait for her shift to end. Fortunately there were no last minute crises and she pulled off her uniform as she hurried to her room. She was in such a hurry she almost ran into the motor bike and sidecar parked outside until Jamie jumped from the pillion and seized her in his arms, grinning at her surprise before he gave her a lingering kiss. Jo waited patiently then gently revved the motor bike as a reminder. Jamie grinned and lifted Rina in his arms to set her down in the sidecar before he settled himself behind Joe.

'You'll not need your bicycle because Joe says we'll bring you back tomorrow evening.'

'I knew he was desperate to see you again, Rina,' Joe called over the noise of the engine and winked at her. She gave him a big smile. Joe grinned. She really cheered them all and he hoped Jim could come to a decision which would help them plan for the future. Almost as soon as they were alone Jamie said, 'If Uncle Jim is grumpy don't take any notice. I don't know what's wrong to make him so irritable.'

'Do you think he could be ill?' Rina asked with concern.

'If he is, he hasn't said anything, but there's something on his mind.'

* * *

As usual on Sundays Maggie cooked the dinner at Bonnybrae so they could all eat together. Rina always enjoyed Maggie's roast beef and Yorkshire pudding with rich brown gravy, as well as roast potatoes and a selection of vegetables. One of Jim's favourite desserts was trifle so Maggie had made a large one in the hope of cheering her brother a little. After they had finished eating Jim asked Rina if she would come and talk to him in the small room next to the kitchen where he kept his animal records and accounts of the farm expenses. It had once been the maid's bedroom.

'Shall I come as well, Uncle Jim?' Jamie asked, rising from the table to join them.

'No, you can help Maggie with the dishes instead of Rina.' Jamie raised his eyebrows in surprise.

'Take a seat, lassie,' Jim said wearily. 'I want to talk to you about buying Bonnybrae. Maggie told me about your talk with Mr MacQuade. I've done nothing but consider what is best for your future if you marry Jamie. The last thing I want is to leave Jamie with a loan he can't afford to pay and a wife and family to keep if times get difficult.'

'I understand,' Rina said quietly.

'Half of me thinks we should take a chance with a new landlord and go on renting but so many people are trying to advise me to buy Bonnybrae.'

'Mr MacQuade and Lord Tannahill think it's a good opportunity, but I'm sure you know best.'

'Don't think I'm not grateful for your offer to use your inheritance, Rina.'

'You have all been kind to me, ever since I first came to Bonnybrae. I would like to help.'

'There is only one way I could agree to use your money, lassie, and that is if you were Jamie's wife and we included your name, with Jamie's and mine, on the deeds as joint owners. Even then I have doubts whether it is the right thing for your future, and Jamie's. So before we go any further I want you to talk it over with Mr MacQuade and I need to know you are certain you want to marry Jamie?'

'Oh yes! I'm very sure about that,' Rina said emphatically and gave Jim her wide smile. 'I've never been as sure about anything in my life. We love each other you see,' she said simply.

'In that case I want you to make an appointment with Mr MacQuade and discuss my suggestion with him. If he is in favour, ask him to draw up the documents we shall need including all three names. It would be simpler if your name was already Sinclair. If you do marry soon there's the matter of where you would live.' He looked at her anxiously, knowing the grand houses she had lived in, in the past. 'I shall move in with Maggie and Joe then you and Jamie can live in this house. Would that be suitable to you, lassie?' he asked anxiously.

'No! Oh no, that would not do at all.' Rina jumped out of her chair.

CHAPTER TWELVE

Rina moved round the desk to stand in front of Jim. Her lovely dark eyes were bright with tears. Jim hastily pushed his chair back and got to his feet, his face filled with concern.

'I'm sorry, lassie,' he said tiredly, 'but it's the best I can offer . . .'

'No. This will never do,' Rina cried in distress and to Jim's surprise she threw her arms around him and hugged him fiercely. 'I would never, never want you to move out of your home. You were born here. This is where you belong. If you would allow me to come to live here with you and Jamie, when I'm his wife of course, then I promise to do my best to care for you as Aunt Maggie has always done. I am not as good at cooking yet but she has taught me how to make lots of dishes and I can learn more. Please, please say you will stay and let Jamie and me live here with you?' Jim felt a wave of profound relief as he looked down into her earnest young face. There was no doubt she meant what she was suggesting. He swallowed hard.

'I'm sure you and Jamie willna want an old man like me living with you,' he said gruffly.

'Of course we shall, if you can put up with us. And you're not an old man. Jamie told me you have been more

202

like a father to him than his own father and you've taught him nearly everything he knows about farming. He would never want you to live anywhere else, I know he wouldn't.'

'Well . . . Well, I don't know what to say,' but Jim couldn't help the smile which wiped the weariness from his weathered features. 'Shall we go and see what the others have to say?'

Jamie was over the moon when he heard why his Uncle Jim had wanted to see Rina alone, and he agreed emphatically that they would not want him to move out of Bonnybrae for their sake.

'Oh well, Jim,' Joe said with a teasing grin, 'you can always move in with us when they fill the house with children.' Rina blushed rosily and looked at Jamie but his blue eyes were dancing and he gave her a hug and whispered, 'I look forward to the opportunity.'

* * *

Rina returned to her work at the hospital with a lighter heart on Sunday evening. She wrote to Mr MacQuade but she knew he would have no objection to her using her money to help buy Bonnybrae. He had suggested it himself, knowing how much she loved Jamie. He drove to the hospital to discuss it with her. He was pleased Jim Sinclair was going ahead with buying Bonnybrae.

'Most of all I'm pleased I was right. He is an honourable man or he wouldn't insist on including your name on the deeds. Few men regard women as equals, even though they have got the vote now.'

One thing troubled Rina. Her mother had shown no respect for her father when she went off to France with Eric Wardle after the funeral, but Rina felt it would be wrong to have a wedding so soon, even though she knew Jamie was expecting it now that his uncle had reached a decision. She wrote to Maggie for advice, explaining she was as eager to be married as Jamie was but she felt guilty at being so happy, and planning a wedding soon after her father's death.

Maggie understood how Rina felt and she respected her for considering her father's memory, though personally she felt he had proved himself a poor parent. She discussed it with Joe and Jim.

'I understand how the lassie feels,' Jim said. 'People are quick to criticise. Jamie is impatient to make arrangements but he knows Rina has to give suitable notice to the hospital, especially when they have treated her so fairly with time off and then promotion.'

Joe proposed they should wait until after harvest.

'Jamie is needed here for that and it takes a while cutting and gathering in the corn. That will allow more time to pass, and Rina wants to give plenty of notice of her resignation from the hospital.'

'That's true,' Maggie agreed, 'but it will still be only a few months since the funeral.'

'I know, but we wouldn't want Jamie and Rina to get impatient, then have to rush into marriage,' Joe said. 'They're young and eager to get on with life, and there's no doubt they love each other. I believe folks will wish them well if it is a quiet wedding in the kirk, if Rina is agreeable to that. The banns would have to be read for three weeks before of course, but people know it's not being done in secret then.'

Rina agreed without hesitation. She longed to be with Jamie — day and night.

'I wouldn't want a big wedding whenever it is,' she said. 'You're my only relative, Aunt Maggie, except for Mother and we wouldn't be inviting her anyway after what she said to Jamie. I would like to have Melissa as a witness and Uncle Joe to give me away — if we still do that when it is a very small wedding?'

'Of course you must do that, dear,' Maggie said. 'Jamie has a lot of relations but they will understand why the wedding should be a quiet one. Then we could have a family party here at Christmas for them all to meet you, Rina. How does that sound?'

'It sounds wonderful,' Rina agreed, 'but will Jamie's parents be hurt if they're not invited?'

'I will write to Emma and see what she says,' Maggie promised. 'You're very considerate, Rina.'

Jamie's mother replied promptly to say they were all a bit disappointed they could not be at Jamie's wedding but if he would bring his new bride to stay with them after the wedding perhaps Rina would not mind if they held a party for family and friends in Yorkshire and she would make new dresses for Jamie's sisters because they were disappointed they could not be bridesmaids.

'Your family sound lovely, Jamie,' Rina said wistfully. 'You're lucky to have brothers and sisters.'

As soon as things had been decided and a date fixed for the end of September, Jamie told Alice and Doug. The country grapevine was spreading the news long before it was time to consult the minister about reading the banns. Only one couple disapproved, but as Mrs Lamont said to Alice, 'I've never known them approve of anybody or anything.'

Jamie received one big surprise. Garridan, the loyal gypsy friend of his boyhood, had heard of his impending marriage and written him a short letter. Meg had enclosed it with one of hers. Jamie was apprehensive about Rina's reaction when he first considered Garridan's suggestion but when he had had time to consider he decided it was a better plan than anything he had thought of himself and he appreciated his old friend's thoughtfulness. He kept the secret to himself, but as time for the wedding drew nearer he hoped and prayed Rina would not disapprove.

Although it was supposed to be a very quiet wedding Jamie and Rina were astonished to see many of the tenants' wives as well as some of the people from both the villages. They were all eager to greet the happy couple and wish them well. It made Rina feel quite emotional and Maggie shed a few tears.

After a celebration lunch at Braeside Mr MacQuade arrived in his car to collect Melissa and take them to catch the train to Yorkshire.

Maggie had made Rina a beautiful new dress for her wedding and she was reluctant to change into her serviceable skirt and jacket but Jamie had been insistent. He said her dress would not be suitable for travelling but she should pack it in their suitcase because his mother and sisters would want to see it and she would look lovely in it at the party his mother was making for them.

As the train drew nearer to their destination Jamie fidgeted and tugged at his collar and tie. He had also changed into his second-best suit and packed his good suit in the case. There were two other couples in their carriage.

'You seem uneasy, Jamie,' Rina whispered. 'Are you regretting . . . ?'

'No! No never that, Rina. I-I just hope you will not be disappointed with the arrangements I have made for our wedding night. Maybe I'm being selfish but I want us to be alone. I want you all to myself.'

'That is what I long for too,' Rina whispered back, her cheeks pink.

'I told Mother we would be arriving the day after tomorrow. That's why I wanted you to pack your dress and my suit in the case and bring a bag with our night things. We'll leave our suitcase at the station and collect it later. We're going to ride the rest of the way on horseback.'

'Horseback?' she echoed, her dark eyes widening.

'Yes, do you mind?'

'Of course I don't mind, but where . . . ?' He leaned closer and kissed the tip of her nose.

'It's meant to be a surprise. But now I'm worried in case you hate it.'

'I shall not hate anything so long as we're together.'

As soon as he had helped her from the train and dealt with their suitcase he took her hand and guided her outside to where a few ponies and traps were awaiting passengers. A fine big horse was tethered to the rail.

'This is ours,' Jamie said. 'His name's Barney. I'll lift you on and jump up behind you. All right?'

'Y-yes, I think so. He's a lovely horse,' she said patting his neck and talking softly to him as she did with Duke, her own pony. 'But where are we going Jamie?' she asked bewildered.

'It's a secret. I only hope you will not be disappointed, or angry with me. I do love you Rina and all I want is to make this special for both of us. I can't wait to be alone with you.'

He untied the horse and jumped up behind her. He followed Garridan's instructions and guided Barney away from the station and the busy streets towards the countryside beyond. They were heading across country and Jamie had been a bit anxious in case he couldn't remember the way, but Barney seemed to know his own way until they got nearer to the gypsy camp and his home, then Jamie had to guide him towards the corner of the next field in the opposite direction to where the gypsies always camped. Eventually they came to a small wood at the bottom of the Common which bordered his parents' farm of Moorend.

'There is a burn near here. We will follow it to the other side of the wood.'

'Oh look, Jamie,' Rina cried in delight. 'There's a gypsy caravan over there, all on its own. Isn't it lovely? It looks as though it has been newly painted.'

'Let's hope you like the inside, my darling wife,' Jamie said but his eyes were anxious.

'Is this where we're going to spend the night?' Rina asked, as excited as a child.

'It is,' Jamie said as he slid from the horse and lifted Rina down. 'Here's our bag, I hope it has everything you need.' He handed to it her. 'I want to give Barney a long tether so he can graze and still reach the burn for a drink. Rina helped him with the horse then they walked together to the brightly painted door of the caravan.

'Oh how lovely it is,' Rina cried so spontaneously that Jamie heaved a sigh of relief. 'How pretty all the china is arranged safely in the polished wooden racks. And see Jamie, someone has made up this big bed with white linen all beautifully trimmed with lace.'

'Ah, so this is what Garridan meant in his letter,' Jamie mused. 'He said the linen and lace are made in Ireland and will bring us good luck. When we leave we must fold the sheets and pillowcases and take them with us. Every year, on this day, we must make our bed with them and be as happy as we are on our wedding night.'

'What a splendid idea, as well as being a lovely gift. The lace is so delicate and pretty.' Rina threw her arms around his neck. 'I never dreamed you would arrange anything so romantic, Jamie. To tell the truth I was a bit apprehensive about spending our first night together in your parents' home. This is wonderful.'

The autumn weather had been beautiful and they could not have wished for a better day to be married but the evenings were inclined to be chilly. Someone had lit the small stove so the caravan was cosy. The fire had burned low but Jamie had noticed a large box of firewood sheltered beneath the back of the caravan.

'There is an outside larder as well,' Jamie said, 'Look, Garridan has left a note for us. He says he stocked it with fresh food this afternoon, with a little help from Meg, my sister.' They went down the steps together like a pair of excited children and discovered fresh milk, eggs, butter and cheese as well as a loaf of new bread. On the bottom shelf there was a pan of stew prepared and ready to heat for their meal tomorrow. 'Good old Dan, he has thought of everything,' Jamie said happily.

'Most likely his wife thought of it and he brought them,' Rina chuckled with a mischievous glint in her eyes.

'Oh, oh?' Jamie cried and swept her up in his arms, 'so you think you can be cheeky now we're married, do you Mrs Sinclair?' He proceeded to carry her up the steps back into the caravan and laid her on the bed covering her face with kisses. Passion flared between them. 'I shall join you in two minutes,' Jamie said huskily, leaning across to draw the crimson wool curtains. He lit the little oil lantern and closed the curtains at the other end of the caravan. It was warm and private. Jamie sent his old friend a silent prayer of thanks as he swiftly removed his clothes and turned to join Rina. She was pulling on the new white nightgown which she had embroidered with tiny flowers, especially for this night which she had dreamed about and waited for, for so long, but Jamie gently took it from her and laid it aside.

'You will not need this for a while,' he whispered as he clasped her in his arms so they were skin to skin, and every nerve seemed alive with desire. He rolled with her onto the wide bed. 'I thought you were the most beautiful girl I had ever seen when I saw you in the kirk today,' he said, his voice deep with emotion, 'but now my darling Rina . . .' he punctuated his words with kisses, exploring her exquisite curves, 'now I think you're a vision of pure delight . . .' He gasped when she followed his example and her hands wandered on a path of exploration over his own body.

It was some time later when they lay together in each other's arms, happy and fulfilled. Jamie leaned across and drew back the curtain.

'See the stars are coming out,' he said as they looked up together at the dark clear sky.

'How beautiful the world is tonight,' Rina breathed softly. 'I love you so much Jamie.'

'And I love you my darling Rina, more than the world itself.'

'Love me again, Jamie. Make love to me beneath the stars and may they always shine on us as they do tonight.'

THE END

THE JOFFE BOOKS STORY

We began in 2014 when Jasper agreed to publish his mum's much-rejected romance novel and it became a bestseller.

Since then we've grown into the largest independent publisher in the UK. We're extremely proud to publish some of the very best writers in the world, including Joy Ellis, Faith Martin, Caro Ramsay, Helen Forrester, Simon Brett and Robert Goddard. Everyone at Joffe Books loves reading and we never forget that it all begins with the magic of an author telling a story.

We are proud to publish talented first-time authors, as well as established writers whose books we love introducing to a new generation of readers.

We have been shortlisted for Independent Publisher of the Year at the British Book Awards three times, in 2020, 2021 and 2022, and for the Diversity and Inclusivity Award at the Independent Publishing Awards in 2022.

We built this company with your help, and we love to hear from you, so please email us about absolutely anything bookish at feedback@joffebooks.com

If you want to receive free books every Friday and hear about all our new releases, join our mailing list: www.joffebooks.com/contact

And when you tell your friends about us, just remember: it's pronounced Joffe as in coffee or toffee!

Made in the USA
Middletown, DE
07 October 2023

40407509R00130